Breaking the Rules

ANIA RAY

ISBN: 978-1-09838-047-2

For my nieces
Madyn, Aubrey, and Karolina

and my nephews
Patryk, Myles, and Dominik

May you always find the good and bring out the best.

Breaking the Rules

Dear Gina,

However many women doubt themselves... here's to breaking that, over and over. Thank you so much. Your work is a compass.

ANIA RAY

Ania Ray ♡

Prologue

The diamond ring came into focus. White gold hugged the stones together, but the image was too pixelated to see how many diamonds there were and how they were cut. As if Marley cared about things like that. But she knew Lily did.

Marley tried to mask her surprise. "Wow! That's…" she searched for the right word. Words mattered to the Cromwells. Everything mattered. "…fast!"

"I know, I know." Lily turned to Logan, who was cooking in her kitchen, and sighed happily. "But when you know, you know, y'know?"

She didn't.

"We'd love…" Lily cleared her throat and bounced her shoulders. "Okay. I'll be honest. *I'd* love a winter wedding. But not when it's dark and dreary. Right before the holidays. All the lights would be so beautiful in the photographs. I know it's fast, but my mother isn't complaining—"

"—for once!" they said in unison and crinkled their eyes. They were always in sync. Mostly. Kind of.

"So it's sooner rather than later," Lily continued. "I don't need Logan realizing he's making a big mistake before it's official." She laughed, clenching her teeth. It was strange seeing this new Lily, who was afraid of losing someone rather than being the one who used to walk away so easily. Marley watched her best friend compose herself on the phone's screen.

"And, most importantly, I need to know if you will be able to forgo your warm Spanish weather for a couple weeks in December for, you know, the bachelorette party and… " Lily blinked rapidly, straightening her torso. "Mar, you've been my girl. My one and only best friend. Would you please be my maid of honor?"

And, though Marley had expected the question, albeit a couple years down the road, she still felt humbled as Lily's eyes filled with tears.

"Absolutely, Lil. Nothing in the world could keep me away."

But promises were easy to make when everything still made sense.

Create Art, Not Conflict

Marley cleared her throat. She had been practicing this presentation for months, but if she were ever going to speak as effectively as Lily or Isabel, she had to practice.

She scanned the empty conference room.

"And so you see, ladies and gentlemen, a million clients is not a ridiculous expectation. But a few thousand is all *you're* going to get if you choose a different agency to develop and deliver your brand. With us—" She shrugged, letting her lips dip into a smug smile. "—that's what we call day one."

Marley tugged at the front hem of her blazer. Maybe she *could* present today. Ezequiel would be so surprised. She wanted to know that she could do it without him or Margaret, his wife, a high school communications teacher, who'd remind Marley to be mindful of her inflection, tone, rhetorical devices, when to smile and when to look stern. Of course Zeke would still be in charge of intercepting any of the pointed questions their colleagues Maria or Isabel would undoubtedly ask. And he'd still have to save her from any of Brandon's passive aggressive snark. But she'd deliver the meat of the material. She had to. It was time.

Marley took a deep breath and looked around. Complete silence— just how she liked it.

She grinned and let something like pride settle through her. This must be what Lily felt every day at work at IceStorm, a start-up that was about to IPO thanks to Lily's grit and vision—which she was not afraid to share with people. Mostly men. At least at Marley's company, La Agencia del Tigre, the ratio of women to men was more balanced. Still, Marley had to give her friend credit for her gumption: Lily had done it all "right." That is, she had graduated from MIT, worked hard as a junior engineer and had become lead architect a few years later. But after years of being Lily Cromwell's best friend, Marley Harrow hadn't quite developed such socially adept and skillful persuasion talents, which really did have to reveal themselves soon if she were going to survive this next round of cuts *and, please dear sweet baby Jesus, hopefully, fingers crossed,* become a senior creative. It was why she left New York, after all. Climbing the ranks in a romantic Spanish town was much more Marley Harrow's speed.

She straightened her back. "*Agencia del Tigre* is the only agency I'm willing to work for. If I don't make your company the kind of success that Spain has never seen before, I'll have to find my way back to New York - and I'm not ready to go back yet." Marley glanced at her binder. *Be personal* was underlined, hard-pressed arrows pointing to the words. What was she supposed to say? That her blood rushed when she heard about the Moorish-influenced architecture and teahouses of Granada - and the fact that a quick weekend in Morocco - *Africa!* - was only a ferry ride away? That this was the exotic adventure she craved because she felt she was the most ordinary, boring human who ever lived? That living in the house with her mother Peggy in Jersey was getting too repetitive and mundane and, as much as Marley loved structure and routine, she knew there had to be more to experience?

And she had been right: that her daily commute took her along cobble-stoned streets and white stone buildings to the sound of the same accordion playing the same version of "Blue Danube" over and over again was equally dependable and made her feel like she had gotten off the hamster wheel - at least enough to make her feel less of a lame-o.

Vulnerability. Ugh. She hated this part. Isabel delivered with such effortless sincerity and "authenticity" - and that reflected in her sales. But it was a skill that Marley desperately needed to learn so that their team's client, Mariposa - and the team itself - wouldn't go belly-up in December - only five months away.

She tried out some of the truth: "This past year has been so much fun discovering all that Spain has to offer the marketing world and I won't let another anniversary go by without doing all that I can to make *Tigre* a success. Not when I see so much potential with you, *Mariposa*." She made sure to roll her *r* and lighten the *a* of their client's company name. She didn't need Zeke reminding her what a gringa she was.

Her heart sank. What did she have to do to have this Cromwell confidence all the time?

Applause erupted behind her. The hair on her neck stood up and she gripped the top of a chair. *Please don't let it be Karl. Anybody but Karl.*

"Bravo," rumbled a low voice she didn't recognize. The tension in her shoulders charged through her arm, and she dug her fingernails into the leather. How much had he heard? Why hadn't it been enough to rehearse in her studio apartment with only Cilantro as her audience?

"It's nice to see some competence in the company. I wasn't sure what I had agreed to when Brandon asked if I wanted to switch teams."

She let go of the chair. *What?* Competence? In her? Was he serious? Marley kept her head down, but looked up through the curls that she hoped were less frizzy than normal. She blew up into the stray hairs and forced herself to look him in the eye: her least favorite thing to do. Ever.

He was tall. Much taller than she. He was smiling, as though amused by the sight in front of him. His hair was swept back, and silver frames brought out the soft brown of his eyes. She felt something within her squeeze. Try finding this kind of one-on-one attention on a New York City street.

"That was a great start," he said. "Thomas Elker. It's nice to officially meet you."

Marley stared at his extended hand.

"Hi," she sputtered. She lifted her hand and shook his. It was the best she could do, considering her heart rate was increasing exponentially. "I'm Marley." She sounded breathless and out of shape. She thought of the rolls tucked in her high-waisted jeans.

How did Lily get people to kiss the back of her hand, like she was some princess?

Because she basically was. Duh.

His grip was strong.

"Small hands," he said.

She pulled away. "I get that a lot." Why did people think that was okay to say? It's not like she felt like she could say, "Wow, what big hands you have" everytime she shook someone's hand.

He cringed. "That's probably something that didn't need to be said." He rolled his shoulders back. "Sorry. It's hard to know what's allowed to say to employees nowadays. I meant to say that it's impressive that such a strong personality could fit in…"

She raised an eyebrow.

"Do me a favor and stop there," Marley snapped. She was being more aggressive than she'd otherwise have the courage to be. But the fact that he was standing between her and the doorway was making her claustrophobic, and that was not good for anybody. She suddenly wished it *had* been Karl who'd walked in. This conversation would be over by now.

He smirked, lifting his hands in mock surrender. Was he always this smug??

The door to the conference room swung open and her colleagues spilled in. Marley spun around, grateful to break off the eye contact. She scooped up the binder that had been waiting for her like a Bible at a pulpit and took a step back to sit in her usual seat: two seats away from the foot of the table and six seats away from the head. It was the perfect place for her to blend in and be invisible. There was a reason she worked with ideas and art. People were a necessary means to an end; otherwise, she could do without all the glib and shallow chit-chat.

She imagined "the group" had traveled together from picking up coffee at Café 43. Isabel would be at the head of the pack with the order of the day, refusing to drink a mocha on a Monday even if the one she had on Friday was out of this world. Marley didn't know what drink was Tuesday's special, but she was sure Isabel had let everybody know. She had probably led them to the bulletin board by the copy machines, where Maria scoffed at the sales report, never taking them seriously enough, especially if Isabel was first in sales. Again.

Before long, Karl would remind them that it was time to be on time for their morning meeting. *Sheep.* They thought having a differently colored stripe here or there would make a difference, but it didn't keep the wool from their eyes. They so often missed a good idea when it was right in front of them. When she had her own agency one day, things would be different. Marley drew circles in the corner of her binder to join the dark marks that held evidence of such meetings. All talk. No action. It's why they were all in danger of losing their jobs.

Within the binder were pages of what she'd brainstormed the night before. Brandon had asked the artistic directors for more ideas *right before* she was going to log off at 5 p.m. She had given her normal shift her all, priding herself on avoiding social calls and social media distractions, so when Brandon asked for *more* ideas, she had already been squeezed of them and needed to find more. People loved cats. Maybe she could work Cilantro into some mock shots? She wanted so badly to lay down, sleep, and not wake up until her alarm rang the next morning. Instead, she had stayed up most of the night pulling out all the creative stops to woo her new boss, which included talking to herself, taking power naps, watching telenovelas, and listening to Lily's run-down of her day. It was finally after fifty jumping jacks, five 30-second plank-holds, and a hot shower that the ideas started flowing. It was a cruel twist of life that creativity followed physical exertion. Or at least she'd read that while skimming through yet another productivity post on her phone some nights ago. Besides. The jumping jacks and plank-holds were good conditioning for the wedding and the waterfall rappelling trip that was on the schedule for team bonding at the start of December.

But now she could barely keep her eyes open.

"*Buenos días, mi amiga!*"

Marley felt her entire body relax as she turned around to face the voice that made her relax - not fight. Or freeze.

"Zeke! Hi!"

"Are you ready to present today?"

All the confidence from earlier was gone. "I sent you all my ideas before I went to bed last night, so…"

Zeke shook his head. "Ay, chica. When are you going to learn that you deserve to be heard?"

Marley shrugged. "Maybe when I stop hearing people gossip about each other everywhere I go."

"So, never?"

"Sounds like a realistic option."

"C'mon, Mar. You've been here for a year. You'll never be senior level if senior level creatives don't know about your work. They can't read your mind. It's time to show off what you can do."

"But they *do* know my work. It's just presented by you. I'll choke, and make an embarrassment of myself. It's safer to be silent than have to deal with all the negative comments."

"Why do you always imagine the worst case scenario?"

"It's better to expect the worst so that if good things happen, I'll be pleasantly surprised. Otherwise, I'll just be perpetually disappointed. People learn self-defense for their bodies; this is self-defense for my mind." Marley tapped her temple. Zeke rolled his eyes.

Marley changed the subject. "Why did Brandon call this meeting, anyway?"

Zeke sighed. "Deborah was let go from the agency. She was taking our ideas, changing *just enough* to make it less obvious, but they were still ours. Later, she used it in her portfolio to 'consult' for others. Shady stuff. Decredits us and puts us more at risk for losing *Mariposa*."

"Ugh, that's awful," Marley said. "Like, if you don't have any ideas, just swallow your pride and wait your turn, you know? It's not fair that some seem to have their lives in the lucky lane while others don't, but still. It's called 'integrity.' Deb will get hers; people are always eventually humbled by life."

"Completely agree, hermana. *Entonces.* They called Thomas Elker on to take over."

She straightened her back and tried to look casual, flipping through her binder, searching for nothing in particular. "Oh? Do you know him?"

"*Sí.* I do. He's worked on other teams in the agency before as a consultant. But I'm sure Brandon will tell us more."

Brandon's clapping brought a hush into the room. Zeke stuck his elbow out and she bumped it with her own. "Maybe you'll surprise me today, amiga. This way I have something to report to Margaret." He winked before walking away to his usual seat, kitty corner from hers. Marley smiled to herself. Zeke was a good friend. Totally different from Lily's go-getter vibe, but part of her tribe all the same.

Part of her listened to Brandon's call to order, but the other wondered about Mr. Elker. She usually double and triple checked her emails so as not to miss anything. Other than the reminders to complete the sexual harassment training, if there had been an announcement of this change in leadership, it had somehow eluded her. She had no idea who this person was. But she'd be lying if she didn't admit that she was intrigued. What did he mean by "strong personality"? "Competent"? No one had ever said that about her before. Where was her dad? If another man told him that his daughter was capable, maybe he'd finally believe it.

"...like to introduce Mr. Thomas Elker, our new Associate Creative Director. He typically works on our *Banco* team, but we need his expertise here."

The room applauded, which meant it was safe for Marley to look up. And when she did, Mr. Elker was staring directly at her. He smiled, and she couldn't resist the urge to turn up the corners of her lips, only to look back down to flip open the cover of her binder. The page inside the transparent cover was green. If she hadn't consulted with Zeke before, this sheet would have indicated to him and her team that she had had a solid brainstorming sesh the night before and felt more comfortable presenting today - *if* she were called on. She wouldn't need Zeke to save her like he typically did. Marley knew that she could trust Zeke to present her ideas as *theirs* so that they could both keep their jobs. She wouldn't have to say anything out loud. No judgment. No negative opinions. Just sweet, sweet neutrality and peace of mind. After all: she created art, not conflict.

Marley knew that Zeke didn't see it that way, but if he understood how much her throat constricted when she was called upon to share her ideas out loud...

She placed her phone on the conference table, making sure the phone was in its ever-present state of vibration-only - with the exception of Lily's calls. Marley promised to answer Lily's calls all the time, no matter what: the Rules of long distance friendship, Lily proclaimed. Hopefully Logan would loosen that girl up. Not that Marley really minded. It was nice to be needed.

Brandon's voice brought her back to the meeting. "Let's talk about these ideas, team. *Mariposa* wants all of Spain to have its eyes on the new recycling campaign they're launching. And we have to be the agency that delivers. No excuses. Seriously. No *Mariposa*, no *Tigre*, no jobs. So let's hear it."

Karl went first. Of course he did. He always did. She had to acknowledge that his ideas were usually fine enough to get started, and she did appreciate that he was often the sacrificial lamb since she could never be, but his eagerness made her so uncomfortable. She would never confess that he stank of desperation, but he did, and it was embarrassing to watch.

At least Karl spoke up, Lily would say.

But whether Lily agreed or not, Karl's over-participation was worse than Marley's lack of it.

Then Isabel, with her bright orange scarf and coffee glued to her palm. She was often second, or liked to wait until the very end to slam-dunk what she thought was an award-winning, bonus-deserving idea. Marley usually agreed with her direction, if only disagreeing with the expected deadlines. The one she proposed today was for the end of the week.

"This Friday? Are you crazy?" Maria asked incredulously.

"Crazy determined, yes."

"Can your nose go up any higher, Isabel?" Karl asked. Marley hid her giggle behind her hand, tucking it away before Mr. Elker had the chance to see where it was coming from.

Isabel set her coffee down on the table and crossed her arms in front of her chest. "Can your head go up any more up your—"

"Alright, alright. Let's calm down, amigos." Ezequiel's voice made Marley lift her head. Soft-spoken, kind, and always willing to help anyone who asked, Zeke was the one Marley - and the rest of the team - respected the most. He gestured across the table to Marley. "Marley and I have some ideas."

"Will Marley finally share them?" Isabel asked. At the disdain, Marley tucked her head into herself, like a turtle within its shell.

"No need," Zeke said. "She's already put in the work. It's my turn to contribute."

She could feel someone's gaze on her, and she turned her head to the side to confirm. Mr. Elker was still looking. Her fingers flew to the bottom of her skirt, fingernails digging into the flesh of her knees. She wasn't comfortable speaking in front of people and she especially wasn't comfortable with being looked at. She wasn't about to start now.

Forcing herself to refocus her attention onto Zeke proved difficult.

Strong personality, Mr. Elker had said. Was it possible? *Did* she have what it took to command a room?

Marley dug her fingertips deeper into her flesh and cleared her throat. She'd whisper "Leave!" to whatever it was that made her feel like her insides were being torn up from the inside out. Today was the day she'd make her agency see that she was Marley Freaking Harrow, and she'd save all their asses so they could keep gossiping in Café 43 and bet on who'd be chosen for what project. They could keep being sheep.

But she'd be the shepherdess.

Zeke interrupted her thoughts. "Mar? You doin' alright?"

She shook her head and pressed her palms to her skirt. "What? Oh, yeah. Totally. I must have zoned out."

"Uh, yeah. I'd say so. Look around."

The conference room was empty, except for Brandon and Thomas in the corner, with Karl hovering around them.

"Huh. The lack of sleep must be catching up with me."

"I worry about you sometimes."

"I know." She patted Zeke's hand on her shoulder.

"I'll talk to you at lunch," Zeke said, patting her shoulder a couple more times. "I saw that green shinin' today. I'm excited to hear what you came up with. You'll get 'em next time. You'll have to, if you want to make senior this year. I know how badly you want it—and you deserve it, too, *amiga*. Don't forget that."

Zeke always said some variety of that after every meeting. Sometimes she wished she could keep her friend in her pocket so he could calm her down whenever she started to feel the spiral into the crippling self-doubt. How he still hadn't given up on her was a small miracle she gave thanks for every day.

Marley smiled up at him and nodded. "I know, I know. I'll see you later."

She gathered her things, grateful that this was the only meeting of the day.

"Marley! Hi!"

Marley tightened her hold on the binder and spun on the balls of her feet. She couldn't wait to be home where the only thing that would startle her would be her cat Cilantro.

"Hi, Karl."

"Someone didn't answer my calls last night," he sang, pulling his chair towards hers. Though the conference room was nearly empty, she felt like she was sitting in the middle seat of a crowded airplane.

"Oh, I'm sorry. I had my phone on silent." Marley was still disoriented. Maybe it was the lack of sleep and over-caffeination. Or maybe she was too aware of Thomas still in the corner of the room. He was looking over at her like he wouldn't let her leave without saying goodbye, but she wasn't sure she wanted a second hello.

Karl drew invisible circles with his finger on the back of her binder. "I guess it was pretty late," he said, defeated. Then, with greater gusto, announced proudly, "I wouldn't have wanted to wake you anyway. But now that I have you! Would you like to join me at Café 43?"

Marley felt her stomach drop. She did not, in fact, have any interest in joining Karl at Café 43. She *did* have all the interest in leaving, escaping, turning around and never looking back, especially now that Mr. Elker was ending the conversation with Brandon and making his way over to them. To her and Karl. She took a step back from Karl. They were not associated. They were not together. Just in case Mr. Elker was wondering.

Why *did* it matter if Mr. Elker was wondering that?

"Marley?" Karl asked.

She nodded in his direction. "Yeah, yeah, that sounds nice."

"Okay, great! I'll see you after work." Karl turned around and greeted Brandon as if he hadn't just spoken with him moments before. "Brandon! My man! Let's talk about this idea of yours!"

Marley barely registered Karl's excitement. They walked out of the room, and Marley went to follow them. *Out. Out. Get out. Irish goodbye. Out!*

But she wasn't fast enough. She was barely at the threshold when Mr. Elker called her.

"What'd you do with Marley?"

Marley pressed her binder against her chest and turned around slowly. He looked so comfortable, leaning against the table with his arms crossed in front of his chest.

"W-what do you mean?" she asked.

"The badass woman who was here before everyone else arrived. Where did she go?"

Was he referring to Isabel? Maria? No... they had walked in after she and Mr. Elker were already in the room. Was he really referring to her?

"Your name *is* Marley, right?" he asked.

"Yes. Oh. I…" Her eyes darted from his face, to the view of Granada behind him, to her feet. Why was she suddenly mute?

"Well, I'd personally like to request a return visit sometime. Maybe not with everyone. But with me? It seems this Marley is more of a… what's a shy animal that isn't shy at all if you call her hands 'small'?"

Marley considered it. She enjoyed games like these. They reminded her of the improv troupe she was part of in college. Her answer was quick.

"A bobcat would complete those requirements." The relief almost flooded her body. She *was* able to speak coherently!

A bobcat. A strong, competent bobcat. Shy, but at the ready if threatened. She loosened the strong hold she had on the binder and let the arm holding it swing to her side. Maybe she *was* worthy of such an identity. Surely, if someone had noticed it within her already, it had to be true.

Mr. Elker grinned. "Perfect. So what makes this Marley bobcat more comfortable? Coffee? Tea? A danish?"

"Oo.." Marley smiled in spite of herself. "A danish sounds amazing. Raspberry or nothing."

Mr. Elker wrinkled his nose. "Raspberry? Cheese is classic."

"I don't trust anyone who doesn't prefer raspberry."

Mr. Elker chuckled. "Hey, don't be mean. I'll rescind my offer."

"You were offering something? And you think this is being mean?" Marley thought of her father who had no qualms about slamming his office door in front of her mother.

"Yeah." Mr. Elker offered a sly smile. Something within her caught. Who was this Marley? More importantly, who was *he*? "I'm a sensitive man."

"You could have fooled me," Marley muttered.

"What was that?"

Marley looked up to see Mr. Elker grinning now, his eyes looking over his glasses in a way that pulled no punches about how amused Marley was making him.

"Oh, nothing. I suppose cheese *is* classic." Marley grinned back. This was like joking around with Karl or Zeke, with the exception that the other two didn't reveal a desire to step directly right in front of them and see what would happen if... But that would be wrong. Marley shook her head of the idea, remembering Lily's warnings to avoid workplace romances above all else.

"And you know, after the danish, it'd probably be good to provide some space. And time."

Mr. Elker's smile faltered ever so slightly. He pushed himself off the table. "That can be arranged."

She heard Lily's voice scolding her: *What are you doing? You know what The Rules say. Surprise him.* Marley could get whiplash from the conflicting advice.

"Mr. Elker?"

He stopped and turned around. Full attention. Eyes completely on her.

"I actually wouldn't mind a chai latte. That might warm me up." To you. To whatever is heating up between us.

"Oh." His grin spread slowly across his face. "That doesn't have to be the only thing to warm you up. Not in Spain, anyway."

Marley felt her cheeks grow hot. Was he flirting with her? Wasn't this sexual harassment? But if he was, and if this was, then why didn't she feel threatened?

Because if it made her feel wanted, it wasn't an unwanted sensation.

He chuckled as he walked away, calling over his shoulder. "'A Thousand Chai Lattes Lure a Strong Bobcat.' Now that'll be a headline for the Times."

Pay Attention to Who Wakes You

The excitement of the morning had passed. Marley was back in her light gray cubicle, where the only other things alive and breathing were the succulents in mini pink mason jar containers, pressed up against her hydro flask. Even the rubber duckie with sunglasses on looked tired. How did Lily make it through a day without afternoon crashes? Exercise and clean food? Who had the energy for *that*?

Marley leaned back in her chair and stretched her arms above her head, the muscles in her back and shoulders much too taut for a Tuesday. She looked around her cubicle's wall to the lounge, wondering what it'd be like if she were confident enough to strut right in and stretch like Cilantro did after a long nap on Marley's lap. Though people around her were wandering the office to make lunch or siesta plans, Marley was rotating the image for a Mariposa project on her laptop for the hundredth time, making sure it rested *just so*. How were people able to get things done so quickly? By the time they finished, she was still analyzing all the things she'd probably done wrong and all the things that could still go wrong.

"Marley! Hey!" Maria's voice made Marley jump. Arms still above her head, Marley panicked out of her stretch and pretended she was reaching for a sheet of paper from the top shelf instead. Maria was senior level and Marley didn't need Maria thinking that she didn't have the endurance to be on her team.

Maria's head popped into Marley's cubicle and then tilted to the side. "Time for a break! You okay, chica?"

"Yeah, yeah, totally fine. Just feeling that midday drag," Marley admitted.

"Why you don't like taking a siesta with us es un misterio. You should try a nap sometime. We have couches back there for a reason, you know." She gestured to the lounge.

Marley winced. She knew what happened on those couches. She wasn't about to lay her body on one of them.

She waved Maria away. "You enjoy," Marley said. "I'll get my break this evening."

Marley gave Maria what she hoped was her most encouraging smile. Maria didn't look as if she believed her, but Maria finally shrugged and left. Marley breathed a sigh of relief. It was cool that her colleagues still practiced the traditional Spanish siesta, but Marley's American-born-and-bred culture of productivity, er, work-until-you-die approach, admittedly made it too difficult for her to step away for a few hours and come back later.

Marley replaced her earbuds and, knowing that so many of her good ideas came when she closed her eyes for just a moment, breathed deeply. In. Hold. Out. Like Dr. Deidre had taught her.

She pictured what would happen when she finally came home: Cilantro would jump on Marley's chest and circle a few times, relieved that they were finally together and safe and tucked away from any potential dangers. They'd curl up and fall asleep, and Marley would finally be able to rest. She tried to steal the peace from a future moment, but it wasn't working.

And how could it? She couldn't possibly relax now. What had Mr. Elker meant by "a thousand chai lattes"? Did he really think she was that high maintenance or high strung that she needed *a thousand* of them to be lured and satisfied? What kind of vibe was she putting out there that he assumed she was some wild cat?

Her eyes sprang open.

Was there anything about her cubicle that gave it away? But what would he be doing looking at her workspace?

Still. Marley spun on her chair and stretched her legs, looking about her. She had a map of the world pinned into the wall behind her, with pink dots showing where she'd like to go and gold hearts revealing where she'd been. She ran her fingers over the golden hearts hovering over Banff and Warsaw and Dushanbe. *Was* she some wild cat? A feline who roamed, always searching for home? Or a wild cat, who pounced on opportunities even when she kept hearing "No"?

A rush of excitement filled her. No one had ever seen her in that way before. Shoot. She'd never considered seeing herself as a creature that was both so graceful and still inspired a bit of fear. That was Lily's M.O. Not Marley's. Not until now.

Marley scooped up her binder and pressed it against her chest. She stood, pushed her chair in, glanced at the black screen of her monitor and ran her fingers through her hair. It was futile, of course, with Granada's humidity overpowering her frizz tamer, but one glance and a fix was better than none at all.

A deep breath in propelled her a few steps forward. She craned her neck towards the creative directors' desks in the corner office, where Mr. Elker had moved in. Okay. He wasn't there. She breathed out. Another deep breath in. She pivoted. What was she doing? She wasn't the kind of person to just go up to someone - especially someone she maybe had a crush on. Probably. Definitely. She shook her head. What would she even say? She wanted to be around him. Soak up some of the ease and power with which he seemed to command himself. Her fear was stronger than her will, though, and she turned back around, shoulders down, walking back towards her cubicle like she'd failed an exam.

"Hey, hey, hey," a voice called. She froze.

Her heart dropped. She spun around.

Karl was standing with a grin. "You okay?"

"Yes. I'm fine. Thank you." *Now let me go so I can keep escaping.* She decided to be honest. "I'm trying to work up the nerve to meet with the new boss."

"What is there to work up the nerve for? He's as human as the rest of us," Karl said.

"Though true, you know that doesn't matter." One *uhm* or *hmm* and she'd lose her father's interest in her immediately. People weren't allowed to be human or make mistakes - unless you were Mr. Harrow, and then you were expected to make allowances.

Karl raised his eyebrow. "Why not?"

"Because that's not the way life works. People judge. People make assumptions. And if you're not one step ahead of them..."

Karl placed a hand on his hip. "Then what?"

Marley thought of all the New York agencies she had walked into for interviews, her confidence deflating the moment her would-have-been-employer scanned her up and down and inevitably asked her that *one* question that she hadn't rehearsed. Obviously the lessons from her father hadn't worked. *Ohs* and *uhms* really didn't pay the rent, and she never got a second interview. But she couldn't admit that to Karl. She wanted *Tigre* to look like her first choice; not a forced second.

"Then you'll always be misunderstood," she finally said.

Karl scowled. "I'm sorry you feel that way."

She shrugged. "Don't be sorry. It is how it is." Besides. It was thanks to those failed interviews that she was in Granada now.

"I hate it when people say that." Karl pointed over her shoulder. "Hey! There he is!" He stepped around her, as if he were going to walk over to Mr. Elker and demand he pay attention to Marley.

She ducked behind him, her forehead centimeters away from his shoulder blades. "Where?!"

Karl looked down at her over his left shoulder and smirked. "Are you for real right now?"

"See?" Marley blinked up at him. "You're judging me 'right now.'"

Karl shook his head. "What? It's impossible to judge you. There's nothing to judge. You have an impeccable record."

"If you knew the thoughts that scrolled through my mind, you wouldn't think so." Her fingers dug into his shoulders, like pulling him down with her would make them disappear. "Stop being so obvious," she hissed.

He turned around to face Marley, causing her hands to drop to her side. "I bet they're harmless compared to what other people decide to say out loud," Karl said.

"Whatever you say." She looked over his shoulder. "Does he look busy?"

Karl looked behind him, then looked back at her. His voice softened. "Even if he is. He'll make time for you. He'd be crazy not to."

"See you later?"

"Yeah, yeah. See you later."

Marley was already moving away from Karl and, as if an invisible conveyor belt was pulling her through, she let herself be carried until she stood steps away from Mr. Elker's desk. She sucked in a deep breath, a gulp of air that never found its bottom.

She didn't know why she was there. Sweat beaded underneath her hair on the nape of her neck. This would be a failed interview all over again; she knew it. But how else could she prove that she was cut out to be a senior level creative?

Mr. Elker was walking out of the adjoining conference room, Isabel close behind. Heat surged through her. Of course Isabel had gotten to him first. And why not? Marley wasn't anyone special. She didn't stand out. Just because he called her a competent bobcat didn't *mean* anything. *You're his employee. Colleague. That's it.* The settling in her heart was heavy, and she resolved to leave, until something caught her eye. A sheet of paper pinned against his cubicle wall.

Her name, scrolled in neatly slanted penmanship, with a few lines marked beneath it.

He had his eye on her. *And* he thought she was some hot shot presenter when nothing could be further from the truth.

But if he thought it *was* the truth, then she might just have a chance at that promotion. She would let him seek her out. After all, she didn't want to appear desperate.

Before Mr. Elker noticed her, she hurried back to her desk.

In the meantime, maybe a small nap wouldn't hurt her.

* * *

A tap on the shoulder jolted her awake.

"Marrlleeyyy," Karl sang. "What-chya doin'?"

Marley stretched her eyes wide and rubbed them. She pushed against the edge of her desk, rolled her chair back, and blew up into her bangs. "It was nothing but a short rest."

"I mean, sure. If you call forty-five minutes a 'short rest.' I came by at three and you looked so out of it, I had the urge to close your mouth so you wouldn't collect any fruit flies."

Marley's jaw dropped. "Tell me I snored."

"Just a little. Cute snores. Tiny ones. It was adorable."

"And you didn't wake me up!?" What if Thomas had been walking by, Isabel in his shadow? They were probably writing reports together, ready to send to Brandon, "Lazy American, Does Not Belong at Tigre" typed in the subject line. Marley slammed her laptop shut. She stood, stuffing her laptop and her binder into her cloth knapsack.

"Whoa. Hey." Karl's hand grazed the top of hers. "I'm sorry."

Marley blew out a shaky breath. "No, I'm sorry. I'm more tired than I realized. I've been staying up late working on Mariposa pitches. I barely had a weekend. I put in a whole day on Sunday and then Brandon had asked me…" Her voice trailed off. "And now that this Elker guy is on the team. I already know I'll be working most of tonight, too." She loved her job, and she'd give it her all, but sheesh. She could really use a break.

"But you're already running on fumes, Mar."

The way he said her name made something in her soften, like a frozen stick of butter in the sun.

"I know. But this is my chance to show that I don't need to be mid-level anymore." Getting the promotion at the hands of Mr. Elker because he knew her *work* was most important. The bobcat validation was just a bonus. She went to leave her cubicle, but Karl hadn't moved.

Karl twisted his hands uncomfortably. "So you probably don't want to go to Café 43 right now."

She snapped her head up. "What?"

"Our coffee date. You said earlier…"

She felt her eyes fold in on themselves. Oh, no. She *had* agreed to go out with Karl, hadn't she? She looked at him with his eager eyes and crestfallen face.

"That's right," she said slowly. "Yes."

"If you forgot, that's okay." But she knew it wasn't. He sounded so disappointed. And he looked so small, with his shoulders hunched, betraying his almost six-foot stature. She didn't want to go anywhere but her own bedroom right now. But she *had* agreed, hadn't she, some time during the meeting earlier? Welp. It was official. She would never get to sleep.

"I didn't forget!" she lied.

"Are you sure?" Karl asked. His sincerity slayed her. Of course she would honor her commitment. Not going would mean she wouldn't be able to fall asleep anyway, what with the guilt eating her from the inside as she'd replay the disappointment on Karl's face over and over again.

"Of course. Not letting down one of my very good friends is more important than going home. And alone? Ha! Who'd choose that over hanging out with Karl Courding?"

Karl's smile wasn't a substitute for sleep or caffeine, but the peace she felt at doing the right thing was worth it.

Besides. Marley always put others first. Why stop now?

* * *

Café 43 was popular, frequented by university students at lunch time, but overrun with tired employees at happy hour. The outside looked like a New York City restaurant along Columbus Avenue that she and Lily used to walk down after school, before Anne would send her driver to take Lily to her internship, leaving Marley to find her way through her favorite hiding places tucked within Central Park.

The red painted maple exterior didn't match the neon insides that blinked in time to the Spanish hits playing in the background. There was something comforting about the dissonant atmosphere. It made Marley feel like there wasn't a specific way she had to be; it was enough that she showed up and paid for a shot of espresso.

"I'll get us some coffee," Karl said, grinning at her while he scooted back a chair for her to sit in. Marley nodded, her gaze following a band member in the corner setting up the microphones.

"I hope this band is good," she muttered.

Karl laughed. "Not if they're anything like last night's burlesque show. It's not like you can really mess up Jazz, right? But those guys." He whistled, then nodded in agreement. "Yeah, anything would be better than last night."

She hoped for her sake that they would be. Watching people embarrass themselves was the only thing worse than being embarrassed herself.

She could tell it made Karl happy that she was there, with his skipping over to the counter. This is what her mom always went on about how it's "not about you" and "your needs can't overpower another's." But what about her needs? Was there a YouTube video about sleeping with open eyes? Marley wondered if Cilantro missed her as much as Marley missed her. Probably not. Her cat didn't need much. And that was a relief. Once she finished living for other people, she didn't have much left for her cat when she came home.

Karl placed an espresso in front of her and cradled his hibiscus tea. God bless him for knowing exactly what she'd order for herself. He sat in the chair across from her, his arms resting on the table in a triangle whose tip pointed at her. His lips twisted up into a smile. "Thanks for coming out with me."

Marley smiled. "Of course." She sipped her espresso and put the cup down. "Wouldn't have missed it."

"I noticed your green page at the meeting today," Karl said.

That made Marley lift and tilt her head to the side. "You did?"

"Of course I did. I always do. It was yellow for a few days." He tasted his tea, then nodded, cradling it in his hand. "Zeke took over in the presentations on those days. But today was green. Why didn't you say anything?"

She gulped. Marley Harrow was *not* a liar. Her white lie to Karl meant she had already hit her quota for the year. For the decade.

"I don't say anything because the very last thing I want to do is give someone a reason to judge me," she admitted.

Marley pressed into the napkin on her lap, as if she were ironing it with her fingertips. Karl's wide eyes betrayed the same surprise that Marley felt at sharing the truth. He reached forward and grabbed a sugar packet.

"Well." He tore the top of the packet and poured half of its contents into the tea. Marley resisted the urge to shudder. She couldn't imagine how much sweeter he needed it to be. He set the other half next to the napkin dispenser. "If you don't share on a day when your binder page is green, what will it take?"

"I guess I would have been ready today - if that Elker guy hadn't shown up. If it were the usual crowd, it would have been fine. But you know how I am around new people." Her phone vibrated. She frowned. "Sorry. One second."

Karl stirred his tea and turned to the television above the bar, one leg crossing over the other so his ankle could rest on the other knee.

She swiped her screen to reveal a text message from an unknown number.

How's the bobcat doin'?

Marley hid her phone under the table and looked around the Café's dining room: a group of young tourists here, an older woman making demands of the cashier and then, *there,* leaning against the end of the bar outside of Karl's field of vision, but very much in hers, was Thomas Elker. It didn't take long for the dread to fill her, the increasing heart rate stronger than the espresso.

"Karl? Excuse me for a second. I need to go somewhere a little more quiet."

He looked over with such concern, she imagined she'd been able to squeeze his face and honey would come out.

She grabbed her knapsack and walked straight past Mr. Elker into the adjacent hallway, convinced that he would follow her.

Thankful for the full-length mirror between the restroom doors, Marley fixed her stray hair in the mirror and patted her skirt. She straightened her back upon hearing footsteps behind her.

When she turned around, a dark-haired man with maroon pants and a bright pink shirt was pushing his way into the restroom. Whatever nerve she had had escaped. The cold sweat in her palm was as familiar as it was unwelcome, and she wiped it against her knapsack's strap. *Don't lose your nerve, Harrow.*

Her phone vibrated again.

She pressed the side to reveal the incoming message.

It's not nice to walk past someone without so much as a hello.

She groaned. This is why she did not do things that could lead to unpredictable results. *Unpredictability.* Ew. Look at all of the unnecessary stress it caused. Marley scowled. She did *not* want to become what she fought every moment of her life. Control meant certainty. Solid outcomes. Security.

She swiped out a reply.

It's not nice to pop up on someone's phone when you haven't officially asked for a phone number either.

She punched the send button and looked up to see a woman following a man into the hallway, only to have them split into their respective bathrooms. She thought of Isabel following Mr. Elker out of the conference room. What *if* she were more unpredictable? She bit her lip as she swiped out a more Lily-esque message. As she did, she felt her heart pounding out of her chest.

Besides. If you're going to pop up, then I have more than a hello waiting for you.

Was it the espresso or the adrenaline pumping through her that was making her so forward? Where was the backspace? *Backspace, backspace, backspace!* But she had already sent it. It was gone. Out of her control.

The ball was in his court. The power literally in his hands. She could feel the familiar mortification sinking in.

Was a roaring fire somewhere nearby? Or a dumpster where she could start a fire, throw the phone in, and walk away like those guys who walk away from explosions? Why was he texting her anyway? Was it for something for work? *Oh, God,* would he report her for cyber bullying or something? She only meant that it was customary to ask someone for their number before texting them pet name messages during happy hour. And why on God's greenest earth did she *have* to know that he didn't think she was the lamest person on the planet? She watched the three dots which indicated that he was replying... then nothing.

And then there he was: Mr. Thomas Elker, striding toward her in such a way that arrested her. Paralyzed her. Froze her in place. The confusion in Mr. Elker's eyes when he approached her told Marley everything she needed to know. He *did* think she was a jerk. And, if Marley was being honest with herself, she suddenly didn't regret sending it. She had watched too many Lifetime movies and telenovelas with Lily to *not* doubt a kind and thoughtful boss when she saw one. Though a creative director might seem harmless, he could totally turn out to be a stalker or murderer or something. *Don't show weakness, Harrow.* Check out her dad's advice coming through.

"How did you get my number?" she demanded. She didn't mean to be rude, but she also didn't have time or energy for his shenanigans.

Mr. Elker leaned against the wall, arms crossed. "Bobcat's a little tense this afternoon."

"Marley," she corrected. "My name is Marley. Sir." She clutched the strap of her knapsack like a tail wrapping around her forearm. She wondered where this confidence was coming from. She waited for him to apologize.

Instead, he smirked. How was he not flustered at all?

"I asked you a question, Mr. Elker. How did you get my number?"

"Of course. And please, call me Thomas." He leaned against the mirrored wall, so it looked like he was leaning against himself. "Yours was one of the first names I put on the list when I was placed on the Mariposa team. And Ezequiel made sure I had your phone number to ask you about the ideas you were hoping to share earlier."

Damnit, Zeke. She loosened her grasp and shifted from one foot to another. "Oh? Zeke gave you my number?"

"Yes, ma'am. But even before Zeke pointed you out, I knew I wanted to be on the same team as you. I've seen your work make it to the top three, consistently."

Ohh… *That* must have been why her name had been underlined at his desk.

Mr. Elker continued. "Most of my job consists of knowing all the work that my artists are capable of doing. And you, bobcat, are capable of very much."

The injection of flattery coursed through her.

He stood straight and uncrossed his arms, letting them swing at his sides, his hands clapping at the top of the pendulum, separating on the way down, meeting again on the way up. "And—" He leaned on the word. "If only the team had heard the speech you gave in that room on your own earlier, I'd bet your designs would be the top choice every time. Zeke giving me your number was just a bonus." He winked, then paused to consider her. "Aw, come on. If I apologized, would you look less upset with me?"

Mr. Elker's lips turned up into a crooked smile and she couldn't help but laugh, leaning her hip against the mirror. "Well. I suppose I could choose to be a little flattered." As if she'd had a choice; she tried not to be too "under the influence" of people she chose to be around, but it seemed she didn't have a choice in how she reacted when it mattered who focused attention on *her*. Especially if that person seemed to be this handsome man totally at ease in his body while she was, you know, trying to figure out which leg was more dependable to stand on.

Mr. Elker gestured up with his hand. "That would be a kind decision, if you didn't mind. I don't like feeling like I've made someone cross."

The tension in Marley's shoulders eased as she took her first real deep breath of the day. "Very well. Let's start over."

"I feel like that would be the best for both of us. I got a little worried when you walked past me with that strong glare. I wouldn't want to mess with you when you're on the prowl, bobcat." He winced. "I mean. Marley. I'm sorry. It just rolls off the tongue."

Marley lifted her head. "You know what? I don't see it doing any harm. Let's keep it."

Thomas grinned, as if what she'd said had made his entire day. And something within her shifted, a realization that she had an effect on him as well.

Someone exited the bathroom behind Marley. Marley caught the woman yawning as she passed.

Marley's hand drew to her face, trying to hide her own cavernous yawn.

"You're tired," Thomas said.

She rolled her eyes. "You don't have to say that again."

Thomas took a step back. "Not like, hey, you look so tired, I can tell by your face. I just noticed you earlier pounding that coffee back like you were taking in tequila. We can postpone. But I'd be lying if I said I didn't hope you'll schedule 'sleep' for this evening and agree to take a walk with me now. I'd like to get to know the designer behind all the work I've been admiring all this time."

She knew the Cromwell Rules enough to know that no one actually cared about what you had to say or what you did for a living; they asked to be polite or to set themselves up for a response. Or to trick you into thinking you mattered, when it was something else entirely they wanted. He had probably told Isabel the same thing earlier. She pictured Isabel leaving the adjoining room of Mr. Elker's office. *Men.* She would *not* fall for it. No, sir. She had standards.

"If you admired my work, why wait until now to randomly show up at a café and creepily text someone who's technically working under you?"

"Sheesh. Tough crowd. Believe it or not, I remember what you submitted for review a couple weeks ago. You're the director who sent in the sketch of the recycling bin morphing into a butterfly, right?"

She pursed her lips. Anyone could have slipped him that file as they were sharing information about his new team. But her breath caught as Thomas leaned forward, arm pressed against the mirror, as if it were solely his strength holding it up. His shirt hugged his muscles.

"Well?"

"Yeah, yeah, that was me."

"I know you have no reason to believe me, but if you really aren't interested, then just say the word and I'll let you get back to watching the game with Karl over there."

Marley bit her lip and looked up at the ceiling, as if it would give her a sign.

And yet, here it was. The opportunity for security. The chance to practice courage. What if she were throwing away an amazing opportunity? Zeke wouldn't have given her number to Mr. Elker if he didn't believe it was a smart and safe idea. On the other hand, she didn't know what the walk would bring. Such unknowns and potentially hidden agendas usually made her nervous.

Who was this man who had wreaked havoc on Marley's natural order of things in only one day?

Mr. Elker cleared his throat, drawing Marley's attention back in. "Very well, then." He nodded one too many times. "I'll see you at work tomorrow. Marley."

Suddenly, the prospect of him leaving without her was unthinkable.

"Ugh. I don't get this. I know you're my boss and all, but you're infuriating, you know that? Against all reason and understanding, I *am* interested." Lily wouldn't be getting married in five months if she hadn't taken risks with a man who made *her* feel something. In fact, Marley would be a hypocrite herself if she didn't follow-through on this - even if she didn't know what "this" was. Yet.

"So you'll walk with me then?

"Yes. I think I actually will."

"An 'actually,' huh?" He chuckled. "You're surprised that you want to."

Marley raised an eyebrow. "Do I have to watch every word I say around you?"

"I'm pretty good at details when I'm paying full attention."

"So you're paying full attention?"

Thomas nodded towards the mirror. "Have you looked at yourself in the mirror lately?"

She felt her eyes widen. "Definitely inappropriate banter between colleagues, Mr. Elker."

He lifted his hands in mock guilt. "I'm simply stating the obvious. It'd be silly not to pay full attention to a woman who commands it." She wanted to search the room for any sights of Lily. But no. He was looking directly at her. How easily he instilled confidence in her, holding up a mirror in front of her that had filters upon filters that she'd never seen herself through before.

"Command attention or not, I might stumble and say the wrong thing every now and then. I'm not perfect."

A man pulled open the bathroom door and stepped out between them. They watched him pass.

"I doubt it, Ms. Harrow. Something tells me you're very careful about what you say before you say it. You wouldn't sit out meeting after meeting otherwise."

She shifted her weight from one foot to the other. The way he was able to see through her made her both elated and uncomfortable. She lifted her phone out of her purse and pressed the side to see her home screen light up.

"It's been a long time back here. Karl will think something's gone wrong and come checking up on me." And the last thing she needed was Karl running the rumor mill tomorrow morning about Marley with Mr. Elker in the back hallways of Café 43. He'd definitely make it sound like the burlesque show had an encore. "I need to find my way back and let him know I'll be leaving."

She walked to the threshold of the hallway and the main room, but stayed hidden behind the wall. She turned to Thomas. "I can't just tell him I'm leaving him for another man." Marley's jaw dropped. "That sounded all kinds of awful." Marley tilted her head back and sighed, running a hand down the side of her face. "How do I get out of this?"

"Well, you can go up to him and say, 'Thomas is saving me from this sorry excuse of a date. See you tomorrow!'"

She shook her head. "I can't say that! No way. He's my friend."

He sidled up behind her, so close that she felt the tip of his shoe hit the back of hers. She waited for the rising panic, but felt nothing except an uptick in her heart rate. What would it feel like if his fingertips grazed her side?

She sucked in a breath and tried to steady her voice. "What's another option?"

He stepped back. "What would be most true to what Marley would do and think is right?"

She was surprised by the question, but liked that he was making room for her judgment.

Marley turned around to face him, tucking her hair behind her ear, suddenly very aware of his proximity to her. She lifted her chin. "Well. I *did* already show up, and if I were to tell him I didn't feel well, he would understand. He *is* watching the game, so it probably wouldn't break his heart if I left." She noticed the clear glass door leading to the street perpendicular to the entrance. She pointed to it. "Why don't you wait for me outside that door? I'll tell him it's time for me to leave and I'll meet you out here in a sec."

Thomas grinned, already walking backwards towards the exit. "A strategizing woman. Definitely an asset to the team." He pushed the door open with his back.

"Do you want anything for the walk?" Marley called.

"Nah. I don't drink coffee. I've already got one addiction." He lifted his hand, a cigarette already tucked between his fingers. He winked. "See you soon, bobcat."

Marley pressed the back of her head against the wall and welcomed a big breath in. The blush in her cheeks would help convince Karl that she wasn't feeling like herself. Because she wasn't. Not really. It was like the part of herself that she had always kept hidden was slowly making its way to the main stage - and she was curious to see who *this* Marley was.

She walked back to Karl, who had been looking over the heads of other guests. He waved when he saw her, arm fully extended and moving to-and-fro like one of those balloon guys who advertised car lots in Brooklyn.

Marley lifted a hand and waved to and fro at her shoulder. She repositioned her knapsack and wondered how she could make her gait look more pitiful. It must have worked, because Karl frowned and walked over to her, abandoning what Marley knew was his prized seat for game watching.

"Is everything okay?" The concern he had for her was almost stifling. She was a grown woman. Even if she weren't okay, it didn't mean that she wouldn't find a way to be.

"Yeah. No. It will be. I'm feeling a bit under the weather. Is it okay if we continue our chat tomorrow? Maybe pick up the coffees before work tomorrow and start our day in the lounge?"

Karl cast his eyes downward. "If you didn't want to be here, you just had to say so, Marley."

"What? Of course I want to be here. I just know I'll be better company tomorrow." She swallowed the guilt of another lie. She didn't want to tell Karl that somebody more interesting was waiting for her outside. Someone who made *her* feel like a somebody.

"Do you want me to walk you home?"

"What? No!" Marley said, louder than she meant to. "I mean, no. It's not necessary. I'm a big girl." She smiled. "I'll see you tomorrow."

"Okay," said Karl. "If you say so."

Marley turned from Karl and walked out of the main entrance. She didn't look through the window to watch Karl's reaction. Sure, he was a kind man who wanted to spend time with her, but on the other side of this café was the kind of man who usually wanted to spend time with Lily Cromwell, not with someone artsy, mellow, and shy. Not with someone like Marley.

But what else was she supposed to do?

A man could have more than one addiction - and apparently there was a bobcat in town.

Make Connections

Marley was grateful for the evening sun in Spain; even though it was only six, the cobblestoned streets wouldn't change from bright red clay to grey stones until Spaniards would gather for dinner after the sun set. This evening in particular, it made Mr. Elker's brown hair shine like the polished maple table in the Cromwells' dining room. It made Marley want to run her hand along it in the same way, if only to press down the bits that were standing up of their own volition. How were some people able to get away with hair that looked equal parts party and perfect? She didn't have a middle ground; she was either "put together" or a hot mess. And even when she was "put together," it wasn't nearly as close to how perfect Lily always looked. She pushed that thought out of her mind and gripped the loose tweed bracelet on her left wrist instead.

Thomas turned towards her, pulling the cigarette away from his lips and blowing smoke up and away from her face. "Got away clean and easy?"

She let go of the bracelet and chuckled. "Mostly. The man knows how to rock a puppy face."

"Some people have a dangerous puppy face, to be sure."

"Yeah? How's yours?"

"I'll save mine for another day. When I need your forgiveness."

"'When'? Not if?"

"When," he repeated. Thomas kicked his foot out. "In which direction shall we venture?"

Marley looked down the road where his body was facing. She pointed in the same direction. Maybe he already had a destination in mind. Far be it from her to ruin someone's plans.

He took long strides, but they were easy, like he wasn't in a rush to get anywhere. She sped up a little to match his gait, taking two steps to make up for his one.

As they walked uphill, she took in the magnificence of the Alhambra, the palace built by Moorish people centuries ago, and wanted to pinch herself for the millionth time, so often did she forget to believe that she was lucky enough to live *here*.

"Where are you from, bobcat?"

"New York City, sir."

He nudged his arm into hers. "Hey. None of this 'sir' stuff. Please. It's embarrassing."

She smiled up at him through a shrug.

"New York City, huh? What made you want to work for an agency like ours in Spain?"

Was this an interview disguised as a casual walk? If it was, Marley knew the answer; she had practiced it over and over and over again before applying for this job.

"There's something about small agencies that I find promising. There's potential for so much growth. I feel like there's more room for artists to have a voice. ...Even if I don't use mine all that much," she admitted. "But at least my art makes it into ads more often than it might if I were working for an agency in New York. Besides, I needed to go in a different direction than everyone else seemed to be going. I want to be successful, but I have no interest in the rat race. Like, my best friend, for example, often works sixteen hour days, only to change clothes — or not — and go out with someone new. I mean, before she met the guy who became her fiance."

Why was she telling him this? Especially since it'd be most honest to admit that she moved away from New York City because the thought of her work being judged by millions of Americans was debilitating. It felt safer to be across the pond from the judgmental Cromwellian crowd.

"Honestly, when I saw the job offer online and wasn't getting responses from small agencies around the States, I sent in my application right away." She sucked in a breath. Admitting that Mariposa had not been her first choice was scary; in her experience, when people didn't feel like a priority, they typically stopped being nice to you.

Thomas nodded, and they walked in silence past a café where a man and woman were deep in debate, a newspaper held down by a cup of chocolate and churros. She felt like she was the newspaper rustling in the wind, unsure of whether she was doing the right or wrong thing by being so open with her boss, but feeling pinned in place all the same. Marley didn't dare ask him what he thought of her for that decision, but it was driving her wild that he wasn't telling her one way or another. This discomfort always felt like it was eating her from the inside. She forced herself to look around, like Dr. Deidre would have recommended. *Grounding*, she called it.

A bookstore advertised a buy one, get two free deal that she'd have to check out later. And there was the boutique where Marley always stopped for stationary and stickers. Part of living abroad was the delight of sending snail mail. She smiled to herself when she thought of the Just in Case letter written by high school Lily to Lily's future self that listed what Lily *actually* wanted in a relationship. Marley had sent it to Lily a few months ago, hearts bordering the small message she'd spent hours crafting: encouraging, but not pushy.

Marley should remind Logan one of these days that he owed her for sending it, prompting Lily to pursue Logan because it's what Lily's heart desired, not because of Anne Cromwell's rules. But no, Marley would never throw it into Logan's face like that. Lily deserved to be happy. Marley was simply following the promise she'd made Lily to remind her best friend of what truly mattered to her - not what Anne Cromwell believed would lead her daughter to her happiness.

Mr. Elker's voice interrupted her thoughts. "How long have you lived here?"

"Sorry, what's that?" Marley pulled the tie out of her hair and shook her head.

He took one more drag of his cigarette and put it out against the traffic stone separating them from the street, throwing the accordion paper onto the street. "How long have you been in Granada?"

"Oh! It'll actually be a year this next weekend."

"Nice! How do you like it?" Thomas asked. With his hands clasped behind his back, Mr. Elker looked like he was on a casual Sunday afternoon stroll on a trail in Connecticut and not in Spain on a busy Thursday evening.

"Do you mean how I like my job, or Granada, or?"

"Sure. Both. Neither. Whatever keeps you sharing what's on your mind."

Heat flushed through her. He was so curious about her. She was not typically an open book like this, especially with someone who was practically a stranger. "You're asking me the questions, so it's not like you're *not* getting what's there to share." Thomas chuckled. "Would you have shared those thoughts if I hadn't prompted a response?"

Marley twisted her lips at the corner. "Probably not." They continued in stride; one step of Thomas' to two of Marley's. His hands unlocked and began to swing at his side. She imagined adding in a few steps to catch up and slide her hand into his, but kept hers firmly at her side.

"Well then. I'll keep asking questions and you'll keep answering and we'll eventually get to the bottom of Ms. Marley Bobcat Harrow."

She squeezed her nails into her palms. "Hope my answers won't be too predictable," she muttered. Why did it matter so much to her that she stood out? That she impressed him?

"Ha!" Thomas barked. "You are anything but predictable, bobcat."

She raised an eyebrow.

"It's true," he assured her. "Like, right now, for instance. I can tell your mind is going a mile a minute. But nothing for those outside the mind to enjoy. I could guess at what you're thinking or how you'll respond, but you keep so much locked up within yourself that I don't even know where to start looking for the key. So I'll keep asking questions, as long as you keep wanting to answer them." His bright smile made her feel like he had just put out his cigarette on her.

"I do have many doors," Marley admitted. "Some with barbed wire over the handle. Most have a complex alarm system. But I'm pretty sure I threw away the keys to many of them."

"Yeah?" The way he breathed out that question made her steal a glance at him. Something about the way he looked back at her drew her in, like he had captured her with his gaze alone. The way he seemed to want to understand her? To really *see* her?

The thoughts within her pushed past the dam, a river ready to cover his feet. "I guess I just like to wonder about things. I try thoughts on for size, you know? Decide whether I like this one or that one better, or how this affects that or… I'm always thinking about how there's more to what I don't know, so how could I ever share it confidently?" She brought her fingers to her lips. "Like, right now I'm thinking I'm just rambling on without any purpose. I need to rehearse something a hundred times to make sure it's perfect."

"Hey. Not everything has to be perfect, or fulfill an objective, or be for a purpose. Sometimes, things can be just to be. Like doors with barbed wire on them. I can still enjoy the door and not necessarily go in. We can enjoy the things around and within us without always attaching meaning to the experience."

How anti-Cromwellian. She'd have to make sure not to have him in the same room with Anne. She decided to try on for size what her best friend would argue.

"Isn't that just a way to say you're making unintentional life choices?"

"Not at all. I intend to make life choices that satisfy me."

"And what satisfies you?"

It was Mr. Elker's turn to raise an eyebrow. "Who wants to know?"

Marley felt her cheeks grow hot. "Not like *that*. I meant, what makes you satisfied? At peace? Happy?"

"Friends. Family. Alcohol. Cigarettes. Baseball. Knowing I made somebody's day better."

Marley noticed that a reference to a *Mrs.* Elker was missing and felt a bolster in her step. But she decided to be sure. "So you're riding solo in your search for satisfaction?"

Mr. Elker chuckled. "What alliteration you have."

"I'm the woman with the words!"

She resisted the urge to slap her forehead. Could she be any more lame?

But he grinned, and she felt herself relax. "You sure are," he said. "And I do 'ride solo'; I really enjoy my alone time. But…" He gestured toward her. "When I find someone who makes time more worthwhile than it would have been had I been alone…" His voice trailed off. He smiled as if to himself, and then kept walking.

Was he referring to her? Was *she* making his time more worthwhile? More than Isabel? More than the other women a handsome man like that spent time with while drinking, watching baseball, and smoking cigarettes?

They turned a corner and Marley bumped into him. Ooh, he was firm. She shook her head of the thought and looked where Mr. Elker's head was turned.

Thomas whistled. "Would you look at this beauty?"

The rays of the sunset hit the window of the shop in such a way that the gold lettering glittered like sunbeams reflecting from a peaceful sea at dusk. Marley squinted, trying to read the shop's name, but it was much too bright and the lights from inside the shop weren't helping. She inspected the golden swirls surrounding the name.

"That is some intricate handiwork," Marley noted. "Check out the detail in the ornate border." The swirls and circles looked like a machine had printed them as a sticker on the window, but Marley knew to look for the tiny crevice where the paint brush had been lifted, revealing a "real-life" artist. She moved to the side to get a closer look when she saw Thomas' reflection grinning at her.

"Like I said," Thomas said softly. "Would you look at this beauty?"

Marley felt the blush crawl up her neck. She forced herself to refocus on the art in front of her.

"It's a jewelry store!" She cocked her head. "You know, I don't think I've noticed it before."

"Would you like to go in?" Thomas asked.

"Oh, I wouldn't want to take any more of your time." But that was a lie. Now that he had admitted all the time he spent alone, satisfied, she felt the challenge of wanting to be the one who made his life better just by being there. What a powerful influence to have on somebody.

"I don't have anything waiting for me at home," Thomas said. "We can go in. I'd be curious to see what catches your eye in here."

Marley couldn't hide her grin. She pushed open the door of the shop. Jingling bells announced their arrival.

The showcase room was in the shape of a perfect rectangle, cases covered in glass that protected the pretty shiny things lying on violet velvet. The lights gave the impression that they were walking through a tariff-free airport. Marley wasn't sure if it had been the short walk here, or the lights waking her up, or the presence of Thomas standing next to her and waiting for her to comment on jewelry that made her feel how she typically did a couple hours after midnight, when her brain was awake, alive, and ready to create.

She nodded at the jeweler behind the counter, who pointed at the cases, identifying the pieces resting within them: "*Arretes, collares, brazaletes, y...*" The woman grinned, passing glances between Marley and Thomas, tapping the ring finger of her hand. "*Y anillos de compromiso.*" She winked.

Engagement rings?! Marley's jaw dropped. "*O no no no! Él no está mi novio.*" *But if he wanted to be my boyfriend...*, she thought, before silently scolding herself. She could have sworn she heard the woman say something like "not yet," but Marley pretended she hadn't heard and moved towards the glass cases that held the necklace pendants.

Marley passed over the howling wolf. A mountain range. A bowling pin? The diamond-bordered meteor. She considered the maple leaf, each edge sharp and precise. But she paused at a waterfall, where turquoise crashed into white diamonds at the bottom. It looked heavy and she wondered what type of person would wear it. Maybe a grandmother who wore loose pantyhose with sensible shoes, but still went out with her friends for brunch and wore purple hats. She chuckled to herself.

Then, she gasped. A butterfly, but different than one she'd ever seen in jewelry before.

Instead of wings tilted up in flight, *this* butterfly had been caught in the moment right *before* it left the flower.

She looked over at Thomas, who was perusing the bracelets. There was a strange surge of pride in realizing that he would come when she called. It made her feel, what, desired? Wanted? Irresistible. Seen. All the things she felt like she typically shied away from.

"This one!" she called over her shoulder. "Look!"

She waited for him, her interest in something pulling his in like a reel. The tug was the same, too, like they were already linked somehow. She didn't move when his arm touched hers.

She pointed. "I love how this one shows what it can still be."

Thomas leaned over the case, but didn't pull back from her either. "What do you

mean?"

Maybe it wasn't attention itself she was scared of. Maybe it was the moment following the attention. On her. Because, suddenly, with him right next to her, she was nervous about how the words tumbled out and what he thought of them. Without a chance to manicure her thoughts before they were shared out loud, people could get the wrong impression. They'd judge her without knowing the story. And then what?

People often left when they didn't like what you had to say.

Her dad was a perfect example of that.

"Hmm," Marley considered, but she got distracted by his hand on the glass, nose almost touching it. Marley cringed a little, knowing someone would have to wipe it at the end of the night. But maybe it was standard practice anyway, and fingerprints were expected. This was not the time to pay attention to something so trifling, but she was Marley, and it was what she did. She decided to shake it off. "Well. Butterflies are typically portrayed with their wings frozen in the opposite direction. It's like a rebel butterfly. Or rebel artist. Whichever it is, I like it."

Marley's gaze jumped from pendant to pendant. Who were the artists behind these creations? Like this pendant that featured an oblong table with small people gathered all around it, the tiniest of amber specks symbolizing the meal they were about to enjoy. It was the length of Marley's thumb and stretched the size of her palm. If her mother were a grand-mother, she'd be so proud of her tight-knit family that she wouldn't mind having it pinned to her chest. Her shoulders drooped as she pictured her mom all alone at the dinner table, no prospect of a future grandchild whatsoever.

Thomas was saying something, but Marley couldn't hear him. Or, rather, she already knew that what he was saying couldn't compete with the ideas firing away in her mind. This happened often, only much later at night, when her mind seemed to make connections faster than at any other time of the day. She knew Lily felt it, too, only in the morning hours before everyone else came to the office. They both experienced the flow when exciting ideas and big dreams collided. They talked more about those dreams and ideas than about people or politics or the latest fashion trends. Their ability to pull something out of nothing was a shared gift they had each stumbled upon and nurtured together in high school — and contin-ued now more than a decade later. It was like being on a highway where one car is driving so fast that it bumps into another, which gains momen-tum and bypasses one just to hit another, until a pick-up truck rams into a semi carrying dynamite and the entire scene erupts in a fantastic, mov-ie-like, mind-blowing explosion. It was like that now—which was strange, since it was the middle of the late afternoon and, just an hour ago, she had wanted to go home and think about absolutely nothing.

At once, the idea came to her. If the goal of advertising and market-ing was to make the client's product stand out, be noticed, and judged *well*, then the advertised product should make the customer *feel* something. And if they didn't have said product, it would make the customer feel as if something was missing. Like they were naked.

"Thomas!" The name felt intimate on her lips. Somehow, she knew it wasn't going to be a name she would say often. Reserved only for moments such as this. For the man who invited her on this walk, who encouraged her to come into this joyería, who *asked* for a front-row seat to how her mind worked.

He must have gotten the same impression, because he straightened his back and turned to her, his hands clasped behind his back.

"Yes, ma'am?"

She clapped her hands together like the little girl in the gif that Lily would send right before she'd come to visit. *This* was her favorite part of calling herself creative: the familiar rush of a new idea being birthed out of *her* imagination. She felt her chin rise higher. She blew her bangs out of her eyes, her breath and heartbeat quickening. Now to get this idea out without stumbling too badly over her words. She reminded herself not to start with "This may be dumb, but…" or "I know this might not work, but…" and decided to own it instead.

"*Mariposa* sells compost bins, trash cans… Anything for garbage, right? Those are not exactly the sexiest items on the market. Even the names of the items we sell sound ugly. But what if we convinced *Mariposa* to start selling jewelry from recycled materials? Or, if that's too big a step, we would at least put designs on the trash bins. 'Bedazzle' them." She knew she was talking fast, but she was on the highway and hitting car after car after…. "People love personalizing things. Or having accent pieces. Why *not* trash bins? We do it for bathrooms, but why not kitchens? Cubicles? Oh!" she squealed. Her pointer finger was dancing in front of her as if she were drawing on a white board with it. "We could highlight the ideas of local high school kids." The finger zigzagged to another invisible idea. "But we would ultimately design them." She took out her phone and shook it so that the camera option would turn on. "We'd make them so beautiful and eye-catching that people will *only* want *Mariposa* compost bins. - I can't take a picture of these, can I? That seems illegal. - If we make the designs on the bins just as beautiful as the ones on the jewelry as the ones in the marketing materials…"

Thomas looked at her with eyes wide and mouth agape. He thought she was being ridiculous, didn't he? Her dad was always shaking his head at her, with that stupid patronizing smile that said, *Aw, you're being so cute, but let's be serious.*

"Sorry," Marley said, dropping her hands and cast her eyes downward. She kicked her foot out. "I get excited. I would obviously have to look at all the metrics to see if it even makes sense for the company..."

"Hey, hey, hey." Thomas interrupted, placing a hand on each shoulder. "Stop." Warmth coursed through her. "You have nothing to apologize for. That is a *really* good idea. And presented with passion - just like I saw before. *That's* the bobcat. Keep her out."

"Yeah? You think so?" His encouragement rested somewhere in her bones, swimming in between her muscles and cartilage, her veins buoyed by his opinion.

"You *have* to present it to the team tomorrow morning," Thomas said.

"What?" Her veins suddenly felt solid - cold.

"Please?" He squeezed her shoulder once more before pulling away.

With dry mouth and shaky breathing, Marley couldn't believe she was nodding. "Yes. Okay. I'll try."

Thomas pumped his arm in jubilant victory. "Excellent! Now take pictures of these before that woman comes back with the engagement rings I told her to get."

"What?" Marley guffawed. "Why would you tell her to do that?"

"Because—. Just take the pictures."

"But what about that?" Marley pointed to the poster of a camera with a bright red X on top of it.

He snapped his fingers. "Quickly now. It's less illegal if people don't see you do the illegal thing. And besides. Taking the picture means you're basically saving the jobs of those at Tigre and those who make the compost bins *and* the budding artists... Not taking the picture would be the less immoral choice here, friend."

Friend?

Marley snapped a few pictures of the pendants. Unfortunately, the sound on the phone was turned up enough for the old-fashioned camera sound to go off, and a disgruntled noise started yelling from the back.

Marley stuffed her phone in her bag, eyes wide. Thomas motioned her soundlessly to the door, and they were out a few seconds later. When the door shut behind them, she erupted in giggles.

Marley pressed her shoulders against the brick wall of the alley. With Thomas in front of her, she suddenly felt conscious of the way her chest lifted when she breathed in. When was the last time she had worked out - not for ideas but for, like, sweat and stuff? The flesh falling over her waist-band certainly told a story. She'd have to start cranking out more dance and spin classes before Lily and Logan's wedding. Definitely before a second date with Thomas. Because this certainly felt like a first one.

Typically, increased heart rate signaled an impending panic attack, or a warning that she was in danger. But it didn't come. In fact, she could swear she could hear her inner bobcat purring.

She was safe. Mr. Elker liked her work. So what if she hadn't been able to talk to the whole conference room this morning, or any other morning before that? Maybe it wasn't about making huge leaps, but taking small steps, one after the other - like a walk, with a person who understood her art - and gave her the confidence to believe she could make more of it.

Be a Good Listener

She'd told Karl that she'd have to stay up late to work some more tonight, but she didn't mind. Her mind was racing with ideas - and she couldn't wait to create the concepts and prepare for the presentation. *Tomorrow.*

So when Marley heard Lily's ringtone, Marley pushed aside her work, excited to update her best friend about all that had transpired. Lily would be so proud of her, stepping out of her shell like this - and all in one *day*!

But when Marley answered, she knew that this was one of those nights when she wouldn't be getting a word in.

"Anne wants to send *another* picture to Firefighter Weekly. It's adorable thinking of Logan as a firefighter, don't you think?!"

Marley swallowed her disappointment and turned on good-friend-listener mode. "Can you be in Firefighter Weekly if you're not actually a firefighter?"

"I mean, he *did* rescue me from a burning building," Lily said.

"True. But you know that doesn't make him a true-blue fire fighter. People work so hard to earn that stuff." Marley held her breath. Lily didn't receive the truth well sometimes.

Marley could hear Lily rearranging her cellphone against her ear. "You're so right." Marley exhaled. *Safe.* "You can't be an idiot and decide to run into a burning building."

"People do idiotic things for love," Marley added. Like take pictures when it was clearly not allowed.

Lily pressed on. "Besides. What engaged man would prance half-naked for a photoshoot, anyway? I don't want another woman getting the idea that Logan West is available. How could my mother suggest such a thing?"

"Maybe it's safer for Logan to hide in plain sight within a fire fighters' magazine than in, say, *The Wall Street Journal*." Last Marley had heard, Logan had been under investigation for sabotaging his company's investment portfolio. She hoped it wouldn't catch up with the two of them later down the road. Few things could mess up marital bliss faster than prison.

"Ha! Too true." Well. If Lily wasn't concerned, then Marley wouldn't be either.

Marley muted herself. She didn't want the commotion of her climb up the creaky stairs, weaving between this neighbor and that, to make Lily feel unheard. Marley hated it when people would pretend to listen to her but would still be looking at their computer screens or cellphones. Undivided attention mattered. Spending time with Thomas earlier had cemented that belief.

Lily continued on about the pros and cons of a calendar modeling contract, especially in terms of how worried she would have to be about other women who would have the nerve to come on to Logan West. Marley thought of her father, who had the wisdom to divorce her mother after realizing that even though he was married on paper, his heart had walked away from their family a long time ago - and that court wasn't a place he wanted his family to be.

Marley unmuted herself. "From what I know about Logan, he doesn't seem the 'wandering eye' type, Lil. Surely he wouldn't put himself in situations where women might get the idea that he was."

"I'm turning on the video so you can see my face," Lily said. Marley dropped her knapsack at the inside of the door. Though she was still a little bummed that Thomas hadn't offered to walk her home and they'd separated soon after leaving the jewelry shop, Marley felt like all the air had finally been let out of a pressure-tight container.

Marley set the phone against the cereal box on the kitchen counter and smiled as Lily's face popped up - then frowned as Lily arched her eyebrow. "I trust *him*, obviously. It's everyone else I don't trust."

Lily was saying something about only being okay with Logan being Mr. December if she could be in the same photo. Marley leaned over so Lily could still see her laugh and stripped off her light cardigan. It peeled off her skin like the soggy backing from a temporary tattoo.

She slid the tie out of her hair, grabbed her phone, and walked a few paces to the bar - if you could call it that. Bottles of various sizes rested on scuffed wood. Did she want liquid the color of autumn leaves, or the stuff with the stiff smells that still made her shudder, or one of the heavy reds?

Ah. The bourbon. The smell of the whiskey wrapped around her, and she felt herself relax.

Man, that girl had a lot of feelings. Going on and on about her mother the same way she had when they were sixteen. The only difference was that now, instead of complaining about how many suitors Anne Cromwell had chosen for Lily, the number of events Lily was expected to bring Logan to were growing in number. Why couldn't she just be happy? Lily was living the life that so many dreamed of. How could she possibly keep finding more things to be so unhappy with?

Marley brought the phone to her desk, leaned it against its back, and settled her chin into her balled up fists, one standing on top of the other.

Marley knew that Lily wasn't really upset; if she really were spiffed, her voice would be lower in tone and a bit more subdued. No, this was the Lily that enjoyed the extra drama. Nothing like the Lily of a few months ago who'd been post-surgery and believing she'd never see Logan West again.

How things had changed.

Something shifted in Lily's voice. Marley decided to tune back in. "I mean, he'd be asked to be Mr. December and then some artistic director like, I don't know, that *Isabel* you work with, will see him and seduce him and it'll turn out that she's a swing dancer too, and I just cannot risk that. He's *my* Mr. December. And why does he even need to be in a magazine anyway?"

"Isabel is married," Marley pointed out. "I think. I actually don't know." Shouldn't it be obvious when someone was committed to someone else for life? Like, there was no doubt Zeke was hitched. Marley stood and walked to retrieve her laptop.

Lily rolled her eyes. "Because that's ever stopped people before."

Marley opened her mouth, then closed it, sitting it back down to open her computer.

"Oof. I'm sorry, Mar. I didn't mean to bring it up."

"No, you're right." She typed in the password. Her dad had proved the frailty of marriage time and time again. She dropped her hands and smiled as Cilantro tapped her thigh. "Where does Anne get these ideas, anyway?"

Lily looked relieved to change the subject.

"Where Anne gets all her ideas from: Claire and her circle. Rose has been extra friendly lately. Even Ashley has been checking in, but I've already texted them; they promised to give Anne an excuse as to why they cannot be in the wedding party."

"Won't their mothers throw a fit?"

"We're so used to mothers throwing a fit at this point, what's another one?"

Marley ran her fingers through Cilantro's hair, reflecting white against the bourbon glass that she lifted to her lips with her other hand. As she set it down, empty, she thought of her mother tiptoeing into her father's study to remove the dirty dishes that had accumulated throughout the day. How Marley had wished that Peggy would have thrown a fit. Yelled. Screamed. Finally gotten fed up. Threw a glass or plate at the perfectly stacked books on the immaculate shelf. Maybe it would have kept her father in line. Maybe he would have had to face what he would eventually lose. Instead, they had hardly made any noise, only fully relaxing when he hadn't been home.

Lily's voice brought her back. "So it's only going to be you and me, girlfriend."

Though she knew that Lily's closest people, like Vanessa, would also be in the wedding party, Marley beamed at the thought of being the only woman from Lily's past to have earned the honor of standing next to Lily at her wedding.

"Who did Logan choose for groomsmen?"

Lily pulled her head back. It was nice to see that even she could have a double chin. She stammered. "I didn't tell you?"

Marley shrugged. "We're busy. It's okay if you forgot."

Lily frowned. "You know I hate using 'busy' as an excuse. It must not have been a priority. I'm sorry I didn't tell you."

It was Marley's turn to show her double chin. "Did you just apologize?"

Lily laughed. "It's the therapy. 'Kill the ego,' Dr. Deidre is always saying. 'Apologize.'"

If someone took a picture of Marley now... Marley leaned forward. "You see Dr. Deidre, too?"

"Yes, ma'am! I figured, if this therapist is the one who helps my amazing best friend always knows what to do and what to say and how to live so peacefully and courageously... then I want to learn from *that* person, too."

Marley didn't know what to say. "Wow. Lily. That's so nice of you to say." Lily was typically the first to point out what was wrong with somebody, not what was right. "I'm so flattered that you think that of me."

"How could you not know that? I had the courage to change my whole life because of a letter you sent me."

"But *you* wrote the letter. To yourself."

"But *you* knew when to send it. And you've always made sure to lovingly steer me into the direction I *should* be going in, not the direction I - or my mother - think I should be heading towards. I know that I didn't make it easy. I owe you so much, Stitch."

"Alright, alright. Stop it now. Bring pre-Deidre Lily back."

With Cilantro on her lap and the bourbon was warming Marley from the inside, making her bolder. She opened the Mariposa folder and opened up a fresh template. It would be time to end this conversation soon so that she could keep working.

"Okay!" Lily had returned to business mode. "Vanessa, Genny, and Jeremiah will be on our side. Katie and Logan's best man, Uriel, will be on his side."

"A bit unconventional, are we?"

Lily shrugged indifferently. "It's not important to have a show of a hundred bridesmaids. I know who I'm close to. Ashley and Rose can suck it."

Marley couldn't help but laugh. "So dignified and classy, our Lily Cromwell."

"For real. I'm so glad we're keeping it small. It's hard trying to be so perfect for everyone all the time. Oh! Hold on. Let me respond to Jeremiah's text real quick. He's on a date with a colleague of ours that he's had an eye on for a while and totally blowing my phone up."

A date with a colleague… Marley's mind drifted to how Thomas had clasped her by the shoulders when she'd apologized for her enthusiasm.

While Lily typed, Marley started dropping and dragging images onto her digital canvas and thought. That was kind of messed up, wasn't it? Apologizing for the way her excitement could have potentially made someone else feel uncomfortable? And did Lily not realize that Marley felt the same about the strive for perfection? The desire to be perfect was the reason she froze when it was time for her to present at work, or why she avoided speaking in public at all costs. It's why it took her forever to say a project was "done." It was because of the Cromwell judginess that Marley knew what people could say about her if she *weren't* flawless - so she just didn't say anything at all. You can't judge what you can't see or hear, right? But she could never admit that to Lily, the queen of control in chaos. Lily handled mistakes with such grace. If Marley attempted the same, she'd have the road rash, burns, and scars that would prove her incompetence. Anne would finally have the proof that Marley had never been good enough to be Lily's best friend.

"Okay. Back. He can't believe that his date didn't want to share the tiramisu. He wants to know if that's a deal-breaker."

"Not sharing dessert *with a colleague* could be a dealbreaker for his *job*, couldn't it?"

Lily shrugged. "Meh. What Greg doesn't know won't hurt him. There's no stopping true love, Marley Harrow."

Marley let this sink in. She thought of Thomas saying earlier that not seeing something illegal made it less illegal. And was it true that nothing could stop true love? Is that what could happen between her and Thomas? She shook her head at the thought. *Much too much, much too soon.*

"Let's rewind," Marley said. You find it hard to be so perfect for everyone all the time?"

"Of course I do," Lily said matter-of-factly. When you grow up with Anne correcting every single thing you thought you did right the first time… you get kind of paranoid. I get how you wouldn't understand, since Momma Marrow is the sweetest woman on planet Earth."

"Yeah. She is." Her stomach constricted as the image of her mother eating alone at the dinner table appeared in her mind's eye again. "But regardless of who your mother is, you're embracing your life as your own responsibility now. Focus on how far you've come."

"That's true. You are the best, Mar. Always putting things in perspective for me. What in the world would I do without you?"

"Aw. Thanks." She didn't know what else to say. Marley Harrow: the best listener of all time. Funny how you got good at what you hoped people would do for you. "Tell me more."

Marley muted herself again. As Lily went on about her day, Marley flipped through her planner. Hours were marked from morning till night. She was paid for her ability to crank out creative idea after creative idea and she knew she could, especially if Mr. Elker would be reviewing them. If Lily ever asked, Marley would tell her that, by the third meeting of the day, she usually felt like running through the streets with no desire to return, or curling up into a ball on her futon and sleeping until the night like Cilantro did during the day, when everyone was sleeping and no one else could disturb her. But then this Thomas Elker guy came and apparently she didn't need to wait until the sun went down to have her lightbulbs go off. He was like her superpower.

Why hadn't Lily noticed the pink in Marley's cheeks, still there from when Thomas had told her before saying goodbye that he was already counting down the minutes until the morning? *He was probably just being nice.*

Marley didn't want to interrupt Lily, but she also really wanted advice: Should she play it cool tomorrow? Should she pretend like this evening's walk and talk had never happened? What was the protocol here? Why couldn't *she* text Lily like Jeremiah was now? Freaking out in real time, desperate to know the next right thing to do or say.

She listened a little longer to Lily mentioning something about going back to the swing club. Marley grinned and said it sounded like fun.

"You sound tired. I've been jabbering on and on and never even asked about your day. I'm sorry." Her smile looked genuine.

Yes, Marley wanted to say. *Seriously*. Instead, she relented. "It's okay. I've got work to do tonight anyway." Preparing for a presentation and *everything*, she wanted to add.

"We'll talk about you tomorrow, okay? Promise."

That made Marley smile. If Lily wouldn't be there for the pregame, at least she was committing to the postgame analysis. "Only if there's ice cream involved," she offered.

"I'll call that one shop - *Geppetto's*? - and make sure they have that gelato you love."

"A month's quota in one day, I hope."

"At least. Nothing but the best for my girl," Lily said. She smiled wide at the camera.

Marley laughed. "If you're not making time for ice cream, what are you even doing with your life?"

Lily laughed. "Exactly."

Others could say what they wanted about Lily, but the girl made anyone feel special when she smiled at them. It was reserved for only her closest people, and Marley knew she was lucky to receive it often.

She couldn't wait to tell Lily about how she would have finally presented in the morning—even if Lily didn't know it was one of her main struggles. Marley would save everyone's jobs *and* ask if her boss would agree to have a drink with her after work. If Jeremiah could ask his colleague out for tiramisu… In fact, maybe if Lily was doing all this changing and growing because of *her*, Marley could step into a relationship with Thomas, just to see where it would go. She would finally let go of always having things under control and see where life would take her. A true adventure.

There's no way she would have ever said any of that out loud.

But for once, she couldn't wait to find out what would happen when she did.

Stand Up For Yourself

Marley stared at the way the conference table curved. It was quiet. The main door to the office opened and shut as people arrived. Marley had already been here for an hour.

Surely it was fine that Marley had woken up two hours earlier than she normally would have. It was understandable that it had taken almost an hour to double-triple-quadruple-check that her makeup wasn't too much, but enough to make her look like a dominant force in the room. It was appropriate that she had scoured online forums that discussed the pros and cons of wearing glasses during a presentation. But what wasn't fine or understandable or appropriate was that she knew she wasn't getting dressed up because it would make her feel good. Not even for a second.

It was that she hoped Thomas Elker would notice.

Why did Lily have to be five hours behind her? Lily Cromwell would never be caught awake at three o'clock, but surely if Marley told her it was an emergency… *No.* Her incompetence wasn't an emergency; it was just who she was. Nobody could fix that.

Marley flipped open her binder one more time and skimmed the answers to the questions that had woken her on her own at the three o'clock hour. She'd texted Zeke then and let him know what she'd need his help with, grateful that he wouldn't hesitate to assist. Three hours of sleep hadn't been nearly enough, but it was more than nothing. She knew the questions each colleague was most likely to ask or challenge her on. Isabel would make a snide comment - for which Marley would have a classy Cromwell answer; Isabel wouldn't realize until later that what Marley had said was actually an insult. She didn't even know why she'd come to work so early. It's not like she felt like rehearsing for the eighth time.

At the same time she closed the binder, a cup with a Café 43 label around it slid into view. She looked up to find Karl grinning in front of her.

"Morning, Mar."

She couldn't help but smile back. "Hi, Karl."

"I brought you some coffee." He beamed like a three year-old presenting a drawing to his mother.

"I see that," she answered. *But why?* "I'm sorry I left you hanging yesterday." A tinge of guilt threatened the confidence she had been trying to summon all morning.

"I don't blame you. Things happen. I just hope you're feeling better. That's why I brought you a little somethin' somethin'. Tu favorito."

She forced a smile. "Thank you so much. I *am* feeling better. You are so sweet." *Too sweet.* There was a "nice guys finish last" category for a reason. How would Lily tell someone like him that he was doing too much?

Out of the corner of her eye, she spotted Thomas stepping into the room.

She forced her attention back on Karl, but he was already looking in the same direction.

Karl nodded towards Thomas. "What do you think about that Elker dude?" he asked, leaning against a chair. But it started to roll, and he started falling. Within seconds, Karl regained his balance, crossing his arms in front of his chest like nothing had happened.

Marley chuckled and stood, gathering her binder. "What does it matter what I think about him?"

"Only because, you know, since he's the new assistant C.D. and someone who has final say on our work?" Karl raised an eyebrow. "Would there be any other reason?"

"Yes. No. I mean. Right. I mean, I guess he's alright. I don't know that much about him." And that much was true. She *didn't* know much about him, other than he was handsome, a good listener, and made her feel like she was ready to deliver a boss presentation.

And now he was walking in their direction.

Marley busied herself with stuffing the binder into her knapsack, but couldn't keep herself from watching him.

Thomas strode next to Karl as if he'd been invited. He looked so at ease, a cup of coffee in his hand. She felt his gaze fall on her, and the heat rose along her neck. His was such an unassuming stare, like he expected nothing but hoped for everything. She wanted to know how to be that comfortable.

Thomas nodded in Karl's direction. "Karl, right?" Marley blew up into her bangs. *As if he didn't know.*

"That's the name behind the brain, yes, sir, Mr. Elker."

Marley cringed for him.

Thomas chuckled. "I shouldn't have wondered where we get all our exciting slogans from. Looks like they all come from right here." Lifting the Café 43 cup, Thomas pointed his finger towards Karl's temple. Marley didn't know whether to laugh or be embarrassed for Karl, so she stood there in silence instead.

"How's my Bob—," Thomas started. Marley widened her eyes. What was he doing? He couldn't call her a pet name in front of people!

Karl frowned. "Bob?"

Marley tightened her grip on her knapsack. She gritted her teeth and bit down on the first idea that came to mind. "Bob is doing fine, thank you."

Karl looked from Marley to Thomas to Marley again. "Who's Bob?" Karl asked.

Marley scrambled for an answer. "My cat."

"Your cat? Cilantro?"

"Yes. I call her Bob sometimes." Marley kept going. "It was good I went home early last night. Poor girl had an upset stomach."

"Exactly," Thomas said with a wink. "I wanted to check up on the cat. Make sure she was doing alright, especially after a night like yesterday's." He offered her the cup with a gleam in his eye. "Here's a good-luck-cup of mojo." She received it with a smile.

Then he turned to Karl.

"See? You're not the only one on the team with rhymes." He winked, but Karl didn't so much as a crack a smile.

"*But is it soy?*" Karl asked incredulously. "She'll erupt if she has dairy."

Marley gasped. "Ka-arrl!"

Thomas looked like he was holding back an eruption of laughter, but he kept his composure.

"It *is* soy," he assured them. He lifted an eyebrow towards Marley. "Soy chai latte, right?"

"Yes!" Marley exclaimed. "You really shouldn't have. Thank you."

"Nonsense. It's the least I could do for all your help yesterday." Thomas smiled. "Can't wait to hear you present to the team. Oh, and hey. Nice glasses. They look good."

He walked away, leaving behind a box of Pop Rocks where his hand had been leaning moments before. She took the box and slipped it into her sack, a small smile stealing across her lips. The glasses had been a good choice. And a strong option through which to glare at Karl, who looked like he'd just found a parking ticket on his car.

"You were so tired, and Cilantro - I mean, Bob? - was sick, and you still helped him out yesterday? Don't let this job steal your soul, Marley. There's a job and a passion, and then there's workaholism, which leads to burnout."

"Oh, it wasn't anything special," Marley fumbled. A rising panic started in her chest. She didn't want to keep lying to Karl, but she also didn't want him to feel like he was second-best. "Just a quick chat."

"And he found a way to hype you up enough to be able to present today? Gosh." It looked like someone had dimmed the lights in Karl's usually bright eyes, but then his smile turned the lumens on and his voice softened. "I'm glad for you. Zeke and I have been waiting for this day for months. We'll be rooting for you."

He started walking towards his seat when he stopped and pivoted. "Maybe give the other coffee to Isabel. I think lattes are her Tuesday days anyway."

Something in her stomach twisted at the thought of Isabel being next on Karl's list if Marley wasn't going to be first. She lifted her latte and smiled at him through gritted teeth. "Will do."

She noticed Zeke waving for her, so she hurried to the front of the room. He tilted the brim of his imaginary hat towards her and she playfully curtsied in response. Everyone settled down faster than normal, probably because it was so rare that Marley Harrow presented. Or maybe they wanted this meeting to be over as quickly as possible. Did that mean she should skip over the detailed parts of her plan? *What would Lily do?*

Lily would proceed as normal, regardless of what others may expect or how they might react. A thousand could-be scenarios didn't run through Lily Cromwell's mind, requiring contingency upon contingency plan. She'd believe in herself and her good ideas and present them as such. Marley would try to do the same.

"Good morning, everyone," she said to the center of the mahogany table. Zeke coughed, so she forced her gaze to focus on the hands above the table—those respectful enough not to be texting under it—and then lifted her head higher, looking right above everyone's heads, just like Margaret had suggested at their last coaching session.

She nodded to Zeke, who pressed the button. They both turned towards the screen.

Then, Marley began. "I'd like to propose a new juncture for *Mariposa*."

A blue morpho butterfly flew from the bottom left-hand corner, passed over the compost bin in the center, and flew to the right-hand corner. It transitioned to a second slide where the butterfly landed on a gold piece that transformed into a bright blue necklace—a stationary figure of what had been in flight moments before. Then, she nodded to Zeke to start narrating the idea just as she had asked him to. He added the flair - the rise and fall of his voice pulling their colleagues in like he had thrown an invisible lasso around each of them. From the corner of her eye, she noticed Isabel put her phone down, something in her eyes glistening. Excitement? A challenge? Marley stole a glance at Mr. Elker, who was leaning back in his chair, his legs relaxed, hands wrapped around the ends of the armrests. And suddenly, it was like someone had turned down the volume on Zeke's voice and turned up the heat in the room. Mr. Elker's posture beckoned something out of Marley. What would it feel like if she climbed on top of him? Would he let her? Where would his hands go?

Zeke cleared his throat and knocked Marley back into reality. She was so not being professional right now, but how could she be with Thomas looking at her like that? Or was she just imagining it? Her heartbeat wasn't helping her figure out the difference.

When Zeke finished, Marley nodded towards Maria, who flipped the lights back on. While others rubbed the dark out of their eyes to let the light in, Marley asked the room for any questions. She held her breath. This was always the part where presenters would find out whether the ideas were passable, good, terrible, or great. But nobody made any sounds. The silence stretched on.

Isabel fidgeted in her seat and looked pointedly at Mr. Elker before turning to Marley. "Who's going to pay for this?"

Mr. Elker raised an eyebrow. He must be so impressed and intrigued by this woman who somehow managed to look both relaxed and in charge at the same time. It's what made all the men stand at attention around Lily, too. If anyone would make senior level first, it'd be Isabel.

Marley squared her shoulders and continued. "Mariposa would cover all the costs. We would provide the marketing on these new products and their audience would come through in droves. The ads would bring in money and Mariposa would keep Tigre on as their marketing agency. It's a win-win."

"So why aren't you going to Mariposa with this? Why show us?" Mr. Elker asked.

Now *that* one she wasn't prepared for. It's not like she could say *because you told me to.*

Isabel hid a coughed-out chuckle behind her fingers. "Great question, *jefe.*"

Marley narrowed her eyes. This is where Isabel and Lily differed. Lily would never patronize a colleague like that, let alone in the middle of someone else's presentation. She looked around the rest of the room. Where was the support that Karl or Maria received after their presentations?

Her colleagues looked at her curiously, like she was a foreign creature. She thought about how Karl made her uncomfortable. Did she have that same effect on others? A pit in her stomach expanded. Standing up here next to Zeke probably made her look like a mouse instead of a bobcat. Who did she think she was assuming this position? The door never looked farther from her.

She tried to calm herself down. This was part of the job. If she were ever going to be senior level, she had to swallow her pride and deliver the product. If she wanted to stay in Spain, she had to keep her job. If she wanted to impress Thomas Elker, she had to square her shoulders and take the hits. *Especially* since they were coming from the Associate Creative Director himself. Even if they were coming from Thomas.

She dug her fingernails into her palms.

"Our gift here at Tigre is making dreams come to life." She took a step forward. Who knew that averting eye contact took *so* much effort? Instead, she let her gaze dart from Karl, to Zeke, to Maria. "We create reality, you guys. Which of us doesn't lay awake at night thinking of what could be possible if we just *made* the opportunities? 'Why wait for the perfect moment when you can create it instead?', right?" She sent a prayer of thanks to Lily. "That's what we're doing here by creating the campaign *first* and then showing the possibilities to Mariposa later. They'll be hooked and creating jewelry and bedazzled compost pins in no time."

"'Build it and they will come', then?" Mr. Elker asked.

"Yes! Exactly!" Marley grinned. But her smile faltered when he didn't grin back.

There was silence. Then, Karl shook his head, looking apologetically at Marley. "That doesn't work, Mar."

"That approach has been debunked," Isabel stated. Her voice was so hard. Was Lily this scary at IceStorm?

That was all the permission to disagree that her colleagues had seemed to need. Others joined in, a cacophony of doubts and shuffled papers.

"Trash and jewelry? How in the world will you sell that?"

She heard Zeke answer. "Have you ever heard of 'One man's trash is another man's treasure'?"

"If we're speaking in cliches, we might as well start looking for new jobs," somebody added.

Isabel stood. "It was a sweet idea, Marley." She nodded towards Zeke. "We should all be preparing presentations like this to see what sticks."

What sticks? How could they not see that this *was* the idea that would save their jobs? They only had to see beyond their own limits.

"Well, this was nice while it lasted." Maria was the next to stand. "I call first nap."

Each doubt was another kick at the bobcat. She pictured it hiding its head with its paw. Marley's shoulders slumped.

As others rose, Mr. Elker leaned farther back into his chair, looking every part the boss.

Brandon raised his hand for attention. "Thank you for your presentation, Marley and Zeke. We'll take a day to think about it and reconvene after people submit their reviews. Any ideas on how to save our asses are welcome, so we thank Harrow and Marquez for taking the lead."

A murmur of patronizing agreement later, everyone filed out of the room. Only she and Zeke remained.

It didn't matter that Brandon had given what sounded like a pity thanks. Marley felt her face burn, and she frantically searched for something for her hands to hold onto. There was nothing. Only space.

"Marley," Zeke started.

"That was terrible!" Marley cried. "I thought this was the idea that would 'save our asses,'" she said, dropping her air quotes.

"No, it was! I mean, it wasn't! It is!"

"Make up your mind," Marley snapped, then softened her voice. "Ugh, I'm sorry."

"It's okay, *amiga*. Your ego is bruised. That happens after presenting sometimes. When they question your darling, it's hard. Especially when it's only been a darling for a day," he added.

"Why the hell did Elker go after me like that? Once he cast a shadow of a doubt, everyone else did, too. He basically gave everyone permission to hate on this without even giving it a chance."

"He wasn't 'going after you,'" Zeke said. "He was giving you a chance to defend your idea even more. It's better to have an ally challenge the idea than a foe, right? Elker was helping you out. 'Coal becomes a diamond under immense pressure.' Or something like that."

Marley crossed her arms. "He planted the coal just to watch me burn."

"C'mon. You don't believe that."

She let her arms fall. "No. I don't. But it made me feel better for a second to think it."

"It's not fair to him."

"Whose side are you on? It wasn't fair to *me*. He knows how nervous I get."

"Does he?"

She paused, thinking about the ways Mr. Elker had seen her yesterday. She didn't express how nervous presentations made her - and all he saw was a confident and enthusiastic Marley.

"No. He'd have no reason to know that about me. He only knows what he's had a chance to learn from last night. Thanks for that, by the way. It was a really nice walk."

"Wait. What?" Zeke closed the laptop and pushed it into his backpack. He zipped it up, but pressed his palms against the edge of the table, as if he'd just heard terrible news. "A walk? You two went for a walk? He mentioned wanting to meet up with you, and I knew you'd be at Café 43 with Karl. That's the only reason I gave him your number."

Marley couldn't lie to Zeke. "I kind of ditched Karl."

He stood, arms gesticulating. "What? Why? Karl is your fiercest supporter - even more than I am. Why wouldn't you keep him around for a conversation with Elker?"

"Mr. Elker - I mean - *Thomas* - didn't seem interested in a conversation with Karl." Why was this difficult for Zeke to understand? "He wanted to talk to *me*. So I gave him a chance to get to know me, without interference. I didn't need anyone to do the talking for me." Not this time, anyway.

"Marley, listen." Zeke's voice sounded harder. "I have to tell you something. I don't want you to have reason to dislike Mr. Elker, but I know him, and I know that I would not have given him your number if I knew he was going to take a *stroll* with you yesterday. I thought he'd just meet you at Café 43 like anyone else would. Be careful with him. He's got a reputation."

She dug through her sack and held on to the box of Pop Rocks. "What do you mean, 'a reputation'? What kind of reputation?"

"He's been around for a few years now, and I don't know if he's changed, but let's just say he's gotten away with a lot. He's either reformed or become an even smoother smooth talker. I noticed the way he looks at you. Remember to set boundaries."

So she hadn't imagined it. Thomas *was* looking at her in that way during the meeting.

Zeke must have noticed the look on her face because he repeated his warning: "This is your job, not a bar to meet one-night-stands. And trust me, Thomas Elker is about as one-night-stand as you can get. Don't fall victim to his charm."

"Are you kidding me? Someone else takes an interest in my ideas and suddenly I'm 'falling victim to his charm' because I finally had the courage to stand up and share them? It can't be that he genuinely takes an interest in my work? In *me*?"

Zeke looked wounded. "I've had an interest in your work the whole time, chica. So has Karl. And Maria."

Marley felt something in her soften, but the bobcat was still out with baring teeth. "I appreciate your concern, but I don't need to be supervised. Thank you for sharing the presentation with me and always having my back." She took a deep breath. "You know? Maybe it's time I stopped relying on you so much."

Zeke frowned, his brows furrowed more than Marley had ever seen them. "Tienes razon. An answer to my prayers. You can start carrying your own weight around here. Act senior level instead of just talking about it all the time. Maybe then, people will finally be able to take you seriously." He swung his backpack around his shoulder and left the room.

What in seven hells had just happened? Zeke was mad at *her*? And Thomas liked her? But Thomas also had a reputation Marley had to look out for? She had suspected that people didn't take her seriously, but it still hurt to hear it said out loud. By one of her most trusted, supportive friends.

And then it was like a tsunami wave hit her, knocking the ability to breathe out of her. She released the Pop Rocks and pulled out her ukulele stress ball. She swallowed long deep breaths in and breathed out shaky shallow exhales. She brought Dr. Diedre's suggestions to mind. *Notice what's around you, Marley. Mark the space. Count backwards from 200.*

The wall was white. The table was brown. Her watch band was light pink. It was a little cloudy outside.

You are safe, you are safe, you are safe, she repeated. But Marley couldn't make herself believe it. And the bobcat was nowhere to be found.

Be Bold

Marley had double-checked that nobody else would be using the conference room for the rest of the day, but she prayed the door would stay closed anyway.

Marley threw what must have been the fifteenth tissue at her feet. The ukulele looked tired and squeezed out of whatever it may have once offered. She leaned her head against the cabinet door that held Tigre's snacks. She hoped the pulled-down shades and closed door would deter any hungry visitors looking for them.

Marley hated her panic attacks. They were always inconvenient, always unwelcome, and never helpful. All they did was remind Marley that she was weak in the face of adversity. Her stomach swam remembering how her dad would shake his head upon returning her to her mom. She'd run into her mother's arms, flooded with relief that she was finally safe again. She no longer had to defend herself against the defense lawyer. She wished she could feel her mother's arms around her now. She yearned for home. But which one? The Spanish flat where Cilantro waited for her, or the house in New York, her two-story bedroom, sixteen again where her biggest problems actually seemed to be Lily's?

She fumbled with her phone, checking her messages. There was a message she had missed from Margaret, a selfie showing her bright eyes, her mouth open in excitement. "You're going to crush this presentation!!!!" was written in white text against a black bar at the bottom of the photo.

Marley couldn't help but smile. Margaret was the best - one of Marley's biggest cheerleaders.

She opened her contacts. Her finger hovered over the picture of her mother's squinting eyes, so big was her smile at being surprised with a trip to Granada to visit Marley. As much as she wanted to call her mother, though, Marley didn't want to give her cause to worry. Besides, there was no way that Marley could explain what she was feeling without her mother asking yet *again* if it wasn't time to come back home for a little while? All it would probably do is start her mother's day on a sour note. Her father had done enough of that to them since Marley was young, and Marley did not want to follow in her father's footsteps. Moving to Spain was Marley's choice, which meant that Marley had to carry the consequences. Marley would only call her mother when she had a good report and felt confident that she had a plan to navigate these stormy waters on her own. More than that, proving that she was strong enough to handle it would prove that her dad had been wrong about her all along. Most importantly, she'd be able to prove it to herself.

She scrolled up to Lily's name. It was weird to think that Lily's name would be lower in her contacts list in December after she'd adopt Logan's last name. Lily West. That made Marley laugh. Sounded like a country singer trying to make it in Nashville.

Marley wiped her eyes. She would tell Lily about this fiasco and they'd laugh about it. Lily would make fun of Karl —*again*— especially after Marley told Lily about Karl's "*But is it soy?*" question. Marley chuckled. Thinking about her best friend being there for her felt like lifting a heavy stone that had been holding her heart down against its will. She was by herself right now, in this moment, but she certainly wasn't alone. And she'd get to have gelato later. All was not lost.

She started to pick herself off the floor when she heard the door knob squeak and turn.

No! *Come on.* Marley gathered the tissues scattered about and threw them into her knapsack. She pushed herself off the ground and pulled her hair into a ponytail, making sure no hairs were scattered about. Her cheeks still felt puffy, so whoever was opening the door had better believe in sudden allergic reactions.

She hid her eyes under her hand in anticipation of the lights being switched on, but the room stayed dark. Her head snapped up.

A man's silhouette sidled inside, closing the door behind him. "Marley?" the voice whispered.

Thomas. It was as if an electric bolt surged through her spine. Her gaze flew to the windows. People of the opposite sex were not allowed to be alone in the same room together, let alone with the lights shut off, shades down, and a shut door. Warnings from Anne Cromwell coursed through her. *Never put yourself in a position where someone would get the wrong idea.* And if someone walked in right now, like Zeke, he would get the totally wrong idea.

Not senior level appropriate.

Not *any* employee appropriate.

She cleared her throat. "I'm here. Had quite the cathartic yoga sesh. Didn't realize I'd fallen asleep and…"

"Hey. Only the truth with me, please," Thomas said. He advanced a few steps until he was standing in front of her. "What's wrong?"

"Maybe we should talk about it another time." She glanced over his shoulder. Maybe she could walk over and open the door just a little bit. "Or in the lounge?"

He tilted his head in question. "Marley? Do you feel uncomfortable being in the room with me?"

"Just saying. It's against company protocol. People might get the wrong idea."

"People would get the wrong idea if a colleague wanted to talk to another colleague about that colleague's presentation earlier?"

Marley considered that notion. It sounded totally understandable from that perspective. Besides - the way he smiled didn't make her feel like she was in danger at all.

"I'm sorry," Thomas said. "I just wanted to check up on you. See if you were okay or needed anything. I can't have one of my best artists locked in a room having a panic attack."

For some reason, she preferred that Thomas had seen the panic rising within her, had left her alone, and then chose to be in the same room with her anyway. If he could accept her in this way... in her sensitive mess... it would be like opening the smallest of windows into her feelings. Maybe even the door that she'd never permitted herself to open before. What did she have to lose?

She turned away, pacing two steps away only to pivot and walk until she stood directly in front of him, her forehead just barely grazing his chin. She looked up into his eyes. Gosh, they were handsome. Hazel. Gentle. Aware.

"Zeke is mad at me," she admitted.

He looked surprised. "*Zeke* is mad? At *you*? Did he say as much?"
"Well. No. He didn't have to. I can just tell."

Thomas raised his eyebrow at her. "O-*kay*," he drawled.

She sounded like a crazy person, didn't she? Marley blew air into her bangs. "Okay. Fine. He's not mad. I just feel like he's disappointed in me." Thomas leaned against the wall. "How could anyone be disappointed in you, Miss Responsible Dependable?"
"I wasn't prepared for today's meeting." Her bottom lip quivered.

"You *were* prepared, though. Your voice was confident. All bobcat, all the way. And those animations were done so well. In one night, no less. Did you even sleep?"

She waved the compliments away. "I slept a little. Three hour siesta. Spanish style."

"Yeah, but Spaniards wake up at ridiculous times to go dancing, not to work."

"Hey, now. Ridiculous to who? It was just a couple of hours though, and then I went back to bed."

"Only to wake up to do it all over again?"

"Precisely."

"I'd call that impressive, but how is that sustainable?"

"It's been working so far."

"If it were, you might be more open to feedback."

"Ouch."

"Hear me out: when people don't get enough sleep, they get sensitive."

"I'm not—. I'm open!"

He gave her a look.

"I am! I'm open!"

He looked over her arm to check her bag, his arm caressing hers. "How many tissues do you have in your bag right now?"

"Hey!" She pushed his arm. "You're not supposed to pry in a lady's bag."

"It's not prying. It's observing." Thomas smirked, but relented. Then, in a quiet voice layered in calm and kindness, he asked, "Can I at least give you a hug?"

Marley looked up at him, earnest brown eyes looking down at her. His question made the scary waters look like a hot spring she could wade in - and his arms extended to welcome her in.

And suddenly it didn't matter where they were or what their job titles were. He was a human being extending kindness to another human being.

"I would love one," she admitted.

He wrapped his arms around her, clasping her to him like they'd done so a thousand times before. She tightened her grasp around his torso. They squeezed just so, and Thomas' hand lingered on her lower back, traveling to her hip and then departing.

It must have lasted for only a moment, but even after he'd released, she could still feel the etch of his arms around her digging deep.

Come back! her body cried. It was like getting a whiff of her mother's cookies before being hurried out of the kitchen — only she was allowed to have cookies after dinner, and she wasn't so sure she was allowed to sink into a longer embrace with Thomas. Zeke had been right, of course. She needed to keep her distance from this man, even if a growing part of her couldn't imagine how that would be possible.

"Thank you," she whispered.

"Of course. Any time. Get some sleep and we'll see you back here tomorrow." He turned to exit. Marley eyed his maroon pants, appreciating the way his shirt tucked just so into them.

Part of her was relieved to have him go. The closer he got to the exit, the more she could relax that she wouldn't be caught fraternizing at work. But there was no doubt that they were becoming friends, and friends were allowed to hug and comfort each other.

And colleagues went out for drinks all the time.

"I could use a drink," she blurted.

Thomas turned on his heels. "Oh?" he asked.

She pulled on the strap of her knapsack. It dug into her shoulder. "Yes. Dinner, drinks, and dancing. That would make me feel better."

Thomas chuckled. "You've had that bad of a day, huh? Dinner, drinks, and dancing. In that order?"

"Not all on the same day! But you're right: if I'm working so hard, I should learn to let loose a little. Especially on a Friday night. It might inspire some creative energy that I could bring to the team later."

"Now you're talking! Which one tonight?"

"A drink. Weren't you listening?" She smirked, and she tucked away this moment to report to Lily later, who'd high-five her boldness.

"Whoa, whoa, whoa. Easy there, bobcat. If I hadn't been listening, I wouldn't have stopped so quickly when you spoke up."

She laughed, glancing down at her feet. On her way back to look at him, she noticed the tissues sticking out of her knapsack. What was all that crying was for if she had three reasons to jump for joy now?

Besides - dancing had brought Lily and Logan together. Maybe such a move would work out in her favor, too.

It was only one drink.

Between friends.

Why the hell not?

Put Yourself First

When Thomas had asked where they would be going for drinks, Marley hadn't wanted to confess that there was only one place on the list. She had always dreamed of being a patron of El Bahama, but thinking of going in there on her own would have been like wearing two poster boards connected by strings with "Obviously Single and Awkward" painted on them.

El Bahama had an unassuming exterior: steel grey with a single red lamp hanging over the entrance. There was something dark and mysterious that lured Marley, like a siren that promised a seductively good time. During her quiet walk from work, she'd pass El Bahama and wonder about the gorgeous women gliding in. Once, she had managed to sneak a peek inside when the steel door was held open for a woman whose body glistened with confidence. Against the tight white material of her dress, her posture had commanded attention - and there was no doubt that she would receive it in that coveted place.

So when Thomas was opening the door for *her*, who was wearing capri jeans and a thin red hoodie, Marley felt that her spontaneous request to bring Thomas *here* had been a grave mistake.

"Maybe we should go somewhere else," Marley said. She pulled her hoodie strings, wishing she could pull the hood over her head and hide her face from the bouncer who undoubtedly recognized her, the voyeur of El Bahama.

As they passed beneath the red light, Thomas asked, "Always wanted to partake in the 'red light' district, have you?"

"What? No! Of course not."

Thomas chuckled and shook his head, placing his hand on her lower back to steer her forward. She felt her cheeks grow warm, but attributed it to the heat coming from the pink neon lights that guided them from one end of the hallway to the other.

She followed the lights with her fingers. "These lights remind me of Texas. The roadhouses have neon signs like this." She wanted to slap her forehead. Idiot. Couldn't think of anything more eloquent to say?

"This place looks pretty amazing. I don't think I've ever noticed it before."

"I've been wanting to come here for a while," she confessed.

"I'm glad to give you a reason to come." Thomas paused and touched the neon lights. "Some Amsterdam out front, some Southern inside... I like when things aren't what they seem. Especially when that kind of magic happens in bars." Static electricity hovered over her skin as his arm reached out in front of her. "And in women."

Thomas pushed the curtain out of the way, and led Marley into the room. It looked like it was covered in ice, everything was so translucent, clear, and blue. Reflections from chandeliers reminded Marley of old speakeasies she'd visited with Lily in Chicago.

Thomas whistled. "Check out that bar!" The four shelves of bottles against the wall were backlit with the same cool blue that made people's shoes glow as they hunkered around the booths along the perimeter. "Thanks for bringing me here, bobcat." He nodded towards the shelves. "You cool with one of their specials?"

Marley nodded, and Thomas waved to the bartender as if he were greeting an old friend, leaving Marley to gawk at the beautiful people, the beautiful space, and wonder where she could make sure that she was just as beautiful, too.

From Marley's knapsack came a string of melody from a violin - Lily's ringtone. To say that Lily's promise to listen to Marley about her day was at a bad time would be an understatement.

Marley winced as she pressed the red button to ignore her best friend's call, slipping it into her back pocket. She started to walk towards the bar but stopped herself. *Boys must never come between us, Marley,* she remembered Lily repeating over and over again - though it was often meant more as a reminder to herself than as a directive for Marley. Marley wasn't the type to even *have* a boy to get in the way. Until now.

Lily *would* be upset if she found out that Marley had screened her call while she was out with Thomas. Especially after the gelato order. Shoot. The gelato order. How could she forget about ice cream with Lily? A voice-mail icon popped up. The gnawing in Marley's stomach grew. It was safer for everyone - Anne and Logan included - if Marley talked to Lily.

Marley opened a text message.

Marley: Out right now (will fill you in later). What's up?

Lily: I need my MOH! Where are you?

Marley frowned and looked over her shoulder. How would she describe El Bahama? *Imagine the Mandalay Bay Ice Bar in Vegas. But Spanish. And cooler. Ha ha.* She scanned the room. It was beautiful. More than what she had imagined when stepping inside had only been a dream. She grinned at Thomas, who raised his arm with a drink in his hand. Adrenaline coursed through her. Lily would have to wait. The phone played again. Marley silenced it, but checked the message anyway.

Lily: Doesn't matter. Text is better anyway. I have news!

Marley sighed, rearranging the weight from her left to her right hip while she waited for the photo that she assumed was on its way. Marley's heart pounded faster. Predictions shot through her mind like arrows. Had Logan turned out to be the scum of the earth? Had Logan been arrested for insider trading? Was Anne sick? Lily wasn't pregnant, was she? If she was, Marley would have to move back to New York and face the facts: her best friend was going to move on with her life and Marley would be left in the dust, alone, lonely, and without any prospects. Unless. She looked up at Thomas, who cocked his head at her, both arms back at his sides, one shoulder lifted in a shrug. She lifted a finger to signal one more minute and glanced at her phone when it vibrated again.

Lily: Look at the gladioli!

Flowers. Marley exhaled the rush from marriage to baby in a baby carriage from her mind.

Tall flowers with red bursts of color jutted from a thick stem. She had to admit that they were very pretty. "Very pretty," however, wouldn't do as the sole descriptor for Lily Cromwell's wedding flowers. Marley knew better than to downplay any of it. Nor did she want to. But surely Thomas' drink would be gone by the time Marley took a sip of her first one.

Marley: They'll look stunning against the white of your dress and the ice in the snow.

Lily: Actually. The dress won't be all white.

Marley: No?

Lily: Nope! My gown has red satin within the folds of the dress. It'll be perfect. Red lipstick.. freshly highlighted hair... your girl is going to *shine!*

What flowers would Marley choose for *her* future wedding? She had never given herself the permission to dream about it, despite Lily's upbringing always bringing it into focus. Lily was the one who was to settle down at a young age. Marley was like the aunt who traveled all the time and, when she visited, would bring fun gifts for the kids.

Something within her turned. Marley wasn't with her very best friend in the whole wide world while she was making choices about her *wedding* day. The guilt growled at her. Instead of being with Lily, Marley had almost ignored her for the sake of what? Drinks with Thomas?

She would be the most supportive maid of honor that ever was.

Marley: You will be radiant! Hope my mom is giving you the family discount!

Lily: Actually. That's why I called.

Three typing bubbles appeared. Then disappeared. Then appeared. It wasn't like Lily to hesitate.

Lily: Please don't be mad.

That made Marley pause. Marley was never mad at Lily. Well, at least not to her face. Had Lily barged into the Harrow household, demanding fields of gladioli be shipped in time for Lily and Logan's December wedding? But how much could Peggy, the COO of a major subscription flower service, actually do?

Lily: We're ordering the bulk of the flowers from Janie's. Remember the woman whose flower shop I stumbled into when I was waiting for the bus from Brooklyn and missed it and met Logan and…

Of course Marley remembered. The fact that Lily had been in a true blue New York City *bus* was enough to mark the moment in history. Janie was the woman who Lily swore brought her and Logan together. Had she not stopped in Janie's Brooklyn flower shop —the story goes— then Lily wouldn't have missed the bus back to the East Side, ending up at Frankie's bakery with Logan.

Marley had met Jane at Lily's IceStorm party last spring. She was a sweet Scottish woman whose late husband, a flower shop owner, had made Ms. Janie do what she hadn't imagined for herself: run a successful flower shop in Brooklyn, New York. Marley caught Thomas' reflection in the mirror in front of her and smiled. The belief of a man in his woman made magic happen. And now, Marley could experience that for herself. If only this conversation would end and she could return to Thomas, anyway.

Marley: I remember Ms. Janie. Super sweet woman. And an important piece of your love story!

But not your life's story, she wanted to add.

How many times had Marley's mom stepped in to be the affectionate, nurturing mother that Anne Cromwell hadn't been? Peggy Harrow was an exceptional COO of a chain boutique company. Lily had given Janie IceStorm's business for the RACES reveal. It was generous. But it was a little hurtful that the Cromwells wouldn't think of hiring her mother's company for the flowers for Lily's wedding.

Lily: So you understand the sentimentality behind it?

Why was Marley always expected to be the one who understood, made allowances, and gave countless benefits of the doubt? This conversation was over. Thomas had waited long enough.

Marley: Of course. We'll talk more tomorrow, yeah? Can't wait!

She'd find more to say later. For now, Marley dropped her phone into her bag and leaned closer to the mirror in front of her. It had a translucent film over it, making it difficult to see whether the bump on her forehead was because of the ornate wax paper or if her acne had found out she wanted to look extra good tonight and decided to sabotage the entire affair.

Marley lifted her sweatshirt over her head, trusting her curls would fall back into formation, and knowing that it didn't matter what was on her face if her girls had some room to breathe.

She'd never wear this by itself at the office, but it felt right to show her red tube top here. She pushed Zeke's warning once more out of her mind. She was After Work Marley right now. Being in El Bahama with a sweater on when she knew what was underneath would have been a cardinal sin - and if she were going to catch up to Lily status, she needed to expedite the process. She adjusted her top, making sure her chest was displayed just so.

In fact, after the rush of the wedding was over and Marley was still at Tigre, Marley would tell Lily that, while they were talking about Lily's wedding flowers, Marley was getting to know someone who might become a more permanent fixture of her future, too. Of course she wouldn't hold a grudge over wedding flowers forever, but right now, it felt good not to care about anyone else's feelings except Thomas'. And her own.

She heard Thomas' laughter, a noise somewhere between a bark and a whoop. Marley spun around to see who had gotten such a sound out of him. The bartender was laughing along with Thomas. It was okay, she assured herself. But then she noticed two women off to the side who were looking over at Thomas, mixing their drinks like cauldrons. A brunette was encouraging the other to go talk to him with pointy elbows that looked dangerous and sharp. Marley realized the other woman was the one in the white dress who often frequented El Bahama.

Marley forced herself to smile. Experiencing dislike was an art; you couldn't show it. Not even in microaggressions. Her father had done it enough to her mother and Marley didn't want to be that way. The Cromwells agreed: You could only show discontent when it was time to command. And even then, you certainly couldn't ever admit that you were *jealous*. The truth was that Thomas *was* handsome enough for such a reaction. The other truth was that he was here because he wanted to spend time with *her*, Marley, even after noticing her sensitivity and witnessing her fallible presentation. That counted for something.

But maybe he was only here because he would have felt bad turning her down.

Was this a pity date?

She swallowed the doubt. She *was* wanted. She was *wanted*. *She* was wanted. Lily was getting married and Marley wouldn't be too far behind.

Marley stepped right in between him and the other women.

"There you are!" Thomas grinned and pushed a drink the color of lavender in her hand.

"Ooh, how pretty!" Marley said.

"A pretty drink for a pretty woman..." Thomas lifted his drink in cheers.

"...and a toast for the man who's able to see it," Marley said, raising her drink. *And then we were finishing each other's sentences by the second date,* Marley would tell Lily later. Or maybe she wouldn't mention how many times they'd gone out, just the two of them. Lily would be tempted to guilt Marley into feeling bad for not telling her right away, but Marley wasn't into creating drama and you couldn't have a war with one person. What Lily didn't know wouldn't hurt her.

Marley straddled the stool next to his and looked at the drink in Thomas' hand.

"You gave me the hard stuff, huh?"

"You had a hard day."

"Something tells me you don't have many of those, do you?"

"Hard days?"

She took another sip, grimaced, and nodded.

"What can I say?" Thomas shrugged. "I'm an easy guy."

"I appreciate that about you."

"That I'm easy?" He repositioned himself on the stool, and Marley forced herself to keep looking at the drink in her hand. It wasn't easy.

"Easy-going, easy to get along with. Would there be any other way to mean it?"

Thomas glanced at something over her shoulder. She looked behind her, and noticed the woman in the white dress laughing in Thomas' direction. This really was the same woman she had seen before when she had been sneaking peeks into the club. Marley shrugged it off. If attracting men was a woman's job, who was Marley to judge? And, if she were being honest, if she were Thomas, she would have noticed the woman, too. Shoot. She *wasn't* Thomas and had already noticed her. Anyone with eyes could see. Besides, she was used to it. Going out with Lily had a similar effect. It was part of the gift of being beautiful: you weren't just noticed; you were seen. And Marley Harrow did not have that gift.

The woman approached Thomas and touched his arm. Marley felt her breath catch.

"Haven't I seen you here before?" the woman asked with a light Spanish accent that made it sound like she could melt chocolate by breathing on it. Marley strained her ears, making sure she caught and translated every word.

Thomas laughed, speaking in Spanish. "No, no. You must be mistaking me for someone else." His Spanish was perfect.

The woman glanced at Marley, then cast her eyes down as she ran her bright red fingernails up Thomas' arm, then across his shoulder and along the back of his neck.

"I swear I've seen you, *guapo.*"

Thomas swallowed, and Marley felt bile at the back of her throat. Or maybe it was the drink. She wasn't used to such strong liquor. Surely this woman was mistaken. Thomas was much too impressed by the club to have acted like this was his first time here. Right? Marley wanted to tell this woman that Marley was working way too hard to be senior level for her to step in Marley's way, but this time, it obviously wasn't about being senior level or even about work at all.

Marley cleared her throat.

The woman pulled her hand back. "Enjoy your time. I'm usually here every night, if you decide to remember that this isn't your first time seeing me." Something clutched at Marley's insides and she wished more than anything that she had the gift of invisibility. Leave. Never come back. What a terrible idea this had been.

Thomas was staring at his bottle in such a way that Marley worried it might shatter. Thankfully, the music was on the lowest volume that it was going to be all night; otherwise, they may not have heard him.

"I assure you that it is," he said. Each word fell hard and landed with power at the woman's red pumps. He leaned his left arm on the bar and leaned over, his lips almost touching Marley's ear. She shivered.

"I'm only here because of this red light." He tapped Marley's side, then retracted his arm. Marley brought the glass to her lips quickly. Her exhale clouded it.

The woman nodded, pivoted, and walked away.

Marley stared at him. That was *not* something a colleague would do.

"Well, that was strange," Thomas said. "Sorry about that." He nodded towards her drink. "Slow down, killer. But. I suppose if we operate according to your dinner, drinks, and dancing plan, that means more than one drink is on the agenda."

Marley laughed, and it seemed louder than she meant it. Had that woman left a mark in Thomas' neck with her fingernail?

"So what will it be?" Thomas asked. The shyness of his smile made Marley want to hug him and simultaneously reach her hand behind his head as easily as that woman had and crash into his lips like the ice had pressed against hers.

She tried to find the words like she was trying to sift gold from the dust in her thoughts. The vodka was hitting her harder than she thought it would. She squinted at him. "What do you mean?"

He grinned. "What drink would you like next?"

"The same, please."

He started turning to call the bartender over.

"Probably wouldn't be wise to mix two things," Marley added, light-heartedly. "I imagine that wouldn't sit too well in the stomach."

Thomas' arm froze in the air like someone had zapped it still. "No," he agreed at last. "That wouldn't be good."

Marley lifted her hand to her mouth and forced a giggle. "I wouldn't want to explode, like Karl had shared earlier. I have a sensitive stomach."

The tension in Thomas' shoulders eased, and he laughed, though it was with less enthusiasm than before. "We definitely wouldn't want that." The bartender slid a full glass of the purple liquid in front of her.

She wasted no time lifting the glass to her lips. Her mind was beginning to cloud. It wasn't often that she was in this looser state.

Thomas' expression brightened as quickly as it had soured, like something suddenly struck him. "Hey. Do you see that over there?" He pointed to the opposite side of the bar, above the doorway. Marley squinted. The door was shut, but painted over the bright blue frames was a lit piano keyboard. Thomas grabbed her hand.

"Let's go!"

Purple liquid spilled onto her hand. "Whoa, hold on!" Thomas stopped and turned around, looking at her licking the alcohol from the back of her hand and along the bottom of her wrist.

She caught up to him. "I wasn't about to wipe my hand on my shirt. Or pants. Or your pants." She was so close to him, it wouldn't take effort to get on her tiptoes and kiss his cheek. His nose.

"That's too bad," he said in a low voice, slipping his arm around her back, leading her up the wide stairwell. If she just turned around, he could press her against the...

Marley cleared her throat and let Thomas lead the way. She took another sip of her drink. It was going down as easily as she climbed the stairs. Going back down would be another matter, but she'd request a couple glasses of water before doing that.

The bobcat would take it from here.

* * *

His fingers caressed the piano keys like pressing down too hard would break them. She couldn't name the melody, but the trills swirled around them, transforming the empty space with unoccupied black seats and a shut down bar into an intimate backroom reserved just for the two of them. The alcohol swam through her and the melody enveloped her like a net that wasn't trapping her, but rather providing her a place to rest. She loved not worrying about whether it was too much or too soon to lay her left cheek against Thomas' shoulder. He didn't pull away, and she loved feeling his body pressed against hers.

The slight lift of his arms as he played added to the spin in her mind, but she closed her eyes and imagined she was leaning against him in a hot air balloon's basket, taking a break from their elaborate charcuterie spread. She wondered what cheese was his favorite.

The melody shifted to a melody she recognized. "Mm..." She straightened like a pin had been placed into her spine, and then relaxed. This one she knew very well. She took another sip of water and pursed her lips. The whistle came out clear.

Thomas dropped his shoulders and, though he kept playing, he looked at her as if he were seeing her for the first time.

"Alright, girl. Get it."

She whistled the beginning of Guns N' Roses' "Patience" like it was just another Sunday morning with her dad. He'd put on the vinyl as he worked in the garage, and she'd pass him wrenches and screwdrivers and hammers while he sang.

"You gotta have patience, sugar," he'd tell her. "It'll all turn out fine."

Marley purred as he brought the song to a satisfying end. Her eyes fluttered open to see Thomas rest one hand on his lap, while the other reached for his bottle of beer.

Marley lifted her head and looked at him. "Wow. That was amazing. Who are you and how can I keep you forever?"

He considered her. "You keep that whistler wet and we'll see if we can work out a deal."

Definitely inappropriate - and definitely turning her on. His eyes shimmered as he brought the longneck back to his lips. She was so jealous of that bottle.

And then her eyes widened. What if he *didn't* mean for it to turn her on?

"I mean. The music. How do I get to keep listening to that music? I would have no trouble falling asleep if I could hear you play before bed." *Jesus, Marley. Bringing up your bed to your boss?!* "I mean. It'd be ten times better than the white noise machine. For real. Where'd you learn to play like that?"

"So many questions," Thomas teased. He glanced at the three glasses sitting on the table next to the music stand. "Sure you'll be able to remember the answers?"

She shrugged. "Not remembering would kind of be a miracle, to be honest." How could she tell him that, despite the buzz, she was committing every detail to memory? It was how her brain worked. She'd remember it all. For better or worse, there was no etch-a-sketch-selective-memory here. It made forgiving and forgetting - especially herself - impossible. She bent her knee and turned towards him, so that her shin was against his leg. "Try me," she challenged.

"I'll start with the easy question. My mom taught me. She'd sing me a song at bedtime, and if I was still humming it in the morning, we would spend the time between breakfast and nap time learning how to play it on the piano. She wasn't an expert, but she had always wanted to learn, so I guess she figured that I was a good excuse to go for it. Over time, she'd clean an extra apartment here and there to have enough money to pay for private lessons. When I got home, I'd teach her everything I had learned."

"Smart. She made sure her money wasn't going to waste."

"Exactly," Thomas said. "You get it."

She grinned despite herself. He was still her boss, after all. Approval meant something. A raise. A promotion. She *got* it. "It sounds like something my own mom would do."

"Yeah? How so?"

"It's not important."

"Okay. If you say so." Thomas turned back towards the piano.

"Okay, okay, fine. I'll tell you." Thomas looked smug, and she didn't know if she found that attractive or a little off-putting. "The truth." She took a deep breath and exhaled. "As a teenager, I spent practically every Saturday afternoon at my best friend's house. Her mom had this… curriculum… that we grew to call 'The Cromwell Rules.' Each Rule was basically a strategy for how to maintain a suitor's interest."

Thomas tilted his head back. "Is that right?"

"Yeah," she chuckled nervously. "Crazy, right? Careful!" She playfully poked his shoulder. "I might be playing you!" Gosh, she hated the way she sounded. Slurred words were never sexy.

He started playing the piano again, a song of mystery this time, like she was narrating a *Sherlock Holmes* story. She pressed on.

"I'd come home and tell my mom the rule of the week. Then, she'd lead me through the advantages and disadvantages of following it. I was only there to support Lily, and both my mom and I knew it, but I think my mom was afraid that I'd 'fall for' the lessons. She didn't want me turning into *that* kind of girl."

But from where Marley was sitting, *that* kind of girl — Lily — had it all: the successful career, the fiance, an amazing apartment overlooking Central Park, and access to any opportunity she desired. In fact, for all the critical thinking done around the Harrow table on The Cromwell Rules, she'd have hoped to have some of the magic rub off on her. All it did was make her aware of all the ways you *could* seduce somebody and all the reasons that *she* wasn't the kind of woman to do so.

Thomas stopped playing and spun to face Marley. "Would you like to dance? Or find a place to have dinner?"

"Excuse me?"

"Dinner, drinks, and dancing," Thomas nudged into her shoulder. "Your idea, bobcat."

Though it *was* her idea and she wanted nothing more than to keep the evening going, she also knew that she had to reject his offer. This rule she knew very well; it had worked for Lily countless times: *Always leave them wanting more.*

"Oh!" She laughed and stood, a bit wobbly, but standing. Thomas stood, too, straightening out his pants and tucking his shirt into them. She forced her gaze to rest on his face. It wasn't easy.

"Why not wait for another day?" She hoped she sounded casual. "Thanks for helping me forget about work."

Thomas' mouth turned down, but something in his eyes glimmered. It made her stand up straighter.

"I don't think El Bahama has a kitchen anyway," she added. She stumbled to the stairs and looked down. This would be a challenge. She stumbled, reaching for the handrail. Thomas' hand reached out and covered hers. "Good thing I asked if you wanted to dance," Thomas said, concern etched in his voice.

"There's no music," she pouted.

"There's no winning with you tonight, is there?"

Marley withdrew her hand, pretending to look wounded. "You don't think you've won already?"

"Touche. Very well, bobcat. I suppose I should be making my way home as well."

She imagined Thomas going to a bachelor pad apartment all alone. She pictured a tattered couch facing a big screen TV surrounded by vinyl albums and sports memorabilia on shelves that were gathering dust. *Alone. How sad.*

She started down the stairs, grateful that Thomas was right there to catch her if she fell.

But she knew she had started falling a few hours ago. For him. For the way he made her feel. The way he claimed her even with a gorgeous woman trying to claim him. The way she yearned to be near him, just to feel his presence.

They stopped in front of the lit up bar, patrons beginning to gather. This was *so* not leaving him waiting, but how could she disappoint the man?

She tugged at his sleeve. "One more thing."

"Yeah?" He turned to face her. So earnest. So attentive. God, he made her feel so *good.* She loved the way he looked at her. The lilt in his voice. The way he made the scene revolve around *her.* How *could* she keep him forever? "Tell me, bobcat."

"It's been about a year since I made the move to Granada," she started. "I know we've already had a few drinks, but—"

"Yeah?" He sounded excited.

She laughed. "Might as well get one more chupito. For the road." Even though she didn't love the slur in her words, the buzz *was* wearing off, and she hadn't kissed anyone since before she'd left New York. Over a year ago. One shot wouldn't hurt.

Thomas leaned over the bar to tell the bartender what kind of shots they wanted.

The bartender was quick, ignoring the throb of people pressing in upon them, even though she and Thomas had approached later than a few of them who had been waiting for a while.

Thomas slid the glasses full of clear liquid in front of them. "I present to you the Statue of Liberty shot. Dip your pointer and middle finger in, and then lift them up. Take the shot, and then shake your fingers out."

Marley's laughter trailed off as she processed his instructions. "What? Why would I shake them out? Where did you learn this?"

"New Orleans, bobcat. Haven't done this in a long time. Dusting off my party tricks." He was so excited. Animated. Like she had been in the jewelry store. Was this part of the reputation Zeke was talking about? That he loved to party? Why was that a bad thing? Thomas rested his arms against the bar and turned his head towards her, smiling. Marley would have melted into a puddle; he looked equally tender, strong, and attractive. The whole package.

"An independent woman who knows the rules to keep a suitor interested, and who also happens to be celebrating a year of working abroad on the 4th of July? It's a perfectly patriotic way to celebrate."

Thomas reached into his back pocket and rested a lighter on the bar.

Marley fished out the Pop Rocks box from her knapsack.

"What are you doing?" Thomas asked.

"I thought we were pulling out things that didn't make sense."

Thomas barked in laughter. That was different. He never *laughed*. He just kind of "Ha!"-ed his way through. She had made him *laugh*.

"I fidget with a Pop Rocks box or crinkle the packet in my hands when I'm nervous. They're kind of like my good luck charm."

Warmth spread throughout Marley. "That's so sweet. I wish I had known earlier."

He shrugged his shoulders. "Now you know for next time."

"Thank you." Then, Marley squinted at the lighter. "What's that for?"

"You're smart. Think about it: why would you have to shake your fingers after taking a shot named after the Statue of Liberty?"

Marley furrowed her brow, then gasped. "No! You can't be serious!"

"As a heart attack. Not gonna back out, are you, bobcat?"

Lighting her fingers on fire? Surely there was a better way to celebrate than melting flesh.

Thomas pushed the glass towards her with his finger. The vodka sloshed over. The bartender had not left any space between pool and brim.

"Alright. Dip your fingers in."

She wanted him to see her as brave, but this was crossing a line.

"Can't we just throw them back like normal? What if my body stays on fire? What if I'm not fast enough in shaking the fire out? Has this been sanctioned by the Bartenders' Association?"

Thomas raised an eyebrow. "Is there such a thing?"

"With stunts like this, there should be."

"How else could we possibly toast to your year in Spain? May this first annual celebration—"

"It can't be a first annual celebration," Marley corrected. She felt giddy. And desperate for anything to delay this madness.

Thomas frowned. "Seriously? You're interrupting a toast —in honor of *you*— because of semantics?"

"It's like respecting the 'n't' in 'couldn't care less.' Someone's got to look out for humanity."

Thomas placed his drink down, lighter next to it. He sighed heavily and gestured lazily towards her. "Get it out."

Keep talking. Distract him. Make him forget about setting you on fire. "The 'Skittles Theory.'"

That made him pause. "The *what*?"

"My best friend and I adopted this theory years ago, thanks to our high school English teacher, Mr. Steel."

"Mr. Steel? Is that real?"

"Ha! You rhymed!"

Thomas rolled his eyes. "So what's this theory?"

"Well, we named it after our nickname for Mr. Steel: Skittles. Guess why?"

"Because he looked hard on the outside, but he really wasn't?"

"Dang, good guess! You must be a trivia guy."

Thomas shrugged. "I do alright."

"I regularly bring down the team average. Do yourself a favor and never invite me out to trivia. Anyway. Mr. Steel wore a different bright pastel color every day, which made it easy to spot him from down the hall. We'd yell, "Skittles!" He'd wave and smile. He was like a cartoon character in a cross country coach's body."

Marley settled into the memory of Mr. Steel. He was one of the only teachers who always seemed to know when Marley needed cheering up. 'Have a day!' he'd encourage her. He must have recognized how much pressure her parents had put on her and wanted to help take the load off. She wasn't ready to tell Thomas all of that yet, though.

"That's quite a teacher."

"Yeah, he was. I promised Skittles at graduation that I'd advocate for the 'Skittles Theory' whenever possible."

"But you never told me what it *was*. You just said why it had the name."

"You don't answer all my questions either."

"Man, bobcat. You get tough when you drink."

"I'm just saying," she continued. "There has to be an inaugural event before you can have an annual one. You cannot have a 'first annual' event." She imagined Mr. Steel giving her a high five from across the bar.

"That's the 'Skittles Theory'? You can't call something a 'first annual' event?"

"Yes. See. I knew you were quick."

"But you've already had an inaugural event: you moved to Spain a year ago. Therefore, this is your annual event."

"But I've never set myself on fire before!"

He gave her a look that said "You're adorable, but please stop talking."

So she stopped talking.

"Shall we continue?" Thomas asked.

Marley gulped. "You promise it won't hurt?"

"I promise. The Bartenders Association just made me an honorary member."

"Just right now?"

"It's easy to get things done in the time it takes you to make a point."

Marley laughed. She couldn't help herself. She couldn't believe she was going to stick her fingers into alcohol. This was the kind of life she didn't know she could experience. The kind that she thought was only available for the Lily Cromwells of the world. It was exciting. It was new.

And she wanted more. She would do anything it took to keep Thomas Elker in her life.

She stuck the fingers of her left hand into the shot glass.

"Thank you!" he said. He looked relieved, and picked up the lighter. "May this *event* be a constant reminder of your strength, your courage, and that anything worth having takes a little risk, uncertainty, and the desire to live so your critics have plenty to talk about."

Marley's smile fell. "Critics? I have critics?"

"No, bobcat. Goodness. Are you really this intent on preventing yourself from having a good time?"

How different this approach to life was from how she lived hers. But he was right. How many times *did* she prevent herself from experiencing life's pleasures?

Marley lifted the shot glass with her right hand. Thomas hit the side of his lighter, until the flame jumped from him to her fingers. Her eyes widened.

"Take the shot! Take the shot!" Thomas yelled, jumping out of his seat. Marley leaned her head back, felt the vodka burn the back of her throat, and coughed as she shook out the flame wrapping around her fingers. She slammed the glass on the bar.

"Oh my God," Marley sputtered. "I can't believe I just did that."

"Now *that's* a celebratory chupito."

Marley shook her head a few more times, the alcohol adding weight to each movement.

"Now you have something to keep you warm during the walk home," Thomas said, sliding his hand into hers. She squeezed his hand, grateful that he'd help her navigate through the cobblestoned streets. He was emergency contact material. Dependable. Trustworthy.

Thomas led them through a much more alive El Bahama club, people reaching over others to get their drinks, others squeezing into the booths. Marley held onto the arm and shoulder in front of her, focusing on Thomas' broad torso, and grateful for her ability to hide her petite body behind him. Despite her spinning mind, Marley felt secure in the hand leading her forward.

When they were outside, Marley shivered and slipped the sweater back over her head.

"What a shame. And here I thought that shot would have done the trick," Thomas teased.

Marley grinned. "Hey. Not everyone gets to see even a glimpse of what you have today. That's why I suggested you had already won tonight."

Thomas stepped directly in front of her, and Marley sucked in her breath.

"Sorry," he said, backing away. "Someone was trying to get behind me."

"Oh," Marley exhaled. "Right. Well. Thank you for coming out with me. I know it was a very last-minute invitation."

"Thank *you* for extending it, bobcat." Thomas bowed. "And for letting me in on what goes on in that head of yours. It's a fascinating place to visit."

Marley tugged at the material at her wrists.

"That's very kind of you to say. Thank you." She meant it.

Thomas reached towards her face. She steeled herself. This was the moment. This was going to be the "Remember When?" of their relationship's story. She tilted her head up...

And suddenly the strings of her hood constricted, which squeezed her face. Thomas grinned and let the strings fall.

"Hey!" Marley stretched the hood of her sweater to expand it again. She laughed uncomfortably, hoping she was masking the disappointment enough. The magic of the evening had ended. "Well." Marley tugged at her knapsack. "Thanks again."

Marley waited for him to offer to walk her home, but only silence ensued. A car huffed in the distance and laughter from a group down the hill seemed to balk in her direction.

"You have a good night, bobcat. Fall asleep knowing you did a great job this morning. You'll win them over next time." He offered a reassuring smile.

She could feel that the smile she returned didn't quite reach her eyes. She waved goodbye and turnt on her heels.

Marley blinked rapidly. She wanted so badly to know what it felt like to feel his lips against hers.

She had lit her fingers on *fire* for him. She had *presented* for him. But him messing around with her hoodie was what a big brother would do - not someone who was really interested in her. There's no way he would have done that to the woman in the white dress, so why did he feel comfortable doing that to her?

Or maybe he was being a respectful boss. As he should be! Even if he had wanted to kiss her, she wouldn't have ignored Lily's stark warning not to. Not while drunk. Not while her head was spinning and she could barely see the next few steps in front of her. Besides: he was just being kind. Playful. A friend. He didn't even offer to walk her home, for goodness' sake.

What kind of a man was that?

And why couldn't she wait to know more?

Break the Rules

She stumbled into her apartment. Cilantro darted around her steps, jumping up on the futon that Marley eventually threw herself onto. Her fingers pawed at her phone until she heard the video call sound like metal balls clinking against marble. A few more pings of the metal balls and a few more seconds of the swirling arrow, and it wouldn't matter how excited Marley was to tell Lily about her escapades. She'd fall asleep, lulled by both the rhythm of waiting and the receding buzz.

Finally, the arrow stopped and Lily's face appeared, bordered between metal bus poles. She could see half of Logan, too.

"My girl!" Lily called. "I was beginning to think you'd forgotten about me!" Marley almost did a double-take. "But I was calling *you*!"

Lily tossed her head back with an exasperated sigh. "All these things you say." She winked and grinned. "I know. I'm just playing. We both know I'm the worse friend. I just felt so terrible about telling you about Janie taking care of the flowers. Your mom had said gladioli were out of season and Janie has an in! Thank you *so* much for understanding. You're amazing. Anyway! How was your day?"

She'd already forgotten about the flowers. And in that moment, she was so grateful to be the type of friend to never make a fuss. It made things so much easier. *And* Lily was in a receptive listening mode. Now that Marley had the attention, she didn't know what to do with it.

Marley recounted, as casually and evenly as she could, about a new Thomas Elker who joined the team, their brief meeting in the jewelry store, and her presentation in the morning.

"Wait, wait, wait. You presented this morning?" Lily asked, wide-eyed.

"Yes."

"Like, in front of people."

"I believe that's the definition of a presentation."

Lily's jaw dropped. "You spoke. Out loud."

Marley rolled her eyes and answered with an exasperated "Yes. And you take the bus regularly now. What's more impressive?" Thomas was right; alcohol did make her a little snippy.

Lily must not have heard her; instead, she woo-ed, right there, in the middle of the packed bus.

"Logan! Marley presented in front of people today!" She moved the phone to reveal a hunched-over Logan reading something on his phone. Logan smiled wide and waved at Marley. Lily nudged him and whispered something in his ear. He looked at Lily with such love in his eyes, it made something in Marley squeeze and look away. Where were those Pop Rocks? She reached over the side of the bed, trying not to disrupt Cilantro lying on her stomach, and pulled up her knapsack. When would Thomas look at her in that way? How long would it take?

Logan chuckled. "I'm being told to give you big congratulations. Way to go, Mar."

Marley turned back to the screen and grinned. "Thanks. It was pretty cool. 'Til it wasn't." She paused. "Hey, Lil? Can you take me off speakerphone?"

"Yes! Of course. Let me put my headphones in," Lily said.

Marley relaxed. "That'd be great. Thank you."

As Lily rifled through her purse, Marley thought of the tissues in hers. How pathetic was she, wearing her heart on her sleeve so much that it took a few *questions* to set her off? Instead of backing down, she should have answered them with conviction. With strength.

When was the last time Lily had cried?

Marley threw back her head and dropped some Pop Rocks into her mouth. The little candies activated, jumping on her tongue like a trampoline.

Lily plugged the headphones in and smiled at her. "Okay. I'm loving this. Tell me more."

Marley shared how terribly the presentation had gone, but something stopped her short of sharing what happened in the conference room. It seemed too intimate to share. Like kissing and telling - even though there wasn't a kiss.

"Our woman of the world is finally letting others know how awesome she is." Lily stuck her chin out like a Shakespearean actor, proclaiming dramatically, "Who is this new Marley Harrow in our midst?"

Marley ran her palm down her face. "I have no idea what got into me."

Lily leaned forward, her eyes beckoning Marley to *go on*. She swallowed some more of the Pop Rocks while they were still jumping. The noise made Cilantro open her eyes and jump off Marley's chest. Marley scooted up onto her elbows.

"I asked my boss out for drinks."

"Ooh, scandalous," Lily smirked. But the way she smirked suggested that Marley hadn't been scandalous at all. Not really. Like, on the scale of scandalous to saintly, Marley still had a ticket to heaven.

"It *is* scandalous, Lil! We have strict non-fraternization policies. I could get fired so fast."

Lily raised her eyebrow. "You wouldn't be the one getting fired."

Marley wanted to laugh at Lily's naivete. "Are you kidding? I'm in Spain, girl. They'd side with the guy and say I was coming on to *him*." Marley dropped her jaw. "Oh God. I *am* coming on to him. This is so no bueno."

"Okay, so maybe it's not the coolest thing ever that the first person you've asked out in, like, years, is your boss." Marley prayed that Logan wasn't listening to this. "But life works in mysterious ways. It's okay to go out for drinks with a colleague. It's less okay for you to bang him."

Marley couldn't believe what she was hearing. Suddenly Lily Cromwell had morals?

"Why did you get to sleep with Nicholas Archer and I'm getting a slap on the wrist for finally going after what I want?"

"Because you're *Marley*. You and I are so different. I-" she cupped her hand around the phone and whispered, "-slept with guys left and right." She brought the phone back to show her whole face. "*You,* on the other hand, made a promise to save yourself for *your man* and have stuck with it! People expect me to mess up. You're the moral compass in this relationship. *You* decide what's good and evil. If you fall to the wayside, the whole world's lost. Besides. I've never had the chance to be the well-adjusted one and I'm kind of enjoying it."

Marley cringed. "Sounds like you 'kind of' get to be the self-righteous one. Is that what I'm hearing?"

"Well. Do you simultaneously wonder if you're a terrible person and are unsure of your actions, but also kind of feel good about them?"

"Yes!" Marley exclaimed. "Yes, that's it exactly."

"That's what living life feels like for most of us on the planet. While others got pummeled by dodgeballs in P.E., you were covering your eyes hoping no one got hurt. Or when you totally had a thing for Roger, but sat out when you knew I liked him, and I had no idea until years after we had graduated. But today, you *participated*. That's amazing. I imagine, however, that it *would* feel like getting a dodgeball to the head just because you decided to play. What you're experiencing is what Dr. Deidre calls a 'vulnerability hangover.' It's what happens when you take a risk and are unsure of whether it was the right thing to do or not." Lily paused to consider her words. "She said that some creatives - like you! - feel embarrassment, insecurity, even shame for sharing who they are.

You did the best you could with the information you had at the time. But let's focus on the positives here: you know you can ask someone out now, and it can turn out well, and you could have so much fun doing so. Just consider redirecting the energy and attention to someone in a safer position. One that won't bring you back here," she gestured to the bus and city around her, "as much as I'd love to take the bus with you."

Marley blinked fast, refusing to let the rising tears fall. But she didn't *want* to give her energy to somebody else. Thomas was the one who showed her attention. He *deserved* some of hers. Especially if he was alone and lonely and - *wait*.

She sniffed. "He didn't even offer to walk me home." What was up with that?

"Yeah, see? You don't need any of that. You deserve a real gentleman, who dotes over you and really shows his affection. Through actions. Not attraction. There's a difference."

She thought of how he had looked at her at the jewelry store, or when they were on the staircase going up to the piano. Was there a trace of how Logan looked at Lily in those eyes? Was Marley just imagining what she hoped she would see?

"Thanks for the advice, Lilo. I appreciate it." And she did. Marley couldn't remember the last time Lily got on her soapbox and lent her perspective for someone else's benefit instead of her own.

"Of course," Lily said proudly. "I've got you, girl. You made moves today. It'll feel weird for a while, but hopefully you fall asleep as proud of yourself as I am of you." She grinned and Marley forced herself to smile back.

"We'll deconstruct this boss man tomorrow so you can put away in your reservoir what you appreciate about a man and find it in the next guy. But for now, put the brakes on this one. Besides - you want to leave him wanting more, remember?"

She tried not to groan. "I remember," Marley said, but it fell flat. She thought she *had* left Thomas wanting more by not going out for dinner or dancing, but it had backfired. He had seemed unaffected - even so far as pulling the strings of her hoodie instead of a kiss goodbye - and now she was the one who was left wanting more. What kind of sorcery was that?

"I'm sorry to cut this off, but this is our stop! Make sure you sleep tonight, okay? Please."

Marley waved goodbye and, after the call had ended, Marley stared at her phone. She put it to the side, facedown, and groaned. Cilantro jumped back onto her chest. Marley pet her absentmindedly, stroking the hair and the tail that coiled itself against her neck.

She squeezed her eyes shut. It felt so good to close them, even if her head was still spinning. She was used to creating art and being in control of it. But today, she had spent most of her time out of control, like a passenger in a sports car doing donuts. Exhilarating. Exciting. New.

Her phone buzzed. She didn't want to look. It wouldn't be Lily.

Zeke would see her in the morning.

She could ignore Karl's messages.

She lifted her chin. But what if it was Thomas?

She flipped onto her shoulder and opened her eyes, the bright light from the phone almost too blinding. Cilantro meowed in frustration and jumped off again.

It *was*. It *was* a message from Thomas:

"I had such a good time tonight. Thanks for being you."

A surge of pleasure coursed through her.

How could she follow Lily's advice to 'put the brakes on'? How could she press the brakes on a car that she'd been waiting to take a ride in for so long? When the wind lifting her hair while she was in it made her feel more alive than she thought she'd ever feel in her life?

Surely Lily would understand that it would be the opposite of self-care to get rid of *that*.

Marley swung her legs over the side of the bed. It wouldn't do to not answer. But it *was* late and there's no way she was following the "Leave Him Wanting More" rule if she responded right away.

She needed a distraction. Or five.

Marley washed her face, scrubbing extra hard at the spots on her forehead. The sugar in those purple drinks wouldn't do her any favors. She sighed, replacing the towel on its hook. Some of the Chinese take-out she'd picked up on the way home splattered on the kitchen counter, so she scrubbed that clean. And when the clothes were in the hamper and the desire to go to the laundromat passed, Marley swiped her phone to reveal Thomas' name. She began to type, deleted, and typed again.

The lamp on Marley's desk was the only light on, and she liked it that way. The setting of the sun had cooled the air blowing into her room and covering herself with the sheet was like a cold compress against the heat of her skin, especially in calming her nerves. She'd see him in the morning.

It was a couple hours after he had sent his initial message, so she was sure he was sleeping. That was good. Did he sleep in boxers? Briefs? She didn't want to bother him - but she also didn't want to leave him on *read*. She would hate to be the reason for any of his own insecurities. What if he was on his fifth Pop Rocks box by now? Tossing and turning, wondering if she had had a good time, too. Wondering if she was mad that he hadn't walked her home or losing sleep because of some stupid rule that she was following? Suddenly, she couldn't take the thought that he could be sad because of something as dumb as a power game. Life was too short for that.

"Aw. You're sweet," she swiped. "Thanks for helping turn my day around. I had so much fun. Very much looking forward to dinner and dancing."

And if he wasn't worried, then he'd have a kind message to wake up to.

She pressed her white noise machine on, remembering how beautifully he had played for her. For them.

Did he have a favorite pillow? She pressed her own to her face and squealed into it. Anticipation. What a beautiful feeling.

It'd be self-sabotage to put the brakes on *that*.

Saturday are Sacred; Protect Them

It was *Saturday*. The best day of the week.

She used to hate Saturdays because that meant she'd have to wake up in her father's house. How many mornings had she been forced to spend sitting at the kitchen table, swinging her legs to and fro wondering when her dad would come home and relieve his assistant Laurie of babysitting duties? At least Laurie would let Marley flip through the travel books that she often brought with her.

But she had to admit that there were some good Saturdays, too. On the best Saturdays, Marley's dad would be in his study and, even though he'd be flipping through papers and making phone calls, she was left undisturbed. The study was dark, so Marley would follow the sun: drawing on the bar cart pressed against the window, careful not to knock over the thick decanters; reading beneath the lap on the red velvet chair; or paint in the sole bright spot on the floor. There was a drawer in his desk, just for her, full of art supplies. She had always been vigilant not to paint off the corners of the paper. Once, she had accidentally dripped paint on the floor and her father had kept the art drawer locked for a whole month.

Later, she knew Saturdays meant laughing with Lily, learning from Anne, and breaking down those lessons with Peggy either at home or later on the phone. Thanks to that, Saturdays became the days where adversity could still exist - the world could still be crazy - but she could enjoy the day and rest in it all the same.

Powering the phone on, she grinned at Lily's solitary message: "Happy Saturday! Chase that joy today!"

Marley knew she was on Lily's schedule, but that didn't bother her; it was better to be penciled in than ignored or forgotten. When she was penciled in, Marley became a priority - and that made her beam.

And her priorities today? Herself.

For most of her life, others had dictated how she spent her Saturdays. But now, there was finally freedom: she could choose for herself, with no one else's input.

She was a grown woman. She had moved across the ocean, for crying out loud. She could do this Thomas thing. She wouldn't allow anyone to decide for her. Not even her best friend.

She sat cross-legged on her bed and looked around her room. The sun was no longer bleeding into the room, which meant it was about to be at its highest. Her skin probably wouldn't take it, but what if she could acquire a tan that competed against Isabel's? Her gaze fell on the one-piece hanging from its strap around the closet knob. How many days had she kept herself home, too embarrassed at the thought of a stranger's disapproving stare? But now that she had caught Thomas' eye, she didn't need to worry about earning anyone else's desirous gaze. Reaching into the back corner of the closet, she dug out the two-piece suit with palm trees whose leaves spread out like ferns across Eve. She frowned at the way the suit pinched her hips, but her butt fit in the bottom half, and her boobs looked great in the top half, so she couldn't ask for more. She zipped up the white coverup, and threw her towel, membership card, water, book, phone, and keys into her knapsack.

Sandals on and she was ready to go.

Probably because she did it so rarely, walking to the pool was one of her favorite journeys. It required crossing the river, passing residents and tourists alike, hearing the Spanish that she could claim as her own but still tripped on words like a misstep on a cobblestone. The humidity was strong today, like there was a dome over the city where there was zero hope of any breeze that could cool the sweat on her face. She matted her forehead with the towel that seemed to be weighing her down the more she walked. Instead of wicking the sweat, it was causing more.

Tucking her earphones into her ear, Marley pressed the speed dial option to call Margaret. Just because Marley was on the outs with Zeke didn't mean the same for his wife.

Margaret picked up on the second ring.

"Bueno? Marley?" She sounded out of breath.

"Are you okay?" Marley asked.

"Si, si, claro. I'm on the last circuit of this workout."

Marley cringed. Margaret had been trying to get Marley to work out with her for months. "Do you need me to call back later?"

"No, no," Margaret huffed. "Now's great. Calling me on a Saturday?"

"Yeah! I wanted to know if you wanted to join me at the pool."

"Ay, sounds fantastico, chica, but I have to grade these papers."

"Always working," Marley mocked her. Margaret always made fun of her for working too much, and now here she was. But it comforted her somehow, knowing her tribe were no strangers to ambition. "I just wanted to say hi and let you know I wanted to spend time with you."

"Next time, amiga. Yo prometo."

And Marley believed her; Margaret always kept her promises. In fact, Margaret was one of the most authentic, trustworthy people she knew. Zeke adored her - and for good reason.

"Sounds good. I'll see you next week!"

"Have fun at the pool!" Margaret shouted, before hanging up.

She must have gotten lost in thought because she was in front of the pool gates faster than the thirty minute walk normally felt. Clenching the towel against her chest while she fumbled with her knapsack to show her membership card, she felt a tap on her shoulder. Marley turned around.

Familiar brown eyes smiled down at her, and the smile jumped onto her face before she could stop it.

"Thomas! What are you doing here?"

She matted her forehead; her hair was probably such a mess.

"Things have been getting pretty hot lately, so I figured what better way to cool it down than taking a dip?" He winked, reaching into his back pocket to pull out his own membership card.

As she watched him, his sleek and firm muscles stretched beneath tanned skin. Seriously, though. What were the chances? Marley was more comfortable being here with the *thought* of him, but now that he was here? Right in front of her? Comfort was not the word she would use.

No. She would not allow anyone to take away her sacred Saturday vibes.

Marley thanked the man in the window and lifted her knapsack while she walked through the turnstile. "Well," she called behind her, "Enjoy your afternoon. I have a thing about Saturdays and spending them on my own."

Thomas laughed. "That works for me, bobcat. Independence looks good on you." He pushed through the neighboring turnstile and walked ahead of her.

She urged her heart to calm down, but it pounded out of her chest with each step he took. Thomas was *here*. Marley watched him walk directly to the bar at the far right corner of the pool enclosure. He was already a casual guy, but today, he looked entirely himself. Single. Free. Open.

Happy.

Before he reached the bar, Thomas dropped his towel and pulled off his shirt, tossing it so that it landed on top of the towel. She felt her mouth form an O as the sun bounced off his tight back. She looked down at her stomach rolling over the bottom half of her bikini. He wasn't supposed to be here. His firm pressing against her squishy was only supposed to happen with clothes *on*.

She forced her gaze away. This time was supposed to be spent focused on her, not him. The only way to recharge and be ready for work on Monday was to forget about anything and anyone related *to* work. She'd never get to senior level if she spent *all* her time focused on the romantic aspects of her life. Taking a page from her dad, Marley knew that acting uninterested was the single-best way to make somebody interested - *especially* if Thomas expected her to be all goo-goo-ga-ga over her. She blew up into her bangs. What a freaking game.

She laid out her own towel, tucking it carefully into the corners of the vinyl stripes of the lounge chair. She'd show him.

She reached into her knapsack for her sunscreen. Her fingers felt the stiff pages of her paperback, the softness of her pack of tissues, her wallet, phone, and keys. She gave the ukulele a squeeze and rummaged her hand through again. Still no sunscreen.

"Shit," she swore aloud. Paying for sunscreen at the gym was not on her agenda. It wasn't in her budget and she didn't have any extra euros lying around. If only Lily were already here, she thought, then Lily would offer to pay for another bottle - even if she had fifty strays at home. It'd always been that way: Marley counting every dime, while Lily seemed to have a mint in her bedroom. Probably right next to her coffee machine.

Nope. Marley couldn't afford the extra expense, and she had already invested too much of herself into this idea and this place to turn back now. Maybe she'd get lucky and not burn like a lobster. She'd been in Spain for a year, after all; an hour or so of swimming and lying out in the sun wouldn't hurt. Besides, she was not about to miss the show that would be Mr. Elker at the pool.

What would make her seem interested, but aloof? Friendly, but guarded? She racked her brain for advice from Anne and Lily, but the only thing that kept creeping back into her mind is that she shouldn't even be putting herself under duress. She didn't adopt much from the Cromwells, but she loved the rule that Saturdays were *sacred*. Men had golf outings, Monday night football, and so many other reasons to get out of the house and ignore the world, so why couldn't a woman have a day to herself? She could unwind, kick back, do what *she* wanted - and needed - to do in order to return to herself. Just one day, Anne asserted, to remind a woman of what *she* likes so that she can do what she *has* to do during the week.

She fished out *Lighting up Her World* and opened to the middle of the romance novel. Before this last week, the book was the only romance in Marley's life. But now? The contents inside were nothing compared to the adrenaline coursing through Marley's body. How could she close her eyes and relax when the object of her affection was *right* there?

Though she wanted to know what was going to happen next in the novel, the way Thomas was straddling the bar stool did a better job of capturing her imagination than the ink on the page did. Marley squinted through her sunglasses, peering over the top edge of the book to get a better look at Thomas. His calves hugged the metal spokes. He was too far away for Marley to make out the tattoo that hugged his calf, but it seemed to constrict when he laughed. He'd readjust his bright blue hat every now and then by pulling on the brim.

Marley put her book down and lifted herself from the lounge chair. It wouldn't do to read about someone else falling in love when her fantasy was waiting to be lived right in front of her. She scanned the pool that was in the shape of a sideways T. In the corner were older women splashing with their pool noodles, following along the best they could with their aerobics instructor. In the other corner, children played Marco Polo. And in the longest section of the pool area, separated by a volleyball net, a group of guys her age were setting the ball to one another. One guy in a white cap spiked the ball down after an impressive leap from the water, showing off a torso that had clearly just done hundreds of crunches in the gym. The volleyball ricocheted off the edge of the opposite wall and flew in her direction; it wedged between the stucco floor and the bottom of her lounge chair. The guys looked at her expectantly - White Cap was halfway out of the pool on his way to reclaim the ball.

She picked up the volleyball and tossed it between one hand and the other. Marley hadn't played volleyball since she had left New York, but she missed the sport. It had been one of the most fun parts of high school. She could never get Lily to play, but she still appreciated a good pick-up game here and there. Marley eyed which guy seemed nicer, but they all seemed like the happy-go-lucky kind, with matte sunglasses, wide smiles, and arms reaching behind and in front of them, pushing water like scissors to paper. An inhale and exhale later, Marley was walking to the end of the T, forcing herself to keep her eyes on the ground, at her toes, towards the water. Anywhere but on Thomas. He would notice her. She hoped. No. He would. How could he not?

Lifting her head, she made eye contact with the one who was sliding back into the pool. "Have room for one more?"

White Cap lifted his hands and wiggled his fingers in a come-on motion. "*Claro. Venga, chica. Jugamos.*"

She grinned and served the ball before canon-balling into the water, imagining the splash hitting Thomas' back. Swimming underwater, Marley came back up once she was on the same side of the net as White Cap, who introduced himself as Jorge. The other two, Red Trunks (Hidalgo) and Farmer's Tan (Rodrigo), claimed the other side of the net.

Marley flicked her gaze to the bar. She could see Thomas still sitting with her back to her, but the splashing and sounds of volleyball would catch his attention soon enough. It didn't matter if people watched; Marley was *good* at volleyball. She had been offered a scholarship to Syracuse but declined. Being a student-athlete in high school had burned her out, and she had decided that university would be dedicated to studies only. It's why she was such a good designer now.

Being back in a game, even a casual one, with her eye on the ball and arms extended, made her feel like she was stepping back into when she had felt like her most confident self. You can't help but feel powerful when the ball you smack almost knocks somebody's teeth out. Jorge received Hidalgo's serve, sending it her way. Marley set the ball for him, who made it look like he'd have a strong swing and hit down, but then changed it at the last second, tipping the ball gently over, giving the other two guys a chance to receive and bump the ball back over. They hadn't anticipated the fake and missed it. Rodrigo hit the water in playful frustration.

And then it was Marley's time to serve. She watched Hidalgo send it back over so that she could pass it to Jorge. He set her up faithfully, and she smacked the ball down with all the energy she had. Jorge whooped in victory and offered her a high five. She laughed and looked over at Thomas, who lifted a bottle in her direction. Marley dropped her head, looking up in humble thanks. She lifted her head in time to serve the next ball.

Marley lost count of how many rounds went just like this. They ended up rotating, so Marley was able to defend the water with each man. With each serve and save and hit and receive, Marley fell back in love with the sport. Though Thomas was there and she was aware that he was watching, it felt so good not to worry about what anybody else was thinking: her only objective was to keep the volleyball from hitting the water - and she was quick enough to save it almost every time.

The sun was at its peak now and Marley was grateful every time she submerged herself under the water. It was crystal clear and as refreshing as it would be to press ice cubes against her skin, rivulets running from scalp to chin. Between gasps of air, Jorge turned to her.

"Marley, *gracias por jugar con nosotros.*" He looked like he meant it; she loved that she could give someone who looked like *him* such a good workout.

She reached up to her ears and rubbed them, trying not to wince. Her skin looked pink, but hopefully it was just a reflection of the red umbrellas deckside and not the start of what she suspected would be a painful bout of sunburn.

As the men left the pool, Thomas sat down to the right of the net, beer in hand. She swam over to him, ducking her head under once more to smooth any recent frizz that had appeared as the sun dried her hair and left frizz in its wake.

She ran her palms from her forehead to the nape of her neck, aware of Thomas' lingering gaze on her chest.

Marley pointed to his beer. "How many is that now?" She must have played at least two hours.

"Easy there, bobcat. We can't all be good at volleyball. Some of us are more skilled at other things."

Thomas lifted the bottle to his lips and took a swig. Marley started to roll her eyes, but then stopped herself. Who was she to judge how somebody else decided to decompress after a workweek?

"True," she said. "We can't all be good at the same thing. You should have tagged yourself in. It would have been fun."

"I could train my whole life and not be able to hit that ball the way you can."

"Oh, please," Marley scoffed. She tapped the side of his knee. "Don't be silly." They both looked down at where her fingers were still lingering on the edge of his flamingo trunks.

Thomas set his beer down and set his arms on either side of him and Marley made space for him to slide into the pool.

Thomas leaned his head back. "Oh, that feels nice."

Marley didn't know if it was the sunstroke or the heat of the moment, but Marley stepped in front of him, wrapping her hands along his biceps. "You'd have figured it out. I believe in you."

"Nah. Some things are better left untouched. Then you don't regret - or miss it - as much when it's over."

"Whoa. Sounds serious. 'The price of love is grief' and all that jazz, huh?"

Recognition flashed across Thomas' face, then disappeared as quickly as it had come.

Though she'd noticed, she didn't want to pry. Instead, Marley traced her hands from his biceps up behind his shoulders.

"Are we still talking about volleyball?"

"Certainly." He winked, and the heaviness of the moment passed. "If I had tried to play volleyball, I'd be nursing my ego *and* my groin. Mostly my ego."

"Oh, poor boy." Marley's hands traveled up Thomas' back and cupped his neck. He bit his lip, his eyes searching hers. She pressed closer against his front, happy to feel his own excitement. Her arm dropped, scraping the edge of the pool. She winced. Her skin looked so red compared to Thomas'.

Thomas chuckled. "More like 'poor girl.' You gotta get some aloe or lotion on that skin, stat."

She frowned. "I don't think I have any."

"I have plenty at home. Let's stop there."

Marley lifted her head. "Oh?" He was inviting her to his house? She wondered if the water would betray the vibrations of her increased heart rate.

"Yeah. It's no big deal. How else would you reach your back?"

Marley grinned, then bit her bottom lip to hide it. She considered the opportunity. It was a gesture of good will. He was right, of course: she'd be able to reach her shoulders and lower back, but between her shoulder blades? It's not like Cilantro would be able to slather her in aloe when she got home. Mostly because she didn't have aloe at home. She laughed at the thought.

"Okay. Yes. You're right. Thank you. Just a quick pit stop."

* * *

They spent the entire walk in friendly banter, sharing what they missed most about living in the States but what they couldn't imagine living without now that they had lived with it in Granada.

"There are no trees," Marley whined. There was no relief from the sun as they walked from the pool to Thomas' house. "Who builds a city without trees?"

"Take it up with the city council."

"How much longer?"

"Just another kilometer or so."

Marley stopped and placed her hands on her hips. "Nope. It's not worth it. I'm going home. I have silk scarves somewhere. Let those soothe me to sleep." She cringed at the thought of Cilantro kneading her skin.

"I'm just kidding. It's right over here."

"What?"

"My apartment. It's up here. C'mon. I forget bobcats are still cats that could whine."

She ignored him. "Water and aloe. That's all I need, and then I'll be out of your hair." Suddenly, the thought of being in Thomas' apartment alone with him made her want to turn around and never come back.

But when would such an opportunity arise again? Just water and aloe. That's it. He was a colleague offering things that a friend would offer. She behaved all day. She could continue doing so.

Thomas opened the door for her, reaching behind her to set his hand on her lower back. She could have crumbled at his touch. Was that a button she always had, or one that only responded when Thomas Elker touched her there? They climbed the stairs and led her through the front door. She kind of processed the living room, kitchen, but mostly on the fact that he was guiding her straight to a bedroom. Eyes wide, Marley followed, too shocked that this was actually happening to say anything.

"Go lay down," Thomas said. "I'll warn you: the pillows are comfortable. Feel free to shut your eyes. I'll be right back."

And then he was gone, leaving her to take in the scene around her. She couldn't believe it. She was in Thomas Elker's *bedroom*, with no one to interrupt them. She didn't feel like she was breaking any rules. If anything, she felt taken care of, like this was the most natural thing to do in the afterglow of such a great day.

Thomas' bedroom was the perfect size. Dark blue walls held up a large canvas of a watercolor sea turtle. His queen bed was bathing in the soft evening sun and his closet doors were wide open to show long sleeve shirts and khakis in neat order. There was a wide chest of drawers that came up to her waist and a mirror that she avoided stepping in front of. What had Thomas said? Some things were better left unseen. Her ego would have taken a hit - and why ruin something nice for herself? He had invited her here. It didn't matter that she probably looked like a lobster.

She set her knapsack and towel on the corner of the bed and climbed on top of it, the soft give of the mattress encouraging her to lay down. The covers and the fleece blanket were too warm for now, but undoubtedly a comfort during cooler mornings. She laid on top of them, her left cheek pressing against his pillow. She sighed. How lucky was she to have such a kind and caring colleague who wanted to make sure she was alright?

Thomas walked in and her heart quickened.

"This feels so nice," Marley crooned.

"Good to hear. I'd hate to hog the most comfortable bed to myself," Thomas said.

"What an injustice that would be." He walked closer and sat on the side of her.

Under her waist, Marley's left hand crumbled up a handful of the fleece blanket.

"Same logic goes for this aloe. The magic should be shared; it's saved my skin many times."

"I'm glad I could help relieve you of the guilt."

"You're not relieving me of anything, bobcat. Don't be telling yourself that story now. If anything, you're making everything tens times harder. "

Marley started to lift her head, but felt the cooling gel of the aloe on her shoulder. She shut her eyes, laying her head back down. "Ohh," she moaned into the pillow. "That's it."

Thomas rubbed the gel into her skin, massaging gently, like pressing a stamp and a sticker onto the corner of a letter addressed to a secret lover.

Marley felt her body tighten, willing his hands to accidentally "slide" underneath her. It took all of her energy not to lift her hips and press them back down onto the knotted ties of the fleece blanket. Maybe then she could feel relief in other ways.

Why was this man not going for it? Had she not put out enough signals letting him know that it would be okay if he did whatever he wanted to her? She wanted to groan in frustration.

But then his hands lifted and there was nothing.

She drew a shaky breath in and opened her eyes. Thomas was looking at her, amused.

"There. That should get you through the next few hours. At least on the way home. I'll give you what's left of the aloe."

Marley flipped over, careful not to have her back touch the covers. Maybe if she made herself irresistible… "Thank you so much," she said. "This was very kind of you. Definitely unanticipated."

"That's kind of my thing. It's when something starts being expected of me…" His voice drifted.

"Oh?" Marley lifted herself up and swung her legs over the side of the bed so that she was sitting next to him, her left leg pressed against his right. "Sounds like there's a story here."

"I went to Italy once and my girlfriend asked me to buy her Prada purses. She had even sent the make and model."

Marley laughed. "It's not a car."

"Might as well have been. I knew then that we'd never make it."

"Because she clearly communicated her requests?"

He paused. "Because she made an expectation instead of just being grateful for what she'd get."

"What would you have gotten her?"

He shrugged. "I don't know. But definitely not a purse."

"So, by that same logic, if I had asked you if you had aloe at home… I probably wouldn't be here right now."

"Probably not. That would have been wildly inappropriate." He leaned in, his forehead nudging hers. Marley drew in another breath. He was so close. His lips were so close. She turned towards him, but it was like he'd hung a thin veil between them.

Expect nothing. Be grateful for what you get.

She stood. "Mr. Elker, thank you so much for this kindness. I really appreciate it. You go above and beyond for your employees, that's for sure."

He stood and straightened his shirt. "Go ahead and put that in my quarterly review."

They looked at each other, he in his graphic trunks and light blue shirt and she in her prelapsarian bikini.

"Or not," Marley coughed.

Thomas smiled. "That's probably best. Thanks."

Marley nodded and gathered her things to her chest. "Have a great rest of your day. I'll see you when I see you."

"I'm sure it will be real soon, bobcat. Rest that body of yours."

And without a second glance at him or his home, Marley left his apartment and leaned against the door, willing her heart to slow down. It was wild: just last night, she was wondering whether he had a favorite pillow or not, and today, she probably had her cheek on it! What Marley thought was impossible was happening at rapid speed. It was a miracle.

Thomas was either the kindest man on the planet, or the most dangerous one of them all. As far as she was concerned, he hadn't necessarily done anything inappropriate: he'd just rubbed the gel on her back that she couldn't reach for herself. Downright a Christian act. On the one hand, he had relieved her in more ways than one: she wouldn't have to pay for a bottle of aloe and she'd figure out a way to apply it herself later. But in others, he had built up a frustration she had never felt before. How could she expect nothing, when he was giving her reasons to want even more? How could she only sit back and enjoy, when he wouldn't touch her when she most longed to feel his touch?

She might come to regret getting involved, but she'd find a way to make Thomas Elker hers. And he didn't need to know that she had any expectations of him at all.

Take Care of Yourself

"**I** will not be coming into the office today."

Seeing the words on screen made her sound strong and final. She sent it to Brandon at Tigre and closed her laptop.

There was *no way* she was going to the office today. If anyone wanted to grill her for more ideas, they'd be too late. She couldn't move without wincing in pain. And *even if* her body had been totally fine, there was facing Thomas that she just couldn't do. There were too many options of how to be - fine, because they had gone out as friends; distant, because she would be playing hard to get; warm, because she wanted to give him the impression that yes, she was interested and yes, he should kiss her, like, yesterday.

She sat on her bed with her back up against the wall. The only good part of going to the office - and it was so strange to admit it - would have been Karl. He would make her feel comfortable, offering his office as a sanctuary with a pot of chamomile brewing. He claimed he hated the smell of it, but if it made Marley happy... How was he so *nice?* She knew he liked her. Why *didn't* she want to spend more time with him?

Even though Thomas didn't brew her tea, there was something about him that made Marley seem to come out of hiding. It's as if *who he was* beckoned a version of herself that she had never met before. Marley loved discovering this brave new way of being. All the advice from the Cromwells about suitors came down to choosing the man who made her the better woman, right? Though it felt equal parts reckless and irresponsible, she also knew Thomas would be there if she took a risk and failed. Karl kept her comfortable so she'd never try. And Zeke basically enabled her shyness. Yes. Right now, the one who made Marley feel like a better woman was Thomas Elker.

But she had no idea what to do with those feelings.

So rather than call the office and tell them that she'd be working from home that day, Marley took the day off. She wouldn't have to be told by Karl later that Maria and Isabel had been gossiping about how poor Marley was at home still recovering from the meeting-gone-wrong. But she also trusted that Karl would defend her regardless of who was speaking. All she didn't know was whether Thomas would join in on the pity Marley train or whether he'd hunker down with Zeke while they volleyed back and forth about the strengths and weaknesses of Marley Harrow as a person and a creative. *Ah, volleyball.* Could they go back to Saturday, but without the sunburn? And also revise the visit to Thomas Elker's home, please and thank you?

Lily was right. Now that Marley had finally gotten over the real hangover, she needed to nurse one from vulnerability, too. Her head pounded, her body was shaky, and thinking about walking to the bathroom let alone to the office left her winded before she'd even moved. She didn't want to be in defense mode today; she needed a day where she wouldn't hyperventilate at the sign of any offense (perceived or not). She needed a day to recharge and figure out what in the highest heavens was going on.

Marley's mom always encouraged Marley to take a nap after school; sleep was the best medicine for a tired mind, she'd say, and a power nap was stronger than a hit of caffeine. "The trick is not to overdo it," Peggy would always say with a wink.

She wasn't sure she could "overdo" sleep today. She *needed* a processing day, as she and her mama called it sometimes. They'd never tell Marley's father because he'd call it weakness, but Peggy had quickly figured out that

Marley's stomach aches were related to her anxiety and not because of a bad egg or potentially moldy piece of toast. When Marley had had a particularly hard day of bullying the day before, Peggy allowed Marley to stay home, lick her wounds, and come back stronger the next day, equipped with some coping mechanisms in her back pocket. But now that she also had in her toolbox this belief from Thomas that she was a bobcat? She didn't feel as weak. In fact, it was like she had uncovered a super power, but needed to sleep on it to charge it up some more.

She imagined lying in Thomas' bed again, the fleece blanket tickling her skin. She really had *tried* the last few days, putting herself "out there" more than she had in who knows how long. She pulled her own sheets tighter against her, imagining what it would feel like to hug his left arm to her chest, her forehead resting against his shoulder. And then she slid into a deep sleep, held by the hope that her dreams could become reality.

* * *

She climbed on top of him, legs clasping around his waist. Muscles she typically didn't use beckoned him closer. He tugged her in, falling backwards, and she gasped, pressing her palms against the mattress above his shoulders. She leaned over him, her brown waves caressing his neck before her lips kissed his throat, and then his chin, and then shallow breaths pulsed against his lips. He growled, and something within her responded to his excitement, urging her hips to press down into him, lifting and dropping, any other thoughts escaping her mind. Thomas' fingers danced along her hip bone, then wrapped around her midriff, the other cupping her hair in his hands and pulling it back, exposing her neck. He snapped at her with his teeth, missing her neck, but making the hairs on the back of hers stand up. He snapped again, this time above her shoulder, and again in her ear. *Just kiss me already*, she begged.

But the snapping went away and a faroff knock interrupted the shallow breaths of her dream.

She stirred, reality sinking in. It had been a dream.

No!

The three o'clock Spanish sun poured in, long shadows cast by the indoor plants lined up on the sill. Her legs tangled in the sheets, Marley swept her hand along the nape of her neck, lifting the hair sticky with sweat. Her windows were open, but the burgundy curtains swayed only when the corner fan turned towards them. Why was somebody visiting *now*? And didn't they know such good dreams shouldn't be interrupted?

The knocking continued. She forced herself to stay in bed. Her naps had often been disrupted on Fridays by her dad's incessant knocking. It was cruel then, and it was cruel now. Processing days demanded solitude. Answering a door was not part of the regimen. She wasn't expecting anyone. She crossed her arms in front of her chest, refusing to move.

But the knocking would not stop. She groaned and slid out from under her thin, high-count Egyptian cotton sheets. The fan rotated towards her, chilling the curves of her body. Goosebumps cascaded down her legs. She rolled her eyes. She'd have to make sure her body was hidden behind the door, because there was no way in hell that she was putting on a bra, too. A shirt would be enough. Suddenly, she pictured Thomas on the other side of the door.

What if it *was* Thomas standing behind the door?

"Coming, coming!" Marley sang. She slipped on the red hoodie from the other night.

She brought her eye to the door's peephole but could only see a brown paper sack held up by a hand. The visitor's face was covered. Her heart rate increased. "Always leave them wanting more" was tried and true, there was no doubt about it. Here he was, standing on the other side of the door, desperate for more. She pushed her bangs up, regretting not taking one last look in the mirror.

She opened the door hesitantly.

The bag lowered, and a boy appeared, the shadow of a moustache shading his upper lip. Disappointment rolled through her. Though it would have been incredibly inappropriate for Mr. Elker to have seen her in this way, that dream felt very real and made her desire more.

"*Buenos días, Señora,*" the boy said, eagerly stretching the bag towards her, as if it held a novel discovery from a long and arduous journey. She took it, thanking him.

"*¿Cuánto debo?*" she asked, already turning back inside for her wallet.

"*Ya pagado,*" he said.

What? She turned back. This was a delivery?

Then, as if suddenly remembering, the boy reached behind him and pulled out an envelope. "*Hay un mensaje para usted.*"

A delivery with a message, too? Lily sent care packages like this from afar sometimes. Lily really was taking seriously her suggestion for Marley to take care of herself.

She thanked him again, and shut the door. She looked at the envelope and saw her name scrawled across the center. Marley walked over to her desk and pulled out the letter opener to release the letter cleanly.

The note was tri-folded. Folding open the parchment, she saw the monogrammed initials TE at the top of the thin sheet. Words filled the page. His handwriting was slanted, but clear, with sharply dotted *i*'s and decided *t*'s.

"Enjoy your dinner. Feel better, bobcat."

Marley felt bubbles of laughter rising to the surface. She pressed the note to her chest. This wasn't an afternoon visit at her apartment, but it did mean that he had probably looked forward to seeing her at work, and when she hadn't come in... She made a mental note to thank Lily for the hundredth time for the osmosis of her Saturday training. She made a second note to call her mother. It was shameful that she hadn't called in a few days - since she had met Thomas, Marley realized. *There'll just be more to report,* Marley reasoned. Marley was living her life. Her mother had always encouraged such a thing. Living life. And now she was. She'd update her mother later.

She kept reading. "Soup never hurts, and a little grease is always helpful for a hangover, in case you're still not feeling your best. When you're feeling better, maybe you can join me for some dessert. I'll be at la Plaza del San Nicolas at sunset."

She dropped the letter and lifted her arms in victory. She loved that he ordered soup - in case she really was sick - but also called her out on taking a day for herself with a hangover. The invitation came with no pressure attached - with no expectations but a soft hope.

There was no question that she would accept Thomas' invitation. Her thoughts were still fresh with memories of the dream she had of his hands against her. At what point tonight would they hold hands? Would tonight be the night they kissed? Would he look at her *that* way?

She opened the soup container to let the chicken soup chill and palmed the torta while she dug through her closet. Since it was so warm today, she'd don her Cromwell class and slip on a sundress, like... she skimmed through the options... the yellow one! Whose skirt hung just above her knee. She held the dress up in front of her, looking at how it would look against her bright-red skin.

Marley didn't recognize the face in the mirror looking back at her. Her cheeks were flushed, but her eyes were bright, like when the Friday night lights of her school had finally caught up to what she and Lily had been up to, sneaking around to mess with the cheerleaders' duffel bags once upon a lifetime ago. It hadn't mattered that Marley had listed every possible disciplinary action that could be taken against them; Lily had simply asked, "Don't you want to live a little?" And she found that Marley did want to.

And now here she was. It was this face - exhilarated, nervous, hopeful - that Marley saw was the same: adult Marley had awoken from a nap, but teenage Marley was back from the dead.

A few long hours until sunset gave her time to shower and finally paint her nails the shade of pink she'd been eyeing for weeks now. She wouldn't even mind the walk up to la Plaza de San Nicolas.

She was about to step into the shower when her phone rang. She lunged across her bed. If it were Lily, she could get her jitters out. If it were her mom, Marley would tell her that she was finally going out! Or maybe it was Thomas, giving her a hint of a location switch because the Plaza was too crowded with foreign exchange students and he wanted them to be alone. Alone, again. With Thomas. Chills racked her again. She looked at the Caller ID.

Zeke?

She pressed the phone to her ear, tugging at her sleeve. "Hello?"

"Marley. Hi." Zeke's voice sounded rough.

"Hey, amigo." She tried to keep her voice light to counteract his. It must have worked, because she heard him breathe out.

"Margaret would like—" She heard him huff. "Margaret and *I* would like to know if you're able to join us for dinner tonight."

"Oh! That's very kind. And unexpected," she added. "Aren't Monday nights usually reserved for you and Margaret?"

They were the kind of couple who dated on Mondays, to start the week strong together, rather than wait until they were drained and desperate for a drink on a Thursday. It was kind of cute. Intense. But cute.

"Yeah, but she was able to tell that something wasn't right when I got home. You know how I can't keep anything a secret from Margaret. That woman smells a surprise from a mile away. She got me to admit that you and I were on the outs. And apparently she likes you or something and doesn't want me ruining her life."

It sounded like he was complaining, but Marley could hear the hint of a smile in his voice.

"Oh," Marley laughed, then forced herself to cough. "I'm sorry, can you excuse me for a second?" She muted herself, as if she were caught in a fit and didn't want to gross Zeke out. Instead, she thought about the choice ahead of her: to spend the evening repairing a friendship that she cherished, or see what would happen tonight at the Plaza. Marley loved evenings spent at the Martinez house. Zeke was a phenomenal cook and Margaret was a kind and patient teacher who smiled encouragingly at Marley's speech faux-paus and corrected her gently to help Marley improve. They'd often go into the night laughing over churros con chocolate, Marley's belly so full that it was often difficult to turn down their invitation to sleep in the guest room. She thought of how many evenings she'd spent with them, laughing and learning around the table on their balcony.

But that was the point, right? She spent so many evenings doing the same things. They were predictable. She was predictable. She knew who she was with Zeke and Margaret. But who could she be under Thomas Elker's influence? Confident. Wanted. Noticed. When would this perfect storm of events ever happen again? It was like the universe was conspiring for her and all she had to do was show up. What was the bigger consequence? To ruin what you had for a chance at something amazing? Or live with the regret of not knowing what could have been? She glanced at the note resting in a sun spot on her desk. An evening of promise lay ahead of her, full of mystery and intrigue and hope. And that's what she wanted.

This *was* taking care of herself. She felt like the protagonist of *Lighting Up Her World*, who spent her days keeping the house of the Glibentz family spotless, yearning to spend even one day as Madame and not a maid.

She unmuted herself. "Hi, sorry."

"You're really not yourself, are you?"

That question took her aback. "What do you mean?" Already? He could sense the change already?

"You sound different than you did yesterday."

She redirected the conversation. "Yeah, I mean, this cough came out of nowhere. I probably shouldn't come over tonight. I would hate to get either of you sick. I mean," she laughed weakly, "I know that you wouldn't mind taking a couple sick days, but I wouldn't want to be blamed for Margaret getting her students sick." Her heart pounded. She hoped he wouldn't see through her charade.

"No te preocupes." Zeke almost sounded relieved. "Feel better. I'll see you when I see you."

"Thanks for understanding. I'll see you tomorrow."

Marley hung up, and then hung her head. She had just lied. Again. To *Zeke*.

She took a bite of the torta that had grown limp in her hand. Oh, well. What Zeke didn't know wouldn't hurt him. He already had Margaret. He didn't know the pang of loneliness that hit her after long days of work and acute reminders every day of her singleness. She didn't have to be a maid tonight. Tonight, she'd be able to feel what it'd be like to be one of *those* girls she read about. The kind of girl her best friend was. The kind of girl Marley wanted to know that she could be, too. The kind of woman she was finally becoming.

* * *

The shops surrounding Marley tempted locals and tourists alike. The colors and textures of art pieces and souvenirs beckoned each passerby to stop and touch, wondering for a moment what it'd be like to wear such decadent Moroccan silk or have *this* scent of tea once they were back in the boring day-to-day of real life. It was quiet, but alive. Marley surged with pride with every step up. Her mother had worried when Marley had announced the choice to move, but Marley had insisted that something greater than her own will was pulling her to Spain. Maybe this was what all of that beckoning was for - for her experiences with Thomas during the last few days. Why else would she have been stuck mid-level for so long, with no attention paid to her ideas, until Thomas Elker came around? He was her key.

And now she was opening the door.

The fears of moving to Granada to start a new life were nothing compared to her climbing the cobblestoned streets towards Thomas.

The yellow skirt swished around her as she climbed on, breaths matching her strides. A guitar strummed arpeggios, not threatened by the chatter of people threatening to overpower the sound. The setting sun casting hues of orange and pink held a beauty of its own, but it was the musicians who made the scene feel like humanity had reached Mount Olympus.

Her shoulders relaxed and adrenaline pumped through her, power rushing through her body in a way that her shallow breathing hid. Where could he be? The Plaza was bordered by stones raised to people's shins, but no higher, so that a misstep would cause a person to tumble over. Hopefully, Thomas had found a spot very far away from the edge.

A small voice within her urged her to go in the opposite direction. *Just go to Zeke and Margaret's. You don't know how this will turn out. It could be a disaster.* She *could* call Zeke and ask if he and Margaret still had time for her tonight, taking them up on their rare offer to hang out with someone other than each other on a Monday. Or she could turn around, stop for some tea and people watch like she usually did on Mondays. How many times had Marley wished that Lily had listened to Marley's advice, and here Marley was, totally obstinate to Lily's? Thomas would never know she was there. She'd be enforcing a boundary; and, if he really did practice this whole "no expectations" thing, that would mean he wouldn't be disappointed if she didn't show.

But then she saw him. On a blanket beneath one of the few trees in the Plaza, Thomas lay with his right leg propped up, leaning on his arms.

He was popping some snacks into his mouth with eyes shut, as if the music were a spell casting him under. He looked so peaceful.

And then it was like a magnet was pulling her towards him. Marley allowed her inner bobcat to lead. Even if she had wanted to turn around- and she really didn't-, she also felt her feet firmly attached to the steps leading her to a future she had never pictured for herself. Although it did feel like something was clamped around her skirt, trying to pull her back, she was going to have dessert with Thomas Elker and that was that. She was making life happen for herself, instead of strolling the streets of Granada with Zeke and Mags regretting that she hadn't backed down or backed out. She couldn't let her worries or doubts or insecurities win this time. She wouldn't. She refused. She had to try.

Her toes covered the corner of his red blanket. The maroon material looked much too nice to be covering the dusty stones. She took off her sandals, as if getting the top of the blanket as dirty as the underside would be as disrespectful as walking into Thomas' house with muddy shoes.

Then Thomas reached for another olive and grazed her ankles. His eyelids flew open and he sat up quickly, almost knocking over a tall glass bottle of wine. She squatted in time to catch it, watching the fruit swirl at the bottom of the bottle.

"Hi," she whispered, a small smile inching across her face.

"Don't tell me I'm dreaming," he said, fixing the brim of his hat.

She smiled wider, hoping it hid the red in her cheeks, as she remembered the feel of his hands on her in her own dreams. "You're not dreaming."

He smiled back and patted the space next to him. "Come sit. The sunset is taking its sweet time and I figure we could, too. sangría?"

"Please," she nodded gratefully.

She sat, spreading her skirt around her. She crossed her ankles, then uncrossed, then pulled her feet underneath her. Something within her squeezed as she took in the image of Thomas in a black baseball cap. She pulled some of the red blanket into a fist.

Thomas tucked his head. "Sorry. I didn't think about how uncomfortable you might be on stone. I could have thought to bring a pillow."

"No worries," she said, keeping her feet tucked under her, even though she could already feel the bones along the tops of her feet being crushed beneath her weight.

He passed her a full glass, chunks of apple and orange falling to the bottom of the goblet. "Thank you." She took a sip and smiled. "Refreshing."

"Glad you like it."

Their conversation felt so stiff this evening. Why? She looked at her full glass and indulged in a few extra swallows.

She picked up her shoulders and exhaled, begging her rising panic to settle.

He seemed to become more handsome with each meeting. "I haven't been here in a while," said.

"No?" Thomas turned his body to face the Alhambra, imposing in its architecture in front of the rolling hills, but at home as the jewel of Granada. Marley cringed as group after group posed in front of the stone borders, her anxiety a prayer for their safety. When the photographer stepped away and the crowd dispersed, she let go of the blanket and picked up her glass of sangría. The smell of fruit swirled memories within her.

"Maria and Isabel brought me here the first week after my orientation. We had taken a tour of the palace, watched a flamenco show, and then we stopped in a deli to buy all the sangría, cheese, and jabon to eat to our hearts' content." She took another sip of sangría. "I thought it was so sweet that they were going out of their way to welcome me not only as their colleague, but as their friend. I didn't realize until we brought someone else on board that doing things like that is typical company hospitality. It made sense why Isabel never took me up on other ideas to go out." She shrugged. "I came up a few times by myself after that."

"Only a few times? I try to come up here as much as I can. Lunch breaks, morning walks, afternoon sloughs."

"That sounds so nice. Maybe I just got comfortable being a resident instead of remembering that I still have permission to enjoy places like a tourist would for the first time. I suppose once you start calling a place 'home,' you stop exploring." She fell silent as she thought about her dad. Family life had become too boring for him, and Marley supposed she couldn't blame him: after defending someone suspected of murder, her dad probably felt that watching a movie with his wife and child was much too dull for a man like him. Once you felt a high, you couldn't stand the low. "After a while, you start to take things for granted."

Thomas raised his glass. "That's a wise observation."

That's it? That's all he had to say?

She sipped more of the sangría, though her hand shook. At least if she accidentally spilled, it wouldn't stain her skirt. "I wish it weren't true. I wish we could always look at each new day as a fresh chance. A new way to be. Even if everything and everybody else is the same."

"But if everything and everybody was the same, it could never *be* 'fresh,'" he countered. "Take this cheese for instance. If I ate it every day, I would cease to enjoy it. But I choose a different treat every time I come up here, which makes it new. Exciting. 'Fresh.'"

Marley bit her tongue. Was she just another treat? A different woman for him for a different night?

She looked from his bent legs to his torso to his neck to his face..

This man was *definitely* not Karl.

"But what of commitment?" Marley asked. "Loyalty. Even to - " She gestured to the cheese. "- cheese."

He shrugged. "That's where commitment and I part ways. Once you commit to something, it loses its luster. And I'm comfortable always chasing what looks enticing. Runnin' with the devil doesn't bother me. Anyway - it's what makes us good at our jobs. It's literally our job to surprise people into looking at life in a different way. Creatives can't stand things being the same. I'm most guilty of that."

Marley bent her legs, crossed her ankles, pulled her skirt to cover her knees and rested her elbows, leaning forward on them. Maybe he just didn't believe in commitment because he hadn't met a woman like Marley before. *Challenge accepted.*

"I mean, yes, but I think being able to see things from all different perspectives and reminding ourselves to pay attention to the world we're living in makes all the difference. My dad - he's a defense attorney - would remind me to examine evidence two, three, four times over, in case I missed something the first time. Every day is like another chance to examine the same thing. This way we don't become desensitized to the gifts literally right in front of us."

"Aw, you don't have to be calling me a 'gift' now," Thomas teased.

Marley rolled her eyes. She set her glass down, but didn't look up to confirm whether or not Thomas was staring at her.

He poured her another glass. "I don't mean to push your philosophy aside. Do you think that would fix a lot of problems, you think? Being able to stay committed to something, regardless of whether or not it loses its luster?"

"I can't speak for the world."

"But if you could."

"And even then I wouldn't. But I can help explain my own perspective: I never got the chance to really settle into a solid routine as a kid," Marley said. "My parents divorced when I was young and, though the shared custody had my daily schedule accounted for to the minute, school brought its own variety." She stopped herself. Did Thomas really care to hear about any of this?

Thomas popped two olives into his mouth and chewed thoughtfully, gesturing for her to continue.

"Let's say we all bought into this whole commitment thing," Thomas said. "You're saying we'd still have to treat what we had in front of us already as if it were brand new? And that would be..." He scrunched his nose. "... enough?"

"Maybe not brand new, but certainly remind ourselves that this, too, could be gone, at any minute." She thought of Anne reminding Lily of this very truth. Lily's father passed away suddenly, and she didn't think Anne would ever get over it.

"But if we treated everything as new, wouldn't you lose that sense of security that this thing - this person - would always be there? How is that not a traumatic way to live your life? Always afraid that this thing or person you love can just - poof - disappear?"

She looked at his still-full glass and smiled. Real conversation. Finally. She leaned into it, and him. "There's a beauty in knowing everything is temporary. It makes you appreciate everything you have, knowing that your sense of security is really a facade, thus making you appreciate your sense of security to begin with. Who provides that security anyway? You? Somebody else?"

Thomas' expression darkened.

Marley swallowed. "Did I say something wrong?"

He shook his head, as if tossing away the thought. "No. You're perfect."

He grinned, but the shadow was still on Thomas' face. She thought of the tears Thomas had seen matted on Marley's face a few days ago, and how he hadn't been scared off like so many others would have been. She wanted to show him that she could do the same for him, but didn't know how.

He pushed the charcuterie board towards her. "Not sure this takes care of the dinner portion of our deal…"

"It's a nice appetizer," Marley assured him.

He laughed. "Okay. I get it. I'll make reservations at a true blue restaurant next time. Mid-day soup doesn't count. Got it."

"Didn't take you for the sensitive type, Mr. Elker." The sangría was stirring up her sass.

"There's a lot that people don't see." She couldn't see his eyes beneath the brim of his hat.

Marley reached out her hand, then pulled it back. "I'd love to be able to."

"Not yet, bobcat." He lifted his head and she saw the hurt in his eyes. "Too many locks on too many doors."

She made a show of pouring more sangría into Thomas' glass. He gave her a pointed look, and she giggled.

"Fine." They looked over at the palace again, munching thoughtfully. Hot air balloons entered the scene, floating over the hills in the distance.

"Have you ever been in a hot air balloon?" Marley asked.

Thomas swallowed. "Haven't had the chance yet. You?"

"No, but I've always dreamed of it."

"What do your dreams look like?"

Her heart pounded. Did he have some weird sixth sense? Marley looked at his hands and gripped and loosened the blanket behind her.

"I typically keep those to myself."

"Well that's no fun," Thomas teased.

"I usually don't remember them," she lied.

He tilted his head back to show the confusion on his face. "What do you mean?"

"Dreams. I usually don't remember them. I'll wake up and wonder why my heart's beating fast, but," she trailed off, remembering the wetness between her legs. "Yeah. Don't really remember them." She was a terrible liar. Then again, she thought of the lies she told Zeke and Karl. Or maybe she was a really good one. The thought scared her.

"Ah. We were talking about two different things."

"Two different… Oh!" She pressed a palm to her heart. "You were asking about the goals and visions I have for myself. Not dream-nightmare dreams." She laughed shakily.

He chuckled. "Correct. I don't remember my dreams either. Kind of sad. I feel like I'm missing out on some key life experience." The Plaza was crowded with people who were probably so much more interesting than she was, and yet. His eyes were on her.

"Tell me about your dreams, bobcat. Young, ambitious, not yet trampled by life. You shine when you give your doubts the middle finger, you know."

Her mouth went dry, but a sudden giddiness possessed her. He *saw* her. He wanted to *know her*. She let her head fall back as she looked up into the sky. "My dreams look like a lot. I want to look back on my life and say that I was well-read and well-traveled. But I suppose what comes up when I think about being in a hot air balloon is where I'll be. I've always wanted to see Scotland. I've heard about their castles and read stories about their history. I imagine seeing vibrant, rolling green hills, stone walls, abandoned palaces, and sparkling waters from the sky would be quite magical. Maybe rent a shepherd's hut and live there for a little while. Adopt a sheep. Name him Gerald." That sangría was getting stronger by the sip.

"Scotland is beautiful."

Her head jerked to attention. "You've been?"

"No, but my family has. 'Elker' is of Scottish descent."

Suddenly, Marley imagined calling her three children home from running around the ancestral Elker home, Thomas giving her a kiss after dropping the chopped wood into the fireplace.

"A Scottish man in Spain. Look at that."

"'By land and by sea' is our family's motto. We can adapt to anything and still get to where we're going," he said matter-of-factly.

What a philosophy. Where had he been when she was young and needed reminders that change was *good*? That *she* could adapt to anything? She could travel and move from place to place, but when it really mattered, the fear of trying typically kept her trapped in place.

"Unless you get stuck on the sand. You know, *sea*... and *land*... *sand*." She snorted, then brought her hand to her nose. "Oh, my goodness." She giggled.

She loved the way he looked at her, like they were weaving a story that hypnotized both of them, a tapestry of their making that was just beginning to take shape. Such attention, she knew from the Cromwells, was rare from a man, and she felt so lucky to have Thomas'.

But what if she wasn't the only one to have it?

She pressed her palms down her skirt. "Thomas?"

"Yes, bobcat?"

This was it. Once she knew, there would be no going back. But if she didn't know, there would be no going forward. She inhaled all the steadiness she could, keeping her eyes on the brim of his hat and exhaled her fear. She had to know.

"Zeke mentioned something to me a couple days ago that I haven't really been able to forget. And since we seem to be becoming fast friends..."

He grinned. "Yes. I've enjoyed it."

"Indeed." She picked at the frayed edges of her sandal, then lifted her head, locking her eyes on his. "Are you just playing games with me?"

Thomas sputtered on his drink.

"Where would you get that idea?" he asked.

Marley steeled herself. "It's a simple 'yes' or 'no' answer, Mr. Elker."

"It's not that simple."

"How is it not?" Marley snapped. "You either are or aren't."

Thomas squirmed, and the Scottish fantasy dissipated. She squared her shoulders.

"All this talk of dodging commitment and bringing a new treat to the Plaza everyday… If you're the type of guy to just go from one available girl to another, then I'm sorry, but I don't know what would give you the impression that I would just go along with it. I took a whole day off when I should have been working on a follow-up presentation. I shouldn't have come."

She stood up, gathering her skirt and knapsack. A few used tissues tumbled out.

"Marley. Wait."

But the bobcat's claws were out. "Why are you encouraging me to share my dreams as if we were building a freaking life from the ground up?"

"Hold on. Please listen," Thomas said.

She didn't sit back down, but she stopped moving. "Fine. Talk."

"You're a feisty one," Thomas commented.

"If 'feisty' means standing up to a man who has women convinced that *they* can open that next door you claim to be hiding, then yes. I am feisty. All I need is for some unsuspecting woman to come knocking on my door asking why I was with you at the Plaza last Friday night."

He threw his head back and laughed. How dare he laugh at her.

"She's not unsuspecting."

That made Marley pause.

"It's not cheating if she found company outside the bounds of holy matrimony first." Thomas spit out the words as if they were poison. His voice softened. "I'm only following her example. We're married on paper. That's it."

Marley's eyes widened. She thought of her mother who had spent what felt like years in marriage limbo because her father wouldn't sign the divorce papers, even though he had been the one to take another woman into his bed.

"Is that why you don't wear a ring?" Marley asked gently.

"Correct," Thomas said. He sounded formal, any indication of his friendship and favor gone. It made something within her feel empty. And panicked. How quickly someone could become used to the warmth of another. It made her realize how badly she didn't want to feel disconnected from Thomas, who'd made her feel so good - herself - and comfortable this week. And they *weren't* dating. This was her jealousy, she realized. And that wasn't right.

She sat back down on the maroon blanket. "I came on way too harshly. I'm so sorry. Here I was encouraging you to trust me, and then I bark at you the moment you actually tell me the truth? I'm sorry."

Thomas shook his head. "No. You're right to confront me."

She turned her head. "I am?"

Thomas slipped his thumb under her palm. "Of course you are. You deserve to know the truth. Not only as a colleague, but as a 'fast friend.' I have genuinely enjoyed getting to know you and spend time with you. I can't tell you the last time I enjoyed someone else's company that wasn't my own. I know that sounds cocky, but I hope you can see the compliment in it."

"I can," she reassured him. "I think," she muttered. "But I'm sorry I don't understand. Why don't you just divorce if you're so unhappy?"

"Sofia and I are practical people. We know our finances are in better shape if we stay together. More money compounds more money, you know?"

"So you're free to see other people?"

He hesitated. "That's what it would look like to other people, yes."

Thanks to the world of the Cromwells, Marley wasn't a stranger to the logistical aspects of finding someone to marry for status or economical boost, but she still couldn't wrap her mind around actually staying in a relationship like that. She thought of her mother. Peggy had *not* allowed her husband to see other people. Marley was certain of that. Otherwise, the night her mother had left a suitcase outside their door with her mom yelling that he was *not* allowed into their home may not have happened.

"You must think I'm a horrible person," Thomas mused. He squinted into the setting sun.

Marley swallowed. She knew she had every reason to get up, leave, and never look back. He had led her on, after all, and he was *married*? But for some reason, she couldn't judge him. He looked too sad to be villain-ous; the men she and Lily judged were much more calculating and manip-ulative. Thomas Elker didn't seem either of those things.

"You'd have been more horrible if you hadn't told me at all," Marley offered. "Would you tell me what's really going on? Why did you meet me in the Café, offer me aloe, send me soup, and why are we sitting in the most romantic place in the world talking about your *marriage*?"

"Investigator Marley, hello," Thomas tried weakly.

"Let's not play games right now," Marley said. She embraced her inner Lily and found her voice hardened as she did so. It felt like she was being mean, but it also felt necessary. "In fact, it'd be quite better that we didn't. Who *are* you, Thomas Elker?"

"This doesn't seem like a conversation for San Nicolas."

"Why, because it's out in the open? Like your relationship?"

Thomas' eyes widened.

Marley resisted the urge to apologize. She was always apologizing. She waited.

"Can we go somewhere else?" Thomas asked. "Please?"

Marley forced herself to look into Thomas' eyes. They pleaded the way she wished her bullies had when they had had their fun. Instead of being called "four eyes" or "teacher's pet," though, he was asking for a private place to talk. Hardly a crime.

She sighed. "Seems like a reasonable request. I'd want to be offered the same." In fact, that is what Thomas had offered her - crying, alone, in the dark - last week. Instead of judging her, he had given her a hug.

"Let's get this all packed up. I know just the place."

Soak in the Serendipity

The strong smell of mint wrapped around them before they had entered the tea house. Lily had always joked that walking into a Moroccan tea house was like bathing in a mojito.

She thought of Zeke who had brought her here the first time, the evening after she had been introduced to the *Tigre* team. How he had sensed her nervousness made her wonder just how much of the stage her anxiety dominated. When she'd swallowed her pride and asked Zeke over a pot of tea just how much she stank of desperation, his face surprised her. She was a girl who traveled away from everything she'd ever known, he reminded her, in order to pursue a dream. That wasn't something a nervous girl did.

And so Marley reminded herself now: she could be cautious and courageous at the same time.

Marley waved to the host at the threshold of the teahouse. Marta was used to Marley's visits here on Monday nights. But instead of a phone, Harlequin, pen and notebook in her hands, Marley had a man with a wicker basket in tow. And Marley knew from Marta's expression that they both looked like they'd seen happier days.

Marley pointed to the back of the teahouse and Marta nodded.

"Follow me," Marley called behind her.

They walked to the room in the back, mint mixing with hookah smoke. Bright colors of teal, orange, and Granada's Moorish influence surrounded them, culture and its colors dancing together like the cobras

Marley imagined hid in Thomas' basket, his words waiting to pop all the hope that had been ballooning within her.

"Here." She opened the curtain, revealing a corner table covered in silk, adorned by pillows that leaned against the wall-pressed benches. The pillows looked full, as if resting on them would cause dust from the desert to tickle the air.

"You sit there." She pointed to one side of the corner of the wall. And then she sat on the other. If someone had built a wall from corner to corner of the teahouse, they may as well have been on opposite sides. She hated feeling so far away from him, but she needed answers.

How could someone turn her and her anger on so much? How could someone have so much power over how she felt? This is why she didn't date. This feeling right here. This righteous anger mixed in with depths of hurt and confusion and insecurity. It did no one any favors.

The curtain swayed and Marta placed a tray with glasses on the table. They watched the tea cascade from high above their heads into glasses wrapped by silver, steam wrapping around them. Marley wanted Marta to pour the hot liquid on Thomas, not caring what she scalded.

Thomas stared at his hands, and Marley stared at him. The chiseled jaw and downcast eyes didn't do her anger any favors. Thomas was in his own world, collecting his thoughts, and Marley was trying not to let hers dictate her next move. Her emotions had always gotten in the way, her father reminded her often. So this time, she was going to stay and listen to what Thomas had to say.

When Marta left, Thomas lifted his head and began. "Sofia and I met when we were young. Both in school for marketing, and we hardly knew the world, but could have sworn that it was ours. We were both dreamers and wanted to be the couple who lived on a sailboat, sailing from island to island, drawing our own maps and building kingdoms that only we would know the entrance to. Except we were both from Brooklyn, broke, and spent more time figuring out what we'd spend our future money on than focusing on how we were going to make enough money for that month's rent."

"I didn't realize you were from New York as well," Marley interrupted.

"Why do you think I wanted to keep hanging out with you?"

She ignored him. Did he really think that she only responded to compliments? What was it about her that gave him that idea? She pressed on. "Being broke in New York is not a good feeling."

"No. 'If you can make it there, you can make it anywhere' hits hard when you're *not* making it there. Especially when you've got big dreams."

She knew the feeling. When she couldn't get a job at what felt like *any* agency in New York following her graduation, it didn't take long for her to start looking abroad. She found internships in Tokyo, Bangkok, and Berlin. Seeing the job opening for Agencia del Tigre in Granada was the perfect chance for a slower pace in a smaller city. When she was offered the position, it felt like all of her prayers had been answered. When had that stopped feeling like enough? At what point had she wanted more for herself?

"So what happened?"

"We basically gave our well-meaning parents the bird, pointed to a spot on the world map, packed up our bags, and ended up in Toledo. Sofia still lives there. I visit occasionally; otherwise, I live here. On my own."

"I know what alone feels like," Marley said. And then it was like all of the locks on all of the doors in her heart broke open.

She wondered how many days Thomas had felt that same way. It made her want to sidle next to him, throw her arms around his neck and tell him he didn't need to be lonely tonight. Or tomorrow. Not with her around.

Marley slid her hand into Thomas'. He looked at her as if she *had* splashed hot tea onto him. His skin felt warm, but like a silk pillowcase that was still cool to the touch. She let go of his hand. They didn't have to go further than the physical. Maybe it was more than enough that they could help each other carry that awful weight of loneliness. And no one would have to know. Lily. Zeke. Sofia. They'd bolster each other up, secret supports where only a glance and a nod across the conference table would reassure each of them that they weren't alone. Two New Yorkers, trying to make it. Two human beings, trying to find the good in the world and bring out the best in each other.

Try as she might, Marley couldn't picture this wife of his - Sofia - living a life of independence on Thomas' dime in Toledo. She couldn't even picture Thomas as a husband. She believed him when he said that he and commitment were opposites: he was too much of a free spirit, doing what he wanted to do instead of what the spirit of the law suggested.

He squeezed her hand.

"If you're not into commitment and you're still married... Why me?"

"Why *not* you?" Thomas asked, bringing her hand to his lips. Her eyes fluttered shut at the rush of tenderness.

"Because I'm awkward. Shy. Awkward," she repeated.

With his other hand, Thomas reached out and tucked a piece of hair behind her ear.

"All that means is that you refuse to play by someone else's rules. You are yourself, bobcat, and that's so rare. I see someone who hasn't recognized how to tap into her power yet. I see someone who's the brightest light in the room at Tigre. But the way your eyes light up when they see me looking at you?" He whistled. She reached for the tea and took a sip. The mint refreshed her, even as Thomas' words charged her.

"But you're my boss," Marley started.

"In the office, yes. But here?" he gestured around them. "Behind this curtain? Here, I'm just a man who has been waiting since he met you to do *this.*"

His arm wrapped around her back and he pulled her in, his lips millimeters away from hers. She breathed in sharply. His forehead and hair was matted with sweat, but she slid her palm against his cheek and hooked her fingertips around his ear anyway. The beard hairs were rough to the touch, evidence of a long day where shaving had happened long ago. He pressed his palm against the small of her back and urged her closer. She bit her bottom lip and opened her eyes just enough to see him looking down at her, making her feel as though she were a treasure he had found in the most unlikely of places. Someone for him to hold on to. Someone for her to rely on. And that's when she realized it: he was looking at her like Logan looked at Lily.

And that was enough. She didn't have to be as bold as the woman in the bar, or as beautiful as her best friend. She just had to learn how to be a woman more open to the world and its experiences. Life wasn't always cut, clean, and simple. It was messy. And why should Thomas be lonely because of a failing marriage? Clearly, she had found *this* job instead of one somewhere else because it led her *here* to *this* moment with *this* man.

"Kiss me," she whispered.

And he obliged.

His lips were strong, commanding, hungry, as if he hadn't kissed someone in years. His hands tightened on her hips, and the pulling of her to him made the table shake. She was certain tea spilled over the edges. Marley's bobcat purred, her claws extending and kneading his shoulders.

She pulled away to take a cooling breath. "Who are you and where did you come from?"

Thomas' grasp around her lower back tightened. They could have been in an igloo, and between the Spanish humidity, the heaviness of their breathing, and the evaporating tea, the walls would have melted.

And when she heard her name, she wished she would have evaporated, too.

"Marley?"

She froze, recognizing the voice. She pushed herself off Thomas, straightening her skirt. Marley didn't want to look - and she didn't have to.

"What a pleasant surprise," Thomas said brightly. "Looks like we all had the same idea tonight."

"Apparently so," Zeke responded. His voice sounded strained. "Marley is usually here on Monday nights. Alone."

"Is that right?" Thomas asked. "I'm glad she didn't have to be tonight."

"Zeke? Where'd you go?" Margaret's voice traveled through the teahouse. At her friend's gentle voice, the pit in Marley grew wider. Fighting with Zeke was one thing, but disappointing Margaret was an entirely more devastating situation.

Zeke pulled the curtain farther back so that when Margaret approached them, she could take in the whole scene. Margaret brought her hand to her mouth, eyes full of concern. Then hurt.

"Zeke. Margaret," Marley started, then cleared her throat. She had no idea what to say.

"We thought you might be here," Margaret said. "If you were feeling sick, Moraccan mint always seemed to make you feel better." Her voice was typically light, so to hear it sound weighed down made Marley want to hide.

Rather than make an excuse or create a false story, Marley stared at her skirt. "That's very kind of you," Marley said to the beads that suddenly felt too coarse. She let go of them, small engravings left in her palm. She didn't know what else to say.

"Glad you're feeling better," Zeke said. "See you guys in the office tomorrow."

He dropped the curtain, separating her from her best friends. It may as well have been a boulder - the weight of feeling alone.

Give Him the Best of You

Marley stopped at the foot of the hill, breathing heavily, wondering where Zeke and Margaret would have gone, unsure of whether she wanted to find them or run in the opposite direction.

Her eyes were scanning and desperate. If she went to the right, she'd get lost in the groups of people climbing up. They were looking forward to dancing or dining or drinking in the views that she was leaving behind. She could blend in with the crowd; she had always been really good at it.

But if she went to the left, she would probably run into them, especially if they were walking home. She could apologize to them, explain why she was making out with Thomas in the back of a teahouse. Beg for forgiveness. Ask for understanding. But that would require confronting the disappointment in the faces of those she respected and admired the most.

And that didn't work when she apologized to her father, time after time. She couldn't imagine it working out with people she'd only met a year ago.

Tears clouded her vision and she wiped them, angry. How could such a perfect moment be so perfectly ruined?

Each step in descent was farther from Mount Olympus. She had tasted ambrosia and, in the same gulp, that same spoonful had been ripped from her grasp. It wasn't fair. Zeke had Margaret. He didn't know what Lonely felt like.

Clutching her knapsack's strap, Marley turned to the right.

"Marley. Marley. Whoa. Hey! Where are you going?" Thomas' voice followed Marley as she stumbled over her feet, sandals clacking against the cobblestones.

She stopped at the fountain of uplit horses spitting water that glittered in the moonlight, only to disappear in the flagons belonging to the stone damsels. Just last week she had been sitting on a bench here after visiting the teahouse, in awe that she lived here, where the architecture seemed so rich, but even someone as quiet and humble as she could call home. Just a week ago, Marley had blushed sneaking peeks at the man spinning a woman as if they were dancing to music only they could hear. Less than an hour later, an arguing couple made her wonder how people could get themselves wrapped up in so much drama. And now she was the one who wouldn't know where to start if a stranger were to ask what was wrong. She surveyed the square. It was mostly empty but for a few tourists taking selfies in front of the jumping waters.

"Marley."

Thomas had caught up with her, his arms extended in question.

"I can't do this," she said.

Thomas took her hands into his. "Why not? What's going on? I thought you and Zeke were really close."

"We were." She breathed in shakily. "We are," she corrected. "But he had also invited me to hang out with him and I told him I was too sick and then he saw me on top of you. Oh, God," she groaned. "I'm a horrible person."

Thomas grabbed Marley by the shoulders. "Out of all the things you can call yourself, 'horrible' is not one of them. Breathe. You can say that you were feeling better this evening, after the call, and you invited me over for tea to discuss the project. One thing led to another and… there's chemistry. That—" his hands slid down to her hips, "you cannot deny."

Her hips lifted and her arms slid around his neck. Natural. It was all so natural with him, like they had done this a million times. "That's a lie, though," Marley said.

He tilted his head. "That there's chemistry between us?"

"No. The entire excuse. What you're saying I should tell Zeke."

He looked down at her, amusement on his face. "Were you not feeling better after Zeke called you?"

They swayed, back and forth.

"Yes," she said.

"And did you not lead me straight to the teahouse?"

"I did," she admitted.

"So where's the lie?"

"But he walked in on us *kissing*," Marley pushed.

"We're passionate about what we do," Thomas smirked.

Marley slapped his arm, but a grin was starting on her face, too. "This isn't funny! They are some of my closest friends and what if they don't even want to speak with me anymore?"

"If they wouldn't want to speak to you after being your own person and getting tea with someone you like, then they might not be the kind of people you want around," Thomas said.

She stopped swaying. Maybe Thomas had a point. Was this why Lily only had a few people she called her best friends? Nobody else understood her, but it was enough that she had her few secret-people in a close-knit support system. Zeke and Margaret were helpful for her professional life, but maybe they didn't have a space in the part that was romantic?

"C'mere," Thomas sighed, squeezing around her hips.

Something in her loosened, but she hesitated, looking around. "Here?"

"Even when we try to hide we're discovered." Thomas' breath tickled her ear. "Why *not* be out in the open? As open as I was earlier. Unless." He stepped back. "Unless you don't want this. Then we'll stop it right now. And take out the treasure chest only when you feel it's safe to."

"'Treasure chest'?" she asked.

"What we can open when we need reminders of how the other feels about us. How we feel about each other. Reminders of our worth, if you will."

So she did make him feel something more than pressure against his zipper. That was good. But she wasn't convinced. "And what is *'this'*?"

"Enjoying each other. No expectations. Sampling life and savoring the flavor."

"Aren't you a wordsmith."

"It's what they pay me the big bucks for." He winked, then took another step back.

"No," Marley caught his hand. "Stay. Please." Zeke and Margaret were mad at her. Thomas was threatening to leave. There was no way she was going to call her mom and confess that she had somehow become the other woman. If she was going to be stuck with the worst of herself, she might as well offer the best of herself to Thomas. She wanted more of whatever was in this treasure chest. If only to finally feel like someone's gold.

He wrapped his arms around her hungrily, and her cheek pressed against his chest. She lifted her head, her forehead resting gently against the tip of his nose. She tilted her head, his lips hovering over hers. Marley's fingernails dug into Thomas' shoulder. She forced herself to breathe deeply. His hand slipped under her ass and he lifted her with ease. She wrapped her legs around him. They were at a fountain in the middle of a Spanish plaza, but it could have been a world all their own.

Suddenly, Lily's ringtone blared from somewhere deep in her knapsack, though it sounded like it was right next to her ear. While Thomas' hands ran up and down her body, Marley wondered whether it was imperative to answer the call or not: listening to Lily would *not* produce the same feel-goods that Thomas was.

Thomas' teeth snapped by her ear, like they were clamping around the radio waves of the cell phone and ripping them in half. She moaned, and the ringtone faded into the distance. His palm slipped under her hair, cupping the back of her head. Her excitement revved *him*. Was this how powerful Lily felt all the time?

Marley pushed gently against Thomas' back and he set her down. She took his hand and led him to a small alleyway. She pressed her back against the stone, grinning up at him, the fire in her eyes reflected in his. His lips bent to caress her shoulder, his nose nudging her neck, kissing her throat. She drove her hips into him. How was he able to make her feel so *good*?

"You taste so good," Thomas whispered, breathing heavily against her shoulder.

She leaned her head back as his fingers dug deeper into her hair and his lips caressed her neck.

"Would you stay with me?" he said.

Forever and a day, she wanted to say. But somehow, she knew that wasn't what he meant.

"When?" she asked.

"I'll let you know. It'll be spur of the moment. Have an overnight bag. We'll have a proper dinner. We'll stay at the Meliá Granada."

"But that's one of the nicest hotels in Granada. You would do that?" For *her*? *With* her?

He gave her a look like he couldn't believe she was still doubting him.

"Yes. That sounds amazing," Marley said.

He wrapped his arms completely around her, squeezing as if he wanted to get every last drop of what she offered.

"Who are you?" Marley groaned, letting herself go slack in his embrace. As his hands roamed her body, she imagined waking up next to him with the sun pouring through the window curtains, stepping around the clothes they left strewn from the night before, turning on the shower for the two of them to freshen up for a lazy Sunday. "Why do you affect me so much?"

He answered her with a crushing kiss.

Get What You Need

Marley felt like she was sneaking back home from a party that she was never supposed to attend.

By herself.

He had to offer to walk her home at some point. Right?

Marley crumpled onto her bed and sat up, pressing her back against the wall. She stared at the ceiling, trying to match her breathing to the rise and fall of Cilantro's white fur, but rest was as elusive as her promotion.

She had ignored Lily's call once, then twice, and then again. Lily knew that Marley went to the teahouse every Monday night, so if Marley wasn't responding, Lily would assume that something had gone wrong. And though something had gone wrong, at least that something wasn't that she had been kidnapped. Or something. Marley's trembling fingers felt her lips. They were still swollen. Marley's heart pound. She opened their text conversation. There's no way she could keep a steady voice if she called Lily, let alone get away with lying on a video call.

Marley: Hey, girl!

Lily: You're alive! I was so worried. Thank goodness. Okay. You won't believe who called me.

The back of Marley's neck suddenly grew very hot, sweat beading at the top of her hairline. As she gathered her hair into a ponytail, she searched her memory. Did Zeke have Lily's number? Would Zeke have called her? Did he see Marley's betrayal of their friendship as an emergency and now Lily was here with her reckoning?

Marley drew a breath in.

Marley: Who called you?

Lily: Nicholas Archer!

Marley: What? I thought Nic had cut off all non-work contact after the IceStorm party.

Lily: He had. So when he requested a video conference with me earlier this morning, I thought it was going to be about work. Speaking of - we have our first official Dove Hospital release next week!

Marley: Congratulations! ...I'm assuming the appointment was *not* a work call.

Lily: Thanks. And no, it was not. TOTALLY out of bounds.

Marley pressed the bottom of the phone to her forehead and sighed. Out of bounds just like she was. Why wasn't she running away from Mr. Elker? What was this hold he had on her, that as much as she desired to stay in her own bed with her kitten laying on her chest, she also yearned to be in his arms, skin against skin, his lips pressing against...

Three dots appeared. Marley imagined Lily typing profusely, so she waited.

Lily: The way he was asking about Logan and how we were doing made it sound like he was scavenging for information. Like, just ask Hugo, Nicholas. Hugo loves Logan. Anne loves Logan. Does he not realize how hard it is to please Anne Cromwell? And now that she's pleased? No way. And that

Mom's boyfriend loves Logan, too? It's adorable. Anyway, I told him Logan was visiting his mom in Illinois right now, and then - AND THEN he had the nerve to ask me to dinner. He asked me to visit him in Utah this weekend! Marley, he KNOWS I'm happy with Logan and wants me to, what, just FORGET I'm engaged? What kind of sick person does it take to sabotage a relationship like that? Even if I WERE fighting with Logan right now, I would never - I mean NEVER do that to him."

Ordinarily, Marley would have wholeheartedly agreed with her best friend, even adding on with something like, "Yeah, I get it. My dad was definitely a Nicholas Archer back in his day."

But then the truth settled, adding depth to her pit. *And now I am, too.*

So, instead, she said nothing. And that was worse than anything else, because now it seemed like she was condoning Nicholas' behavior instead of rising up against it like she normally would, defending Lily to the end.

Lily: Mar?

Marley: I'm here.

Lily: Isn't that the sickest kind of behavior?.

Marley: The sickest. He's got to have no life whatsoever.

She had to have no life whatsoever. She laid on her right side, the weight of holding her hypocrisy suddenly too much.

Lily: None. That guy's got a serious problem. Thank God we're not like him. Anyway. No need to dwell on him. I feel so much better already. Thanks so much for listening."

For all of Lily's judgment of Anne, there was quite the resemblance between them now. They didn't know Nicholas or what he might be going through. What if Nicholas was being courageous, reaching out to Lily before she fully committed to Logan?

Tears welled in her eyes, but she blinked them back. What was wrong with her? Defending Nicholas? She must have a serious problem, too. Why else hadn't she walked away from Thomas the *moment* he had confessed that he was married? Most pressing, and a growing weight around her as she tried to scramble some thoughts together for Lily: how could she ever tell her best friend about her predicament *now*?

> **Lily:** You've been busy this week. Does this mean you've had the chance to celebrate the one-year Granada-versary with your Spanish friends?

Marley sat back up.

> **Marley:** You remembered?
>
> **Lily:** Says so right here in my calendar reminder!

She hadn't expected anyone to remember. That's why she'd asked Thomas for that last minute celebratory shot.

> **Lily:** Zeke and Margaret didn't ask you out? I called Margaret and made sure they'd do something special for you this week since I wouldn't be in town. At least for a little while longer. I'll be there before you know it.

Marley's jaw dropped. If Lily had remembered with her million to-do lists of professional and social activities, then the Martinezes would have, too. *That's* why Zeke and Margaret had invited her for dinner?

Marley flushed.

> **Marley:** Lil. That's amazing.

Her best friends. How dare she claim loneliness? The Martinezes had welcomed a shy American girl into their country, into their home, and into their lives. Shame on her for disrespecting them by placing her wants above their hospitality. And for basically throwing Lily's generous outreach on her behalf into her face. Marley felt the pit widen.

Lily: Aw, yay! You're surprised! Let me see your face!

Marley's heart pounded in her throat. If Lily had a chance to see Marley's face, there's no doubt she'd see her flushed face, wild eyes, and pink cheeks. They were thousands of miles apart, but they were still best friends.

Marley: No! I'm not looking my best. Please save me the embarrassment.

But something about Lily's enthusiasm and warmth gave her courage. This was her chance. Thomas was right: the people who loved her would support her, no matter what. And if they didn't, then maybe they didn't have a place in her life. She swallowed.

Marley: But you're right. I do feel a little higher on life than normal.
Lily: Aw, I love that. How come? Did you hang out with Zeke and Mags?

Marley squeezed her eyes shut. *Now's your chance, Marley. Tell Lily the truth. Just spit it out.*

Marley: I did see him, yes. Margaret, too.
The *whole* truth, Marley reprimanded herself.
Marley: And Thomas.

Lily: Your boss? Oo. Are you being good?

Marley's eyes widened in annoyance. Marley wanted Fun, Reckless Lily on the phone, not the Lily of near-death experiences and therapy. She wanted the Lily from a few months ago, *before* Logan, who saw men as playthings and ways to feel good.

Lily: Marley… Tell your girl what's up.

It was different, this change of dynamic in their friendship. It was usually Marley waiting to hear about the trouble Lily had gotten into, not the other way around. Marley suddenly understood why it took Lily days, sometimes weeks, to admit what was on her heart. Vulnerability was scary.

Marley: I had tea with Thomas.

Lily: …You're SURE we can't chat on video?

Marley: I'd really rather not.

Lily: Fine. Let's talk about the facts: you went out for TEA to celebrate your one-year anniversary. But also, don't get wrapped up in that workspace drama. Seriously. Girl. You can do better.

Memories of her extinguishing her Statue of Liberty shot came to mind. She straightened her spaghetti strap. Remembering the heavy breathing by the fountain made her skin break out in fresh sweat. She looked down at her skirt and the shame of needing to pull it down in front of Zeke made her want to hide and never come out ever again.

Marley: I know. I know I can.

She pulled her pillow underneath her head.

Marley: You know, I'm actually really tired.

Lily: I don't like your spirit, Stitch. We're just going to have to fix this. I'm booking a ticket to come visit so we can celebrate properly. I get an extra day off for my birthday. I'll tell Greg it's finally time for me to take that two-week vacation I've been putting off. It'll be a surprise. We'll go to a club, find some sexy men for you to dance with, and wake up the next morning wondering why your sandals are on your hands. It'll be wonderful. Hm… Oh, shoot. My period will be there around the same time I will be, but what's a better excuse for ice cream?

Thomas had invited her to spend the night, but she didn't know when that was either. Besides, given the choice, she'd *obviously* have to tell Thomas that they'd have to reschedule. She typed eagerly, happy to know she meant it.

Marley: Yes! I'm so excited to see you!

Lily: I'm excited, too. The IceStorm party was fun, but my trips to Spain are way better. I love that I don't have to worry about a thing when I'm with you, Stitch. What a gift. Have a great night!

Marley smiled sadly. She used to be able to say the same.

When had Lily gone from being her safety net, to a spider's web Marley didn't want to get trapped in?

And since when had Marley become so good at spinning her own web of lies?

Most importantly, why wasn't all of *this* reason enough to stop?

She groaned and picked up her phone again. Even though it felt like things were okay with Lily, she had a feeling that sleep wouldn't come until she knew things were okay between her and Zeke and Margaret.

"Please pick up," Marley begged. "Please, please, please." It was almost two in the morning, but according to Spanish time, that meant they were finishing the last of their tapas and about to go dancing. It was only the American ego, Zeke had taught her one day, that made her feel like everyone was thinking about her and judging her when Spaniards were busy having a good ol' time.

Zeke's voice echoed for the fourth time. "Bueno! Deja un mensaje."

She threw her phone across the room, the movement and noise making Cilantro jump off and shake her head. The phone landed with a thud on the cushions of her pull-out couch. She guessed they could be sleeping, but how could they sleep soundly with their friendship on rocky ground like this? She wanted to apologize and hear the forgiveness in Zeke's voice. Especially Margaret's. Would Margaret meet Marley for churros con chocolate in the afternoon and Marley could tell her everything? But if Zeke had already told her his side of the story and Marley wasn't getting a chance to share hers…

She sat up, pressing her back and leaning her head against the wall, the memory of Thomas' hands around her just hours ago.

"Unfair. This is all unfair," Marley said into the darkness, stroking Cilantro's back until her butt raised in the air. "Why does everyone get a chance to find love in normal, happy ways, and my story has to have such a bullshit mess that Thomas and I have to sift through?"

Deep breath in. Shaky breath out. Reason it out, Marley: Zeke was a Spaniard, which meant he dealt with conflict differently than an American might. He probably *was* sleeping, while their relationship might as well have been a body at their feet that was bleeding out with each passing second. Instead of freaking out about this, she needed to cool down and get her mind back in control.

She knew who to call. Her father was totally fine with people being unhappy with him. It came with the territory of being a defense lawyer.

Though he was typically the last one she wanted to talk to, Marley knew her father would understand.

She typed out a text: "Dad, can you come to Granada this week?"

She set the phone down and picked up Cilantro, whose back legs straightened as if ready for a pedicure. Marley giggled and felt herself relax. Marley didn't actually want her father to visit - and she knew that he wouldn't - but asking for a trip would ensure that she would at least get a phone call.

It wouldn't take long to receive a response from him. Her father's assistant, Laurie, received his texts, checked his schedule, and ran more of his life than Henry Harrow III did. She could imagine Laurie clicking frantically from browser tab to browser tab, double-checking Henry's schedule and to either make the trip from New York to Spain work or find excuses for why it wouldn't.

Sure enough, a text from Laurie came in: "Hi Marley. Sorry. Your dad can't make it out to you this week. He's got an important case heading to court. Can I leave a message?"

What message could she leave her father? *Hi, Dad. Wanted to give a quick update: Finally presented at work. Love the way my boss' body feels against mine. Boss is married. I've lied to my friends. I believe you may have been in a situation that's similar. Please advise. K thx bye.*

She wasn't going to type a response. Something about Zeke ignoring her calls made her angry. Her father wouldn't get away from her this easily this time. He owed her. She punched the video icon on her screen.

A few rings later, there was a slight shake in the camera's view as the phone passed from Laurie's hand to her father's. Marley watched her father press down on the cowlick that usually lifted at his forehead - just another habit that didn't work out the way he hoped it would. It was what her mother first noticed about her father, the story went. Marley had to admit it did make her father look more youthful, balancing out the grey hairs that were starting to show.

She caught her father furrow his brow at Laurie in disapproval and Marley felt herself shrink. He cleared his throat.

"How's my girl?" Her father's gruff voice attempted enthusiasm. Someone in the office must have been eavesdropping, and it wouldn't do for someone to think Henry Harrow was not a decent father. "I don't have too much time, wrapping up the details for this case and all...."

Marley forced a smile, pulling at her split ends. "I know you're busy. I appreciate you taking my call."

"Of course. How can I help you today?" Like she was just another client.

She felt the familiar sinking feeling. What had she been hoping for? A fireside chat where her dad would finally relax and share a whiskey with the daughter he had always wished had been a son? Maybe her half brother Vince would be the recipient of such a gift when he grew up.

"I actually wanted to ask if you would do some digging for me."

That made her father pause. "Are you in trouble?"

"No. Well. I haven't been feeling my best, but I'm definitely not in trouble. At least I don't think so. I don't mean 'digging' like, private investigator stuff. I mean 'digging', like, through your memories."

He scowled. "Well. That doesn't sound like a quick check-in between work tasks."

"You might have to come out here for a visit for a longer chat." She gritted her teeth. She couldn't imagine something worse than hosting her father in Granada. Shoot pigeons in an open field in Granada? She didn't love manipulating her father like this, but *needed* to know what had been running through Henry Harrow's mind leading up to his decision to betray her and her mother. She needed to know if, despite her greatest attempts to be different from her father, she was really the same. And was he really that unhappy with them that he had to leave? Did they not love him the way he needed to be loved? Because maybe then she could finally accept that her father was better off as a wild, sow-your-oats everywhere kind of man.

"I'll make sure Laurie books a flight for me the moment I win this case, baby girl. And then we can have those churros you're always talking about."

Was he serious? *Abort mission!*

"I can't possibly take you away from your work. The added pressure of traveling after a high-stress case doesn't seem fair."

The amount of relief that crossed her dad's face was the same when Marley had told him years ago that she'd prefer to spend most of her time at her mother's. She wished he would have fought for her, even just a little bit.

"Want to give your old man a hint about what you wanted to talk about?"

"Honestly?" She harnessed the anger she felt at Zeke and the frustration she had with herself and the universe and spit out the truth. "I want to know what was running through your head when you cheated on Mom."

"Marley." She saw him fumble for the button that would take her off speakerphone. "I thought we had let the dust settle on that."

"*You* may have." *With your fancy house and big dog and son and wife that you could cheat on whenever you want.* "But I haven't made my peace with it. Especially not now, when I'm in the position that I figure Valerie was in."

Her father's face transformed, understanding dawning upon him.

"Oh. Well. I know from her that it was not easy."

She could see the wheels turning in his mind, struggling to know how much to say and how much had to stay hidden. It sounded like he really did know that it wasn't for Valerie to wait on the side while her dad figured out how to leave his original family. Maybe Marley and her mom *had* been keeping him from happiness and ease.

"Marley…" he started. "If I've learned anything, it's that whatever the heart thinks it wants is typically a need that hasn't been fulfilled. Figure out what you really need. What is making you attracted to this person that you could actually do for yourself?"

And then he looked at her like he was seeing his daughter for the first time.

"I hurt you and your mother terribly. There's a way to get what you need without wreaking havoc in the process."

Someone called him in the distance.

"I'm sorry I have to go. Remember to think before you act," he reminded her. And then he smiled and said what he always said before hanging up: "Be a good person. Make good choices. Try and have a good night."

And then he was gone and she was alone again.

She had expected to receive answers, but now she had more questions. So he'd messed up a bunch of lives in the process of getting what he wanted - which ended up being what he needed, too, apparently. Look at him now! He was living his best life. She and her mother had eventually gotten over it. And then Marley felt a flood of indignation: she was worth happiness, too, even if others suffered. Marley and her mother had been devastated in the beginning, but ultimately happier with Henry out of their home. Marley didn't know Thomas' wife, but if they had already agreed to separate…

She turned off her phone, hiding it in her knapsack. She had disappointed the Martinezes, she had lied to Lily, and she had called her father before reaching out to her mom. She didn't need a mirror to see that she was slipping backwards instead of propelling forwards. Her company was failing and she wasn't any closer to senior level. But she had hope. With Thomas' help and confidence in her, she would be able to figure it out. She would reconcile with Zeke, make sure her next presentation this week at work was a hit, have a magical night with Thomas, *and* reconnect with Lily, where Marley would finally tell her everything. And if she didn't like it… Marley swallowed. Well, they'd cross that bridge when they got to it.

Yes. Marley deserved to be happy. To feel alive. And if others were a little sad in the beginning because of that, well, the ones who were meant to be in her life would stay.

This compass wouldn't change direction just because someone wanted it to.

A compass was only attracted to one thing - and as it so happened, Mr. Thomas Elker was her magnet.

Love Hurts

Karl bounced into her cubicle.

"Hey, girl, hey," Karl sang, bouncing into her cubicle.

Marley quickly hit the minimize button on her screen. She wanted her plan for next month's team meeting to remain a surprise, especially from Karl. He would tell Brandon right away, but swear that Brandon wouldn't tell anyone. This idea was too big. This would be her chance at the promotion *and* the honor of saying that *her* ideas saved an entire company from going under.

She spun around in her chair.

His eyes widened. "Whoa. You are *burnt*."

She rolled her eyes and pressed her back into the chair, only to wince and pull her torso straight up. "I know."

"Like, to a crisp, are you actually bacon, burnt."

"Is this supposed to be making me feel better, Karl?"

"I'm still talking to you despite your stop sign skin, aren't I?"

"*Que quiere decir?* What the heck is that supposed to mean?"

"Just saying. If someone were driving and they saw you, they'd hit the brakes."

She glared at him.

"Come on. That's not even a little funny?" He flopped down into her bright yellow smiley face bean bag chair.

"No." She turned back to her work. Even the spin in her chair moved her blazer *just so* and the pain flared again. She would *never* let herself be outside in the Spanish sun without sunblock *ever* again. "Is that all you wanted to say?"

"No, it's not. I just couldn't ignore it."

She was hoping Thomas would be able to. This was *not* the condition she wanted to be in if their hotel date was going to be sooner rather than later.

"I've never gotten *this* sunburnt before. I would have probably saved so much money by just buying the dang sunblock at the pool instead of—" She gestured to the used bottles of aloe on her desk. She wasn't surprised that Cilantro had lain on her stomach last night; her skin was probably as warm as a heating blanket.

Karl frowned. "It really does hurt, huh?"

She scowled. "Yeah. It does."

"I'm sorry, amiga." He bowed his head. "Let us have a moment of silence for your smoldered epidermis."

She swung to kick Karl but the shooting pain made her groan. "What do you want, Karl?"

Karl hesitated. That wasn't like Karl, and that made her nervous. What did he know? Had Zeke told him? If Karl told Brandon…

"Well, spit it out then."

"You're fighting with Zeke. What's wrong with you?"

"What's wrong with *me*?" Marley stood up despite the pain. "Why do you assume something has to be wrong with me?"

"Um. Because you always say things like, 'What's wrong with me!?' and when you say it enough, people start to wonder what *is* wrong with you. Really, I'm just being a good listener."

Marley unplugged her headphones from her laptop and turned up the speakers. The local radio station flowed through the air and created a barrier between them and anyone who might try to listen. She stood up, pushed her chair in, grabbed her *Be Brave* coffee mug and sat next to the beanbag chair. She lifted the back of her blazer so that she could rest her back against the cabinet, the metal handles cooling her scorched skin through her camisole.

"Zeke has every reason to be upset with me."

"I doubt it. Zeke gets prideful sometimes. I'm sure whatever you did wasn't anything compared to what other people do on a daily basis."

She didn't know what to say. Why did everyone think she was perfect? Like she wasn't capable of being the kind of person who would do what "other people do on a daily basis"? Like she wasn't capable of kissing a man she *knew* belonged to someone else?

She stared into her coffee cup. It was darker than she liked it, but she hadn't wanted to use somebody else's creamer and she had forgotten to buy more for her stash.

"Just because a sin is relatively less severe doesn't mean it isn't hurtful," Marley said.

Karl considered her. "This is why I love you."

The words should have shocked her. It was the first time he had said the words, but she had known he did this entire time. Chamomile in his office, lattes in the morning, frequent check-ins in her cubicle were love in action.

"Thank you," she whispered.

Though she was usually annoyed with Karl's logic, she found his light-hearted presence comforting this morning. After all the knotted messes she had caused this weekend, she was grateful knowing that Karl was still on her team - both professionally and as a friend.

He lifted her chin with his fingertips, then quickly tucked his hands under his thighs. "And just because you don't believe it doesn't mean it isn't true. Not to mention your boy is saying it, which makes it doubly true. I don't just spread my Karl-sized seeds of love everywhere."

That made her laugh. She set her mug on the desk, the magic of laughter waking her up more than the coffee had all day.

Karl reached out and squeezed her hand. Marley hadn't realized her hands had been shaking.

"You don't have to tell me what happened," Karl said. "I'm on your side, no matter what. Don't forget that I'm here for you." He grinned, a smile that reached his eyes. "I'm a really great listener."

"If you say it enough, you think people will finally believe you?"

Karl's jaw dropped, then he laughed.

Marley felt a pull in her shoulders as her body relaxed. "I know you are. Thank you."

"Hugs?"

Before she could finish nodding, she felt Karl's arms wrap around her. He was gentle, not pressing or squeezing too hard. Friends like him were hard to come by, she knew, and she wished she could match Karl's enthusiasm for hanging out with her. She hugged him back regardless, grateful for his affection.

Karl tapped her back a few more times before stepping away. "Can't wait to see what you come up with next. You don't need Zeke. You've got everything it takes right inside of you."

She smiled. "Thanks, friend. We'll chat later."

"No doubt."

She picked up her mug, smiling into it and looking over the brim as she took her final sip of the day. Any more and she'd never fall asleep tonight.

Marley hoped that Karl was right. But just because you said something to yourself or someone said it about you didn't make it true. Words only took someone so far; actions were required - and right now, Marley's actions were not matching how people perceived her, and that was causing an internal chaos that she didn't know how to settle.

* * *

There was no way Marley was going home. Taking a day off on Friday and spending all weekend cuddled with Cilantro in bed feeling bad for herself meant she couldn't waste another minute when she could be working.

But wow was the singular copy machine running in its rhythmic motion lulling Marley into a stupor.

It was after seven o'clock in the evening, but in order to protect the element of surprise, she had to wait for everyone to leave the office. She hugged her arms to her chest. She had work to do. At least that's what she told herself. Maybe this is why her father had spent so much time at work: one felt in control in the office. The work didn't care what kind of person you were. You could stay away from needy colleagues, or blame their bad attitudes on things outside of your control. But at home? The people you lived with were direct examples of how who you were as a person affected everyone else. And the truth was that Marley and her mother weren't happy when Henry was around; in fact, they both seemed to breathe easier without him around, even if they were also holding their breaths waiting for him to finally come home. Even though Cilantro wouldn't change her opinion of Marley - as long as Marley fed her - it was Marley who couldn't imagine sitting at home by herself - with herself.

300 copies would take a while, but folding the paper into butterfly origami might actually take forever. Ordinarily, she'd have asked Zeke and Margaret and they would have folded them in a few hours' time around their bright yellow kitchen table. She frowned and hugged herself tighter, the pit growing in her stomach. What she'd give for Margaret's paella or

Zeke's sangría. Had she ruined it forever? Would she ever get a chance to laugh in that bright orange kitchen again, at ease in the knowledge that she was seen and still accepted? Was being turned on by Thomas really worth trading that in?

She considered how much potential they had. His casual approach to life and her drive? They'd make *Tigre* the top agency in Spain. Marley unwrapped her arms and lifted her chin. The way he believed in her - desired her - gave her more confidence than she'd ever felt in her life. More than when she played volleyball: she won respect by dominating the other team. Here, she had earned respect because of who she was. There was a difference. And then, at once, an idea.

As if Lily had been listening to her the whole time, Marley's phone vibrated in her back pocket accompanied by Lily's ringtone. She swiped to reveal Lily's fifth "I'm so excited!!" message. Marley grinned. So Zeke and Margaret weren't around. That was okay. Lily Cromwell had been, and would be around, forever.

Marley: I think I finally understand that stuff about walking in confidence.

Lily's response came in hot.

Lily: ?!

Marley felt someone walk into the room. She turned around to see Isabel. Why did she always look perfect? And so late in the day? She shook her head and turned back to the phone. Marley typed quickly, like she needed to be done before the copy machine was so that Isabel wouldn't get frustrated with her. Not that she would. Marley was the hurried American, she reminded herself. Spaniards had all the time in the world.

Marley: Remember Mr. Steel teaching us Latin roots? Con-fid-ence… with faith or trust. I always thought you walked with confidence because you had everything together. But maybe that's not necessarily true. Maybe having confidence doesn't mean you have everything together, but that you trust that everything will be okay *despite* not having everything together. Anyway - can't wait to see you this weekend! Love you!

The copy machine stopped running. An arm wrapped around her stomach. She jumped, thrusting the phone onto the top of the machine with a crash. The surprise of being touched so intimately in such a public place had been enough to shock her, but add it onto the sharp pains of her sunburn, and it was almost too much to bear.

"Hey, bobcat," Thomas whispered into her ear. His breath grazed her neck, tickling the skin around the spaghetti strap of her camisole, tucked beneath her blazer.

She spun around, eyes wild, looking for any sign of Isabel or Brandon or any colleague who could pass by at literally any moment. She stepped back. "Are you crazy?" she hissed.

"I've been thinking about doing that all day." He nudged his nose against her forehead. "I double-checked the hallway before I walked in. Promise."

She wanted more than anything to wrap her arms around him and pull him close. She wanted to breathe him in again and again, the feeling of home wrapping around her. Is this what her father left them for? This peace that he couldn't find anywhere else?

Marley's phone pinged, violin strings that signaling Lily's response had come through. Marley drew up her shoulders, tucking her elbows into her sides, then pushed them out to push him away.

"We can't get too comfortable," she said. They needed to be at a distance that would communicate to onlookers that they were only colleagues;

that's it. Even if the pounding heart and shallow breathing between made it totally obvious that they weren't.

"You're right. Or…" He looked over her shoulder. "The machine needs more paper, huh?"

She ran a hand through her hair and eyed the exit. She heard someone walking past the copy room. All it would take is someone walking in and they'd totally be able to tell that Marley was flustered - and that it was Thomas who had caused such a reaction.

"I guess it might. I can take care of it. Or leave it until tomorrow. It's getting so late anyway, you know. I always do this to myself." Her pitch kept increasing, matching the frequency of her heart rate. Someone was going to walk in and she'd be sent home. All her stuff wouldn't fit in one box. She'd need a second trip up and she couldn't face the shame or Zeke when that happened.

Thomas stepped in front of her. "Hey." He clasped Marley's hand and tugged her towards the supply closet. He shut the door behind him and turned off the light. She flipped it back on in a rush.

"What are you doing?" She hated when her voice got like this. Closed spaces were only okay when she was in one alone. Her voice was rising in panic now. She wasn't one of those girls who got it on in the supply closet of the office. "I thought we were leaving it for the hotel."

His shock almost looked natural. He slipped his arm around her back. "I had a dream about you last night."

"You did?" Marley elongated the "i" in did, a sing-songy voice she didn't realize she had. Thomas looked down at her with eyes that looked like they were drinking her in.

"I did," he nodded, his nose brushing hers. His lips were so close. She should be finding a way to slow this down, but being this close to him again… she shut her eyes, memorizing this moment. This feeling. Tingling traveled through her body and her hands ached to explore every inch of this man.

She leaned her head back and tilted it up. "But you said you never remember your dreams."

He smiled, still swaying, his palms holding her hips. "This one is one I couldn't forget. Maybe I had fallen asleep imagining it and then it became a dream."

"What was it about?"

He dipped his head lower, his lips only centimeters away from hers. He pushed his lower half into her and she gasped.

She grasped his hair, trying to hold on as a tornado swirled within her.

"Well?" she whispered, knowing her breath was tickling his lips. She hoped she tantalized him as much as he did her.

"I'm here right now, aren't I?" He pulled back just enough to push against her again. "I woke up knowing I couldn't wait. I'll do what I really want to, then, but right now? I can't possibly wait. Not when I keep remembering how good this felt…"

And then his mouth was finally covering hers. She quivered in his grasp and held on tight, as his power both overwhelmed and steadied her. Any resolve, any worry, any fear of being caught disappeared, and all that remained was the hunger that drove Thomas to this moment, too.

She moaned, but only loud enough so he would hear. In response, Thomas' breathing grew ragged, almost panting. It felt so good knowing that her pleasure increased his own. His thumb played at her waistline, rotating in circles at her hip bone, a tease of where else it could happen, if only she said yes. He slid his hands around to Marley's butt and lifted her, pressing her back against the metal rack. Her sunburnt back seared in pain. She bit her hip, trying to suppress a squeal and a demand for release. Each time he pushed against and into her it was as if a paddle whacked against her, rattling her nerves until even her head throbbed. The cold of the metal against her neck and the way the edges dug into her skin made the moment more intense than anything she had ever experienced. She willed herself not to scream. It was more pain than she had experienced in her life, but she didn't dare complain or tell him to stop. Maybe it was supposed to feel this way. Many of the movies that had been popular as of late had suggested so. But she did not like this. It did not feel good. Speed and intensity did not equal pleasure.

Her breathing became labored and Thomas thrust against her, again and again, undoubtedly urged on by her reaction. His lips found her neck and she leaned her head back, squeezing her eyes shut tight as the pain of the shelving unit against the softness of his kisses fought for her attention.

She suddenly wished he had brought her here only for a hug - to comfort her and tell her everything would be alright. Marley retracted her left arm that had been wrapped around his neck and reached behind her own. She pressed her fingertips against the tender area and pulled them back. No blood. Could have fooled her. Man, makeout sessions had changed a lot since she'd been in the game. Did Lily experience this? Surely Logan wasn't as rambunctious a lover as Thomas…

Thomas must have felt a change in her. He ran a hand up her back and cupped her head in his palm. The relief was immediate and she sighed into him, laying her cheek on his shoulder. He pulled her closer to him and held her, her legs still wrapped around his waist, her breathing still much too strained to be walking away from a storage room in the copy room. In the office. As if her restart button had been pressed, Marley remembered where they were. She pulled on his arm and he set her down.

Thomas turned around, fixing his pants. She smiled to herself, relief and pride turning to satisfaction. *She* did that. Not the woman at Bahama's. Not Isabel. *Marley Harrow did that.* She fixed her own hair and blazer, stretching out her capri pants, trying to peel away the material.

She looked up to see Thomas looking for the paper on the shelving units.

He took a knee and it took her breath away. She gripped the edge of the machine as desire clutched her heart. So he was a rough lover - who cared? It was probably just the sunburn that made it so. How she wanted to be asked by *him* to be by his side, to be chosen, to be his. Their days would be spent talking about creative things, she sharing her ideas and he challenging her lovingly until they'd get it *just right*. They'd sneak in kisses, just like this, and go home to do what they had wanted to all day. They'd never take their hands off each other. Nothing would ever get done at home, but wasn't that what home was for? There would be *love* waiting for her. And not just the kind people settled down in marriage for. She'd have the *exciting* kind. The "Seriously? You're not newlyweds?" kind. The imaginary ring she pictured him lifting towards her was replaced by the paper he'd pulled from the bottom shelf. Marley tried to steady her breath.

He pushed himself off the ground. "You can take it from here?"

"Yes," she exhaled. "Definitely." She reached for the ream and her heart caught in her throat as he squeezed her hand before letting her have the weight.

He winked again, then spun before almost running into Isabel at the doorway.

"Have a great night!" he called over his shoulder and left. Marley spun around, fixing her hair, praying that Isabel wouldn't ask any questions. But Isabel walked by and then it was just Marley, alone, trying to gather her thoughts like a hundred push pins that had spilled around her.

She heard Zeke's grunt and looked down the hall to see Zeke swinging his backpack over his shoulder.

Marley lifted her arm, hoping that a few days apart were enough for them to miss each other and keep living like nothing had happened. Pretend normal. She was good at that, having observed how her father did it after he'd left them for Valerie. How he kept doing it after he'd served Peggy the divorce papers and told Marley she'd be a big sister later that day. How her mother would smile and sit at the kitchen table with Marley over tea after school, though Marley could see Peggy's blotted out tears and swollen cheeks. Pretend normal was how one made it through life. "Fake it 'til you make it," people always said.

And so it wasn't ridiculous for Marley to expect Zeke to wave like he always did, with reminders to rest easy.

But this time, he avoided any eye contact and walked out.

And though there was no door between them, Marley felt the slam against her face - and it hurt more than the sunburn.

Damn Thomas for having the power to weaken her knees with just being himself.

And damn both of them for having the power to walk away.

Make Him Wait

"Tonight."

That's all that the text message from Thomas Elker said.

It's what she'd been waiting the entire autumn for. And now it was happening! Tonight!

Though there was so much to do, the time dragged like the days had in high school: with Marley's head down in work, coming up for air only to see how many hours were left until the weekend. Lily still hadn't visited, but that was fine with Marley. She helped plan Lily's wedding shower from her cubicle, exchanging emails with both Anne and her mother. Regardless of all the work that Marley was pretty used to by now, the difference was that, for two months, she rode the high that was the magic of stolen encounters with Thomas around the office.

When she wasn't forcing herself to focus on the presentation she would give to Mariposa's team, she was plotting her next route to the kitchen or the copy room. Sometimes, she'd see Thomas' back as he topped off his water bottle and look forward to when he'd lean into her like that, pushing buttons that gave sweet release. She'd have to force herself to look away, only to have him directly in her way in the hallway for her next break. She'd go to the water cooler after him only to find a small box of Pop Rocks tucked behind the water cooler. Sometimes they'd be in her mailbox, by the coffee pot, in her desk drawer, or waiting for her in her usual spot at the conference table before meetings. They could be all the way down the hall from each other and she just knew that he felt it, too. The attraction was something she'd never felt before. The needle of her compass pointed directly towards him, and all of his little signs and signals meant directly for her kept her locked and loaded in his direction.

Before she knew, she was one of *those* people on the couch in the lounge. They'd steal time together in the copy room, in the conference room, in the lounge. In the alley behind the building. Anywhere that felt safe and dangerous all at once. Marley got by on caffeine, carrot sticks, and power naps at her desk. The ukulele stress ball had ripped into pieces at some point in that time. Though dangerous, it felt worth it.

Once the working day was done, typically around 7 or 9 in the evening, she'd throw out her takeout and venture straight to her home closet. Between figuring out what to wear to work every day and whether her overnight pack was perfect (in case Thomas finally told her it was time for their hotel date), there was admittedly a mess in her room. And her life. But mostly her room.

Marley tiptoed around the room, avoiding the piles of clothing strewn around her studio apartment while Cilantro's midnight zoomies knocked shirts over as she leapt over them. She set her smeared plate into the sink and looked around. She had always been such an efficient packer. Until it was time to pack for *one* night. Did she want the oversized t-shirt so that her cheeky panties would show a little of the bootie that Thomas was becoming familiar with? Or her maroon hipster panties to go with the black tank top with a push-up bra that would help her respectably-sized rack look a little more impressive?

She frowned at the thongs lying pathetically in sad humps. She hadn't bought new lingerie in years. There hadn't been anyone to impress. Besides - It was uncomfortable and impractical. She wasn't the type to wear tight pants and what happened to getting it on in the dark anyway? She bet Lily got it on with the lights on. Marley was definitely not that type of girl. Or maybe she was and just didn't know it yet? But seriously: what *was* Thomas' type? Wasn't that what a caring, loving, generous girlfriend worried about?

But were they even *dating*? It was this question that had kept her awake last night. She was getting kind of worn out of the whole "no expectations, only enjoy the present" thing.

Lily would be so mad the moment Marley would tell Lily that she still hadn't put the kibosh on the hots she felt with her boss. And it wasn't just like it'd been going on for a few weeks or something. This had been stretching out for months now. Lily would ask something like, "Seriously, Mar, is his dick magic or something?" and that was a conversation Marley did *not* want to have. Not before a night like tonight, full of anticipation and wonder and - *Oh, God.* She pressed her hands against her face before running her fingers through her hair. Thomas wanted to have sex with her, didn't he?

Why hadn't that occurred to her before? What were they going to do otherwise? Swim in the pool? Play Marco Polo? *That's* what Thomas had meant about not wanting to wait. Would he still want her if she admitted that she hadn't been with a man *like that* before? Did she even *have* to admit such a thing? And, really, what was the rush?

Because Marley *did* want to wait. While Lily had been sleeping with goodness knows who and how often, Marley was the complete opposite.

What had Anne told them about self-respect once? "Leave any situation or person that doesn't serve you, isn't for you, or leaves you wanting more."

"I thought wanting more was a good thing," Marley had interjected once. It didn't matter that Lily had shot her a look not to get into it with her mother.

"It is," Anne had said sharply. "Wanting more is ambition. Wanting more in a relationship is a sign that you shouldn't be in it. It means it's not satisfying you. Don't put permanent feelings onto a temporary person, darling."

Later, Marley had complained to her own mother about it all. "Didn't Anne literally say that we should 'keep a man wanting more' just last week? If that's self-respect, it sounds mean. I feel like love *is* showing that you can't get enough - that you're willing to do anything for the person of your affection."

"It doesn't have to be mean," Peggy had said. The way Marley was stretching her eyes open now in fatigue reminded her of how wide her eyes had grown then when she had realized that Peggy Harrow was agreeing with Anne Cromwell. "You can care for others very deeply and completely lose your sense of self-respect."

"You can?"

"Oh yes. Your father lost his when he started caring more about what felt good instead of caring about doing the next right thing."

So what was the next right thing? To call off the hotel date? She was willingly choosing to go spend time with someone who was *married* and hadn't expressed wanting a commitment beyond tonight's date. A clean hotel room would be so nice compared to what was going on in her room right now. It was never this messy. Her *life* had never been this messy. She didn't know which way to turn.

It was time to call her mother. She needed to hear Peggy's side of the story. Her father had rocked their world by admitting that he had been having an affair. She was too young to feel the extent of that admission, but if Marley asked her mother to recount those emotions now, maybe it would be enough to stop Marley in her tracks. Maybe she'd have the courage to call Thomas, say they were moving too quickly - with zero direction -, and then spend a night in her own bed, cuddle with her cat, and sleep all night, ready for the presentation tomorrow morning and Lily's arrival the next day. Besides. If she called off the evening, she wouldn't have to choose among all these clothes lying around. Suddenly, cleaning her apartment sounded a thousand times better than tonight's unknown.

She picked up the phone and found her mother's name on the homescreen. Before she could change her mind, she pressed the green phone symbol. It was so long since she had called her mother that Marley wasn't sure what Marley would be interrupting in her mother's life on a Thursday afternoon.

"Hello?" Her mother sounded out of breath.

"Hi, Mom!" Marley forced enthusiasm in her voice.

"There's my sweetest girl! How are you?" The love she felt gushing from her mother almost overwhelmed her. Marley scooped up her pillow and buried her face into it, squeezing it as if it would hug her back if she hugged tightly enough.

"I'm so good," Marley forced. "So, so good."

"Yeah?"

It was no use. She couldn't lie to her mother.

"No. That was a lie. Not so good. Not so good at all."

It sounded as if her mom was moving around, clearing the space, making room for her daughter like she would in person, urging her onto the couch, cup of tea not far behind.

"Tell me about it, sweetheart."

"I feel like I'm at a crossroads." Even though she'd been at one, over and over again, the past few months.

"Ah," Mom said. "I know what those feel like. What's got you trapped at the crossroads, baby girl?"

Marley pushed the piles of clothing under her futon mattress and laid on her back, propping her left leg over her right knee. "Okay, so, to my left, I have my normal, usual life. I know what to expect. I know who *that* Marley is. But to my right is this new, exciting life that is showing me who I could be, based on circumstances I've never really been in. Going to the right requires me to throw my caution to the wind. If we're honest, I've been going down that road for a while now. But I'm not loving this new Marley. She's kind of wild."

"That sounds like so much to carry all by yourself. Thank you for calling and sharing that with me. I've been wondering what's been going on. I was about to call Anne."

"*That* desperate?"

Peggy laughed. "You know, she's been quite different since Lily met Logan. She reached out to me a little while ago asking about the flower designs I would recommend."

Marley scowled. "I thought Janie was taking care of the flowers?"

"That's what's kind of cool about it. Anne asked if I would be willing to work with Janie - a collaboration of sorts - so that Janie can get on my list of florists."

"That's a lot of opportunity for Janie."

"Exactly."

"Whoa."

"I thought it was so cool, too. Logan West has been wonderful for that family."

"I've noticed it in Lily, obviously, but look at Anne looking outside of herself!"

Like Marley used to.

Suddenly, asking Peggy to revisit painful memories appeared too self-serving. Did Marley really need someone to remind her what it felt like to be hurt so that she wouldn't hurt someone else? But what had Thomas said? That his marriage was as good as dead, anyway. Right? She had no reason not to believe him.

Marley sighed. "It's funny how one person has the power to totally change a family's dynamic, isn't it?"

"That is so true." Her mother fell silent. She knew more than others how someone can change a family - happy and complete one day to totally shattered the next. "Choice is power," her mother continued.

"'Choice is power,'" Marley echoed. Here was her mother, the guru. Marley loved her for it. She decided then: Marley couldn't bring her mother into her drama, no matter how confusing it became. Peggy had already been through enough heartache; Marley wouldn't invite her mother into the chaos of hers.

"It's the truth. Even not making a choice is essentially making one to stay the same. Every time you make a choice, you make a bet on yourself. Even if your circumstances change around you, I hope you know that the essence of you will *not* change, Marley."

Marley thought of how good she was becoming at lying. "How can you be sure of that? Isn't Anne changing, now that she's helping Janie instead of exploiting her like she may have before?"

"Right. But Anne is returning to the person she always was, especially when Richard was alive. Lily's father wouldn't have fallen in love with the prissy woman she became following his death. Anne got a little lost, but she's finding her way back. People will slowly reveal who they are over time. The truth will always eventually come out. Lord knows that's what happened with your father."

Marley's heart squeezed. Marley had called her mother so that she could feel convicted - get that little bit of shame so that she would have the courage to call off her night with Thomas. Instead, according to what her mother was saying, Marley wasn't changing; she was a late bloomer, only showing now who she had been all along: a liar. A cheat. Manipulative.

Maybe Marley had resented her father for so long because she *was* her father. Her true self had been repressed this whole time. And now she'd met her match. The way Thomas anchored her when her worries were speeding out of control or how he was able to convince her that she could do what she was most afraid of… it was like having a magic pill for the difficult parts of life. Somehow, he numbed any painful parts and made her stronger as an individual.

Or at least that's what she'd keep telling herself.

She didn't know whether to thank Thomas or curse him for having the key that unlocked the type of person she had been all along: hungry for more and desperate for love. Lily was right about one thing: she *was* a compass - but not for morality. Her needle pointed towards adventure that was wild and alive and *hers*.

And she couldn't wait to be his tonight.

* * *

Marley loosened her grip around her bag. "This place is gorgeous," she marveled.

The four-poster maple bed in the center of the room looked more fit for a castle than the hotel chains Marley typically stayed in. The matching writing desk against the wall looked like it belonged in the writing room of a dedicated author, so heavy and austere was its presence. The windows were exposed, heavy cream curtains tucked to the sides, heavy and ready to fall to hide them from Granada's view. Light scones waited to be turned on, ready to highlight the play that would soon begin.

"They promised it was their finest room," Thomas said, pressing his palm against her lower back before walking ahead of her to set their bags down. The door shut behind them. Marley inhaled sharply, suddenly aware that they were alone, finally, with no more reasons to hide or be nervous of getting caught. But instead of feeling relaxed, it made her more nervous. She set her bag next to his on the wide cream ottoman at the foot of the bed.

Light poured in from the balcony door, leaving long shadows that made Marley think of the way shadows would grow longer the longer she stayed in her hideaway in Central Park so many years ago. Was it possible that Thomas would become that cave for her now? A place where she would be protected, held, and encouraged to return when the world became too big and scary for her?

A sharp pain hit her abdomen and she leaned over to cover it. She keeled over discreetly and rubbed the flesh under her waistline.

Trying to ignore the pain and discomfort, Marley picked at the strap of her worn sandal while Thomas unzipped his bag and started tossing items on the neatly made bed.

She wondered again about the state of his bachelor pad. And the mess that she left at her own apartment an hour ago.

"Making it home already?" she smirked.

"Hey," he stopped rummaging and looked over at her. "I keep a clean house." He turned back to his bag. He bounced his shoulders. "Mostly," he added.

She lifted an eyebrow. "You good?" she asked. Because she was *not* good.

This sandal strap would not loosen, and this random nervous or hunger pain was not what she needed. She pushed into her flesh again, as if she could push the thorn back from whence it came.

Thomas huffed. "I will be once I find my toothbrush."

She laughed, and both the cramp and sandal strap loosened. She pushed herself off the floor, kicked off her sandals, and stepped onto the cool wooden floor. "If you're worried about bad breath, your kisses in the elevator…" she trailed off, making her way towards him.

She flipped over the flap of Thomas' bag and sidled in front of him. She wrapped her hand around the back of Thomas' neck, pressed her forehead against his, and breathed gently on his lips.

"Your kisses are my favorite."

"Yeah?" His hands wandered down to her lower back. He clasped them around her. They swayed to and fro, looking into each other's eyes.

His brown eyes seemed softened with an inner glow. She pressed her right hand closer against the back of his neck while the other squeezed his shoulder. She tipped her head back and closed her eyes, soaking in the safety and security she felt. It was like he'd always be here, a rock just for her to stand on. No one had ever been able to help her feel that way. Not completely. She could fall and he'd catch her. She trusted him - completely.

His nose caressed hers, with a warmth that made her weak in the knees. Marley breathed out. "Yes. It's like…" she paused, desperate not to rush from this moment to the next but rather savor each second, committing each moment to memory.

"Like what?" His nose nudged her cheek and she returned the affection with her forehead against his chin, their nuzzles reminding her of a wild cat's with her mate.

"You kiss me like you mean it. Like it's the last one, every time. It's like, while your lips are touching mine, your hand reaches deep within me, scooping up all the parts of me I thought were dormant. It's a feeling I've never experienced with anyone else."

Her cheeks grew warm. Though it felt scary to admit, it was true, and the admission thrilled her. She wanted this feeling from now until kingdom come. Was it possible? If she asked, would he really be all hers? Or, though considering it made her heart deaden like a weight within her… *was* he the kind who only committed to the chase?

And if he was…

Thomas wrapped his arms tighter around her, bringing her hips against his. She gasped as his lips covered hers again. They kept their lips pressed together as if they were only allowed one kiss. Like asking for more wasn't a possibility. It created a craving she already knew she would never be able to satisfy.

But they needed to come up for air sometime. They disconnected and she stood on her tiptoes to peck his cheek.

His hands pressed against her head, his fingers in her hair, covering her ears, his pinkies cupping her chin. He kissed her forehead. "I'll be right back."

He walked into the bathroom. Thankfully, there was a frosted window that could be slid to cover a bathroom visitor from spectators, but right now it was half open and she saw everything but from his hips down.

She nodded, in a daze, and sat at the edge of the bed, watching him. Was being the object of someone's pursuit really the worst thing? Wasn't it the ultimate compliment? Cromwell Rule reminders floated into her mind, especially one that her own mother couldn't refute: A relationship that's alive will always have each partner chasing the other. Endless pursuit. *Always leave them wanting more* didn't apply to one partner. It was a requisite for both. Lily and Logan were a perfect example of this: Logan never stopped chasing her, and she couldn't forget about him. They always wanted just a little bit more. They were so busy chasing each other that anyone else was peripheral. An after-thought. Water after whiskey.

His voice interrupted her thoughts.

"There are no extra toothbrushes here!"

"Oh no?" she asked. She leaned against the doorway with her arms crossed against her chest. She wanted to tell him that there usually weren't, but she thought it was cute that he thought there would be.

"Maybe the front desk has one. I'll be right back, bobcat."

At the threshold, Thomas wrapped his hand around her hip before leaning down to kiss her squarely on the lips.

Marley pulled away and wrinkled her nose. "Ew. You're right. It's so much worse than it was. Go get yourself together."

Thomas laughed. "I love it when you don't take yourself so seriously." He glanced in the direction of the shower. "You know, I wouldn't be mad if you got first shower."

"It would probably be quite the motivator in getting you back up here faster."

Thomas nodded, his eyes bright. "You're figuring me out real quick." He kissed her once more.

She watched him leave and turned to the mess of clothes on the bed. Pajama bottoms and floss sticks, headphones and paperbacks littered the bright white comforter.

If she was figuring him out so quickly, why did it feel like she didn't really know anything about him at all?

* * *

Cold water cascaded around her, rinsing off the soap that she'd gingerly rubbed into her skin. She let her head fall back, lips parting slightly into a slow smile. She turned off the water and stepped out, wrapping herself in a towel.

A sharp ringtone rang from the other room. Towel wrapped around her torso and tucked in right under her left armpit, hair wet and tickling her shoulders, she crossed to the bed and saw Thomas' phone pulsing next to his bottle of toothpaste.

Marley knew she shouldn't look, and maybe she wouldn't have, but she thought of her mother, and how many times Peggy had called her husband to see when he'd be coming home. And he wouldn't. Not for a few hours after the workday was done, probably with who knows who in a hotel on a Friday night. Marley's stomach pinched in pain. She took a deep breath and flipped over his phone.

Isabel? Seriously? Marley rounded her shoulders and curled inward. She felt her mouth dry. Another colleague on his contact list? Was Isabel penciled in for tomorrow night? Marley pictured herself picking up the phone and both demanding Isabel to explain herself and explaining that, yes, Marley was the one Thomas chose, and if she had a problem with that, then she could just…

On the other hand, if she picked up, Marley would reveal that she was with her boss, and everyone knew that Isabel was a gossip. It would get her fired faster than Deborah had been; instead of stealing someone's work and calling it her own, Marley was stealing someone's husband. Which was worse?

Tears threatened to rush to Marley's eyes, but she shook her head, urging them away. Why did this have to be so complicated? The desire for Thomas - for them to be together, like Lily and Logan were - was so strong. But did she really have what it took to simply enjoy the carnal and forget about the emotional ties? Because isn't that all Thomas wanted her for?

She heard the hotel room's door open and shut. It was a faint clink, and even though the door didn't slam shut behind him, it felt loud. Intrusive. She fixed her towel to ensure that it would cover up the annoying bloat that was beginning to come out of nowhere. She hadn't experienced stress stomachaches for a while now, but she supposed it was possible that a new man who brought with him a multitude of new experiences for her would make her and her body freak the heck out.

"Got a toothbrush!" Thomas exclaimed, before drawing in a breath when he saw her. "You took my recommendation. You look stunning."

She drew the towel tighter around her, burying the phone into its folds. The last person to have seen her with only a towel on was in a hostel in Tokyo, and she had scurried away before he could get a closer look or come up with any ideas.

Thomas set the toothbrush down and reached around her. He clasped at her other hand. Thomas stopped laughing, his face hardening, the soft light in his eyes extinguished and replaced with something harder.

"Why do you have your phone in my hand?"

She had the phone clutched in her left hand like she was about to detonate something, keeping it just out of reach of his grasp.

He lifted an eyebrow. "Find anything interesting?"

"No! I mean. I wasn't looking through it or anything. It rang while I was in the shower." She watched his face carefully. "I only managed to see that it was Isabel."

If he had been hiding anything, his microexpressions didn't betray a thing.

"Oh, that's weird. She's probably asking about the meeting I canceled for tomorrow."

That sounded like a lie.

She pushed the phone into his hands, mumbling apologies, desperately wishing he would leave and wait for her to look adjusted and, well, Lily-Cromwell-perfection. This was all turning out to be nothing like the movies and romance novels she had watched and read.

Thomas tucked a stray hair behind her ear and kissed her shoulder. "Nothing for you to worry your pretty little head about, bobcat. It's us time now. Phone turning off…" he pressed the power button and the screen went black. "Now."

She was relieved to have the commitment of his present attention, but she couldn't shake the feeling that, once things were done here, he'd go to the next available contestant.

"I'll leave you to your refreshment routine. We have dinner reservations for about thirty from now. I'll get dressed out here and leave you to your steamy lair."

Marley nodded, her throat tight. She grabbed her duffel bag and went into the bathroom, sliding the frosted window shut. What was she doing here? She was so uncomfortable. When had Marley become so *easy*? Her stomach tightened in response. Maybe she was just hungry? She always became all sorts of cranky and suspicious of her own thoughts and emotions when she was hungry. It wouldn't take her a full thirty minutes to get ready. Shoot, it wouldn't even take her a full five. She wasn't one of those girls who men had to wait for.

She looked covetously at the outfit for later tonight, after dinner. Her light blue long sleeve and white draw-string shorts were comfortable, loose, and, quite honestly, the closest thing she had to pajamas. And, if she was supposed to pretend throughout the entire dinner that she wasn't nervous for the moment he'd unzip her out of her red dress later, wasn't it better to just get this over with now? This way, they could enjoy the entire dinner, in the afterglow of their first time. Her first time.

She was a go-getter now. Lily would be spontaneous. Unpredictable.

Impulsive.

Brave, she corrected.

She tried to be okay with her nipples lifting the blue shirt. Extra lift from the extra bloat.

Thomas sat up the moment she stepped into the room. Marley grinned, straightening her back and lifting her chest. Was this what Lily felt like? Marley had witnessed many a man almost lose his head because Lily had walked in and the craning heads couldn't follow her far enough.

The drawn out whistle made her blush. The way he looked her body over...

"Oh, wow."

She tugged on her shirt. "It might not be a lacy number, but…" She stepped closer to the side of the bed, every step closer to a person she had never imagined she'd be: Reckless. Spontaneous. Exciting.

"No, I love it. It's so you."

What did *that* mean? She didn't wear lingerie so she was, what, homely? Boring? Ordinary? When would the second-guessing *end?!*

She didn't have time to think or ask him about it. He stood and scooped her up into him so that she was straddling him. The rising mound of his excitement pressed against her. She leaned her head back and moaned. Marley squeezed her legs around him, hoping that her core strength would be enough to keep her up. She placed her hands on either side of Thomas' head, right above his shoulders. She moaned as his hand traveled up her back and around her neck so that his forearm was between her breasts. He squeezed her neck, his fingers pressing against her throat. She gasped. Did it always hurt a little when you were being loved? Her mind thought again to Logan, who had saved Lily from a burning building and made sure she had a chance to breathe, not have it taken it away.

"It's not a hug unless my hands are in the right spot." His breath tickled her neck.

"I've never had this kind of hug before."

"You've never had Thomas Elker as your lover before."

He sat down on the bed, his back against the headboard. He pulled her onto him so she was straddling him. She hadn't considered how thin her shorts were, but it was like wearing nothing at all. She swallowed.

He went to kiss her, but she pulled back. "Your name is perfect for you, you know."

"Yeah? How's that?"

"Mr. E," she stated. *Like I don't really know who you are.*

"Mr. E?" he said, searching her eyes. "I like that."

"For extraordinary." She kissed his forehead. "For exciting." His cheek. "For elusive." His lips. "Mr. E…"

"Like 'mystery,'" he added.

Ah, he got there. She kissed his lips, then sat back on her haunches. "Indeed. That's what you are to me. A wife you claim doesn't want you… Isabel calling you…"

"That was nothing. Work related."

"Sure. Next you're going to tell me this is work related, too." She didn't mean for bitterness to discolor her tone, but it was undoubtedly there. She shut her eyes and pulled the covers into her grasps. Marley needed reassurance. She needed to know there wasn't a woman out there waiting for him to come home - and that Marley wasn't the reason why he wasn't there. Or that she was just another hit on his list, a plaything for a while that he'd toss away once the thrill of the chase was over.

"Hey. They don't have anything on you, bobcat."

His finger traced her face from her forehead down her cheek until it hooked under her chin, tugging her towards him. She obliged, her body slinking down next to his, one arm propping up her head, while the other traced his torso, up and down, never quite making it to the place she knew he wanted her to be.

"If only your hugs weren't so…"

He raised an eyebrow. "So what?"

"So enticing."

"You know it's only you who gets them. I haven't been able to focus at work because I know you're somewhere down the hall. If I really had wanted to talk to Isabel, don't you think I would have remembered to bring the phone downstairs with me? Did I invite Isabel here with me or you?"

Marley's stomach muscles loosened. She hadn't realized how tightly she'd been constricting them. Okay. That was all she needed.

She bowed her head and picked it up, hoping this wouldn't sound too cheesy.

"We have some time before dinner, right?"

Thomas glanced at his watch. "Twenty minutes."

"That's four times longer than we typically get. Let's take advantage and have our bodies take over the talking for now."

His eyes brightened. "Yes, ma'am," he mumbled, loosening the string of her shorts.

She leaned her head back, and the next thing she knew, Thomas had flipped them over, so her head was sinking into the thick pillows, the scent of fresh cotton mixing with the lilac conditioner coating her hair. Hands reaching around his neck, she pulled him to her, but he wouldn't budge.

"Keep trying," he whispered. "C'mon. You can do it."

She laughed, self-conscious of the pullups she knew she couldn't do, but did her best to pull herself up so their lips could join once again. Once, twice, and again, he held himself back. When he finally let her in close, his hand pressed against her chest. This time, her wheeze became desperate. Her heartbeat in her ears, Marley pushed up and against his hand, but he kept her down. Breathless, he crashed his lips against hers.

"What..." she gasped, "the hell.. was that?"

"Mr. E," he grinned. Fingertips traced from the back of her knee, up her thigh, and over her shorts.

She lifted her hips. This was it.

White stars crossed her eyes as she felt his fingers enter her. She tilted her head back and moaned. Though he slipped in easily, his fingers felt stiff, unrelenting, stretching her in ways she hadn't anticipated. Maybe this is how he loved: he made it feel painful so that the pleasure would be tenfold, she reasoned. The tips of his fingers hit the wall inside her, again and again, and she didn't know if the sounds escaping her were because of pleasure or pain or both. He retracted, allowing the pulsing to match the throb growing in her mind, clouding out anything else than the physical sensations running through her body like unrelenting waves. She lifted her arms above her head as Thomas' fingertips started grazing her stomach, on their way up...

"Oh!" he gasped, blinking rapidly. She tilted her head, and then looked down to see what he was staring at. A streak of bright red ran from her stomach to the bottom of her breast, wrapped around Thomas' fingers.

"Oh, no," Marley's voice cracked. She shook her head vigorously, like doing so would cool down the burning in her cheeks. "Oh, no no no no. I'm so sorry." She ran to the pristine bathroom and shut the door, trying not to retch at the disparity between the gleaming white marble and the deep red she couldn't control. Her bottom lip quivered. Sitting on the toilet, she opened drawer after drawer, desperate for something to quell her panic and her flow. Of course there weren't any tampons or pads in a hotel bathroom as ritzy as this one. A cold sweat beaded on the back of her neck. It was so unlike her not to remember to pack any extra sanitary napkins. Instead, she had worried about the clothes that would lead to *that* moment. *That* experience. And they had!

The universe was conspiring against her. Lily enjoyed night after night of passion and excitement, an amazing career, and a condo on prime real estate, and Marley had to have her night ruined by her fucking *period*.

It wasn't *fair*.

She squeezed her eyes shut and forced them open. She leaned her temple against the wall. Now, instead of just her stomach cramping, her head was beginning to throb, too.

"Thomas? Thomas, I'm so sorry."

He didn't say a word. Obviously the last thing they would have expected to happen was *this*, but reassurance that she hadn't totally messed up the evening would have been nice. The Cromwells were comfortable in silence, but that's because their confidence allowed them to be. Marley was on the opposite end of the spectrum.

No answer. Marley opened the door a little wider to reveal an empty room. For someone she had pegged as comforting and encouraging, what if Thomas was the type to say "I thought I'd give you space"? She shuddered. Such a cowardly response instead of embracing the opportunity to create connection. Marley's dad used that excuse all the time when Peggy really needed him: "Oh, honey, I thought I'd just give you space." Gag.

What if he *had* left her? Sayonara, see ya later - and she wouldn't have blamed him for a second. A cool man like Thomas would never willingly choose to handle a mess like her. At this point, she kind of hoped he had left. She could quit her job, go back to the States, and never see him ever again.

But then she heard him cough. The door to the balcony was opened and she saw him standing there, leaning his forearms on the railing, a cigarette in his hand as if they really had just copulated and he was waiting for her to come back and join him for one in a moment. How she wished that would have been the ending. Thomas probably hadn't slept with anyone in a while, so broken up over his wife he was, and now here she was, a respite for him. She wanted to be that for him. And she'd ruined it. She ruined everything.

She rifled through her bag, eyes wide and searching. Finally, she found it. Heaven in a plastic applicator. She cleaned up quickly, washed her hands and then her face, but it was no use. Even though she could walk around without worrying about staining her dress, there was no "going back" to the moments before. There was no way she could look him in the eye, let alone try and hold a conversation with him as if she hadn't died the moment he looked at his hand with such disgust. *She* had made that scowl appear on his face. The universe was screwing Marley over, but she knew it was doing Thomas a favor. Zeke walking in on them in the teahouse had been a sign she'd tried to fight. This one she couldn't ignore.

The purple capri pants and flowered blouse she had worn to work were still folded on the bathroom counter. Her eyes never left Thomas' back. God, he was handsome. It made jumping into her clothes more difficult, but she yearned to have them on and be gone before Thomas finished his cigarette. She didn't want to watch him fumble for the right words. She didn't want to hear the placidity in his voice. And she *really* didn't want to hear the pity in it, either.

She was about to turn around when he turned and made eye contact with her before Marley's gaze flew to his feet. She was sure he had never had a less attractive, less passionate evening. What would they do now? *Cuddle?* He shut the glass door behind him.

"I'm sorry," Marley blurted, talking to the floor. "I'm so sorry. I'll gather my things and call a taxi."

"Now why would you do that? Room service is coming up with a hot fudge brownie."

"What?" This time she couldn't keep her eyes off him. "You want me to stay?" she asked incredulously.

"I'd seem a little bit the dick if I didn't, wouldn't I?" He launched himself onto the bed so that the covers around him fluffed up like a cloud settling around him.

So was he offering such hospitality in order to save face, or because he really didn't want Marley to leave?

She didn't want to ask. She wouldn't want to know either way.

He patted the space next to her. "Would you like to lay down while we wait for them to bring up the food?"

Though she knew someone like Lily would have already forgotten about the snafu, Marley looked for stains on the white bed sheets. Why did hotels risk getting their pristine sheets dirty? How embarrassing would it be to fall asleep and wake up staring at the mishap that cost her such a magical evening?

She sighed. She crawled into the bed, pressing her back against his front, his arm wrapping around her, cupping her chest and bringing her tight against him. She'd stay for the brownie, maybe enjoy a cuddle here, a few more kisses there, and she'd finally have the courage to say that she couldn't be with someone who still had a wife. He wasn't what she thought he was. And she wasn't who she thought she wanted to be.

She closed her eyes and imagined what she'd say: *I'm sorry, Thomas. This is moving way too fast for me. I thought I was ready to jump in, but that's just not me. I like the idea of taking it slowly. Building on a bedrock of friendship. Maybe we can try again after December. When I'm let go from Mariposa and Tigre. When you're not married anymore. When you're ready to settle down.*

More than anything, she knew she wanted to be able to look Lily or her mother in the eye and say that no, of course she wasn't a home-wrecker. She'd do it all the right way. If it was meant to be, it would all work out. What was meant for her would always find a way. The moral compass within her demanded it.

But sleep often robbed a woman of a good idea.

He Needs to Go

Come *on*. Where *was* it? Marley looked through her overnight bag, again, but it was useless. She stuffed it in the corner of the supply closet. How the mighty had fallen: judging people for making out on the lounge couch and now she was storing her dirty underwear in the office's copy room. Classy, Marley. Real classy. She couldn't just run home. She'd be sweaty and gross by the time she came back and, she glanced at her watch, the presentation was in *twenty minutes!*

But seriously. The day of her big presentation was here and she had *forgotten her binder at home!?* The binder was her ticket. Color-coded, words bolded, everything in order. Her room had been a mess before she left for the hotel, but her work was ready. The color in the front pocket was *green*. She was Lily Cromwell confident. Almost. It was like losing her floaties in an ocean. It was already terrifying enough with the binder, but without it, she would drown. She wished she could call Cilantro and have her deliver it. Damn the single life sometimes. You really did have to have all your shit together all the time. No one else would help you pick up the slack. She'd have to print out her files and create a de facto binder. But that would take too long!

Had she gone home after last night's debacle, she would have her binder now. But she also wouldn't have the memories of their strong kisses, sweet, sweet cuddles, and the promise of more - right after this presentation.

"Where were you last night?" Zeke's voice sounded hard. Unrelenting. She turned to face him, clutching the edge of her desk.

He looked like he already knew the answer to her question.

She lifted her chin. "I was with Thomas," she said. If a man like that was able to stay with her and soothe her, making sure what he ordered for breakfast from room service wasn't going to hurt her cramps any more than they already had… then she was going to own it.

The hard V of Zeke's eyebrows softened. "Who are you, mija? Has he really changed you in such a short amount of time? You go from worrying about everything to worrying about nothing, huh? You think that's a good way to live, too?"

"I still care!"

"I know you do." Zeke sighed. "But when's the last time you had a good night's sleep?"

Marley jerked her head back. "I don't know."

"A good breakfast?"

"I grab some snacks from the kitchen with my coffee."

"You think what you're doing right now is sustainable? This is the biggest presentation of your career and you spent the night before doing what? Hoping to convince your boss that your body's more important than your brain? Do you really know this guy, Marley?"

Marley hated that he was asking all of this. It's not like she hadn't wondered the same. But not knowing the answers was adding more insecurity to the kind she already felt. Floaties in an ocean. And there was definitely a hole in one of them.

She plopped onto her seat and ran her hand through her hair.

"You wonder this, too," Zeke said.

"Of course I wonder. Any sane human would. I don't understand why he has this effect on me. I want to keep pursuing a relationship with him, but I feel like I doubt myself up until the moment we're being, *tú sabes*, physical. Up until then, it feels wrong, which is so messed up because it's the physical that's the wrong part. I know that. But not wrong enough to stop. I've never had a true blue addiction. At least not until now. I can't help but want more. It makes me feel so weak, Zeke. It does. But please try to understand."

"Ah, there she is. Marley's in there somewhere. You *know* what's right and what's wrong. You've just gotten caught up in the excitement of it. But excitement isn't peace, amiga. The truth is - I don't understand. You can't be doing this. Please. You can love something so much and it can still be so bad for you. Like cigarettes. Like drugs. You have to put a stop to it." He swallowed. "Try to be done with this by the company field trip, yeah? If you don't stop, I refuse to be your partner."

And suddenly, she was six years old and could hear her mother saying the same to Henry: *if you don't stop, I refuse to be your wife.*

"You don't mean that."

"Desafortunadamente. Si."

"So you would just throw our friendship away if I continued exploring my relationship with Thomas."

"If you continue to see him, Margaret and I do not feel comfortable having you in our home."

"You are asking me to choose between my happiness and our friendship."

"I don't know how else to make you see that he doesn't bring you happiness. Look at yourself, mija. You don't have your binder. You're *always* prepared. You always do the right thing. But not now. You're lost. Not completely. You can still figure it out. But you've got to cut him out."

"You don't have the right to do this, Zeke," Marley struggled. "It's my life."

"It's my family y la cultura de mi familia. I do have that right."

"No. I'm not arguing that. I'm saying you don't have the right to tell me that I have to choose between someone who could be the love of my life and the loves of my life who I cannot imagine a life without."

"You can't be serious that this guy is your future, Marley."

"Why not!?" she said, louder than she meant to. "Why can't he be?"

"Because he's *married*. He's already accounted for! He's been *claimed!*"

"But they're unhappy. He's unhappy. The wife has basically given him permission at this point."

"Then why can't he wait until he's officially divorced? I know you can see. Keep your eyes open. Keep asking him questions. Catch him in a lie - before you find out that you're the one he's been lying to."

"It feels like he's been telling the truth."

"Feelings aren't facts."

The blood within her ran cold. "Who told you that?"

"A 'Lily Cromwell' called me last night looking for you. She said something like that and I thought it was a cool phrase."

"Lily called *you*?"

"Si. I appreciate you making me an emergency contact."

Her head was swimming. Lily had called Zeke? *Why*? She wasn't scheduled to land until tomorrow morning. What if something had happened? Marley's phone had died sometime during the hotel stay, so she wasn't around. What if something happened to Logan or Anne or, she panicked to think of it, her own mommy?

No binder. An emergency call from Lily. All the trust issues surrounding Thomas. Ultimatums from Zeke and Margaret. *And* she was expected to give a presentation that would save not only her job but the jobs of her colleagues in front of people from Mariposa?

"Marley! You ready?" Thomas called.

"Yes, sir!" she yelled down the hall. "Zeke, I'll—"

Zeke rolled his eyes and nodded before backing away. "Don't worry about it. You'll do great. Just don't make me lose my job."

Her heart lifted at his smirk. There was hope. It was faint, and only a moment, but she had caught a brief smile, and that was enough for right now.

"Bobcat!" Thomas' voice was near. A Pop Rocks box flew in the air. She caught it. Here went nothing - and everything.

* * *

Marley took a deep breath and looked at Thomas. He nodded at her. Like he had last night when she had asked whether she could unbuckle his belt.

"Please open your butterfly origami," she ordered the room. Like she had zipped his jeans open. She lifted a few Pop Rocks into her mouth.

The rustle of papers both invigorated her and filled her with dread, but not for long. As the Pop Rocks animated within the cave of her mouth, she pushed doubts of her colleagues not understanding the idea away from her mind. Her colleagues made eye contact with one another, curiosity piqued and enthusiasm high. Like when Thomas had looked at her last night with anticipation and she hadn't really known what to do next.

She hadn't been expecting the sounds of awe that filled the room, but one quick glance at Zeke and Karl confirmed that this was her cue. Her mouth was calm. Ready.

Like last night, when her tongue had touched Thomas and it was she who had made him lose control.

Now *that* was power.

* * *

Thomas pressed his lips against Marley's, caressing her cheek with his thumb. When they had both exhaled, he released. "You did an amazing job. You should be so proud of yourself. I saw the Mariposa director. She looks so excited."

"So you don't think we'll all be fired next month?"

"Quite the opposite. I think there are promotions to be discussed."

"That would be exciting. Wasn't I so different from normal?"

"Yes, ma'am, but in all the best ways. It felt good to let go and get away, didn't it?" Marley smiled. "Yes. It really did." Thomas slipped his fingers between hers, their knuckles gently knocking into each other. His reassurance was a warm cup of tea in her hands.

He stepped back. "Here. I was walking along Calle Meson de Paredes a couple days ago and saw a mural that reminded me of you. I don't know why I didn't think to show you earlier this week."

"Oh yeah? What'd you find?" She sat on the table and let her legs swing, watching Thomas search through his phone. The stubble on his chin was coming through. So she had forgotten her binder at home, but what was that compared to the memory of that stubble pressed against her neck, her chest...

Sure, they may not have gone all the way, but this Thomas Elker really did earn the title of Creative Director.

"Ah, yes. Here."

She took Thomas' phone and felt her breath catch. The mural was of a girl reaching over her open window, caressing a daisy in a bed full of them.

Marley swallowed. It was beautiful.

"She's so innocent," he said. "She could be spending her time doing anything: making a hurried call, scrolling mindlessly on her phone, watching a TV show. But she's not. She's interacting with nature outside her window. When I said that your clothes were 'so you' last night, that's what I meant. You don't put on airs. You're not out to 'get' anybody. You just do your best to be the best version of yourself at all times. That's rare."

"But you don't know if she's about to pluck them."

"Why do you always look for the worst in yourself? Do *you* think that's what she's going to do?"

The fight left her. "No," she admitted. "She's probably making room for *that* one. It was probably all scrunched up and—"

She swiped to the right, thinking there'd be a zoomed in picture. Or another mural.

But instead, she saw a photo of the woman in the white dress that she recognized from Bahama Club. But this time, she was in a white bikini, chest lifted the same height as her martini glass. She scrolled again. Isabel? Her wavy hair covered her bare chest, kissy face. Marley swiped as quickly as she could, hoping to go back to the photo of the mural of the innocent girl whose only crime was that she wanted something beautiful for herself. Instead, she saw a picture of a redhead who was looking up at the camera with *those* eyes. The Lily-Logan-love eyes.

Thomas lashed his hand out to retrieve his phone. "Slow down there, killer."

Marley snapped her head up. "I was thinking there'd be more photos of the murals. I'm sorry."

Thomas relaxed his shoulders. "No. Yes. You're right. I'm sorry. I'm just not used to people looking through my phone. What if I had a picture of a gift for you in there?" He winked.

"That's a good point. Sorry again." She wouldn't have liked it if people went through her phone either. But she couldn't unsee it. And the truth settled in like lava around her heart.

She wasn't the only one.

"No harm done. Let's get you home, bobcat." He placed his hand on her lower back to lead her out of the room, dropping it as they crossed the threshold.

There was no reason to continue the charade; they weren't going to develop into anything more.

Marley Harrow was just another photo in Thomas Elker's camera roll. Nothing more.

"Would I be your person?"

Thomas stopped and scanned the hallway. But she didn't care who heard anymore. "Would I be your person?"

Thomas ducked his head and walked back into the copy room. "What do you mean?"

"If you weren't married. Would I be your person?"

The silence was unbearable.

"Please answer me," she whispered. It came out more like a whimper.

"Maybe."

"'Maybe'?"

"I'm not sure what you're asking."

"Do you think we would be an, I don't know, thing. A couple."

She hated herself, she hated herself, she hated herself. The insides of her body were turning into mold and she was disgusting and -

"Oh, Marley. I'm so sorry. I don't think so. Marriage is kind of a no-go for me. I tried it once. I don't want to do it again. It's legalese that doesn't mean anything. Not really. It steals the joy and life out of so many people. Too much compromise, not enough freedom. I'm not built for it."

Any anger, any frustration, even any jealousy flooded out of her. *Maybe.*

So it had all been in her head.

"I think it's time for me to go home."

She needed time to herself, to decompress, to process everything that had happened: especially the pictures she just saw on Thomas' phone. Who *were* those women? And why wasn't she enough?

Listen

She was so tired.

Each step was a trial, but she knew she could rest the moment she opened her door and lay on her futon. Thank goodness it was a sacred Saturday. She'd sleep and then call Lily. Her best friend would help heal her. It would be hard for Marley to hear, but Lily would know just what to say. Marley mostly needed Lily to do her Cromwell thing and say all the things Thomas was - because Marley was too kind, even now, to say them out loud.

So it was too much too quickly to see Lily lying on Marley's futon.

Cilantro meowed.

Marley dropped her bags and took in the sight. "Lily! Wh-what are you doing here? How'd you get in?"

Lily sat up and leaned on her elbow. She blew up into her bangs, hanging loosely from a high ponytail. How those two phenomena could coexist was magic only Lily Cromwell had access to. "You gave me an extra key last time I visited. Happy to see you, too?"

"I'm sorry." How was she going to explain an overnight bag? How badly did she smell of betrayal? "Of course I'm happy to see you."

"I wanted to be your relaxation after wrapping up the project! Where *were* you?"

Marley fumbled for an excuse. She wasn't ready for the truth. She wanted it to come tomorrow, not tonight. She already had too much on her plate. Late night at the library? Phone finally died for good?

The words tumbled out. "My dad came into town," she said.

"Oh yeah?" Lily stepped around a pile of clothing to the mirror. She fixed her lipstick. "Which hotel was he staying in?" Lily asked.

"Oh, you know, the one he always stays in. I don't remember the name of it."

"Well, *I* stayed at the hotel down the street and was getting really worried about you, Mar. I even contacted Zeke and—"

"How did you get his number?" Marley interrupted.

"I didn't. The staff directory on your webpage has a contact form. He emailed me back and then I called his number directly." Lily rolled her eyes. "I can't keep this up, Mar. How long do you plan on lying to me?"

Marley felt the heat crawl up her back, making her face feel like it was going to pulse off. "What do you mean?" she asked weakly.

"Zeke told me you were probably with Mr. Elker. You know, your *boss*."

There was no other way out of it. Marley had to trudge through the truth. "Yes. I was."

"What else have you lied about?" Her usually fierce eyes fell in their strength and fervor, a look of hurt that was quickly replaced by a hard look that Marley had only seen on Lily's face after Roger would no longer speak to her in high school. Marley kept silent. She didn't know what to say.

"Even though Anne is awful in her own way sometimes," Lily continued, "it's always from a place of honesty and, ultimately, love. But this? This is self-protection - and not for empowerment or courage. This is cowardice of the worst kind, Marley."

A coward? She was *tired* of being labeled as a product of her sensitivity. She was not a coward be*cause* she never gave up despite the intense fear that would threaten to paralyze her. She was not protecting herself; she was finally advocating for herself. There was a difference.

"I have never judged you for *anything* you've done or said, Lily Cromwell." Marley's voice shook and she hated herself for it. Another sign of strength that would be perceived as weakness just because it didn't match her father's or her best friend's definition of strength. "You're going to judge me so quickly? You didn't even ask me how I'm feeling about it. In fact, you never ask me how I'm feeling or how I'm doing. It's always what you think, what you want, what you feel. I'm tired of it. I'm tired of being the one who always cares more than everyone else around her. So I finally did something for myself! Sue me!"

"Are you serious right now? What delusions have you been *under*?" Then, with more gentleness than Marley thought Lily had in her, Lily asked, "What has this guy done to you, Mar?" She furrowed her brow and sucked in a breath. "You know what? I don't even want to know. Mom was right: you Harrows were even more dysfunctional than we were. At least our family was broken because of death. Your family is broken because of—" Lily gestured to all of Marley in a circular motion "—everything you don't have the courage to fix."

"How am I supposed to fix the fact that the man I would want to try to have a future with is married?!" Marley yelled. She grabbed the clothes from the floor and threw them into the corner, her hamper overflowing. "Tell me," she cried. "How can I have what you have?"

"Get out." Lily's amusement at Marley's mess was too much. Marley bit down on her lip. Hard. "He's your boss *and* he's married!?"

Marley crumpled. She reached around herself, arms hugging her back. She heaved, trying to catch her breath, though it grew increasingly difficult to fill her lungs. She would die, right here, like this. At least her best friend could tell her parents how she went. Maybe Thomas would feel bad for…

"Get a hold of yourself! How can you have what I have? I don't spend my time thinking about how I could get things. I just get them. I don't let anyone or anything stand in my way. People either work for me or against me. You are not that way, Marley. We are different people. I thought we knew that. Common knowledge and all. But now I don't even know who you are. If you've always been more worried about how you appear to people than actually being yourself... maybe you should sit this wedding out."

"What?" Marley sniffled.

"I can't live my life wondering if my best friend wants to sleep with my husband."

"Lily, I—"

"Isn't that what you meant by wanting what I have? I have to do what's safest for my marriage. If that means cutting off—" Lily choked on her words. Marley looked up to see Lily wiping her eyes. "If that means cutting off my very best friend in the whole wide world, then that's what has to happen. I love Logan too much. Jesus, Marley. What happened to you?"

Lily opened the door and looked around once more. "I hope you find what you're looking for."

Marley sat on the edge of her bed, absentmindedly petting Cilantro.

And then Marley's phone buzzed. Was it Lily, asking for forgiveness? Admitting that she'd gone overboard?

It was Thomas. "If you're not doing anything later..."

She looked longingly at Cilantro. And her room. And the storm she'd made. Would she really throw more lightning into the mix? Maybe just one more time?

She picked herself off the floor. Yes. She was going to go after what she wanted.

It was better to be in the eye of the storm with Thomas than to have to clean up by herself the damage she'd caused.

Anything was better than being alone.

But first, she needed to nap.

How to Say No

The nap ended up being a full night's sleep.

She picked up her phone and smiled at Thomas' insistence that she NOT bring him coffee (apparently he was too civilized for it), right before he sent his address. Then, another message, not to worry about visiting. Such a tease. The image of Isabel's photo in Thomas' camera roll burned in her memory like the morning sun was searing through her window. She groaned and stretched her head back and Cilantro jumped onto her chest with a gentle thud. She opened her Instagram. Her finger hovered over the search bar. Looking up Isabel's social media photos would *not* help right now. So what *if* Isabel was interested in Thomas? Marley was the one he took out for drinks and hosted in a hotel room. Marley was the one who had his address.

Suddenly, an Instagram notification from Lily slid across her screen. Marley sucked in a breath. Lily was holding up a white garment bag, from a few weeks ago - it must have been - in front of her and pointing to it with a wink. "Saying no to this dress would have been sinful," her caption read, "and I'm trying to be good!"

Marley squeezed her eyes shut, turned off her phone, and tucked it under the covers. Cilantro climbed on top of it, paws hooking over the side of the futon, eyes bright. Marley scratched the fur behind Cilantro's ears and sighed.

After picking up the clothes around the floor, throwing in a load of laundry, taking a shower, and washing the dishes, Marley assembled two breakfast sandwiches. Preparing a meal for two felt right. She grabbed the blue silk robe peeking out from her closet.

It'd only be a twenty minute walk, and it'd be easy to fit both the sandwiches and her robe in her knapsack. She imagined the plan like a check-list:

knock on his door, walk in like she owned the place, tell him he had to stop entertaining all these other women and, most importantly, make it crystal clear that if he didn't want to lose her, he'd have to choose her.

And they'd live happily ever after.

The robe and sandwiches would fit somewhere in between.

∗ ∗ ∗

She pressed the third button from the left and waited for the buzzer. When the doorknob shook, she opened it, inhaling sharply. This was it. Marley Harrow was creating her perfect moment.

She climbed the stairs and turned to Thomas standing in the doorway, basketball shorts revealing calf muscle tattoos and a solid black shirt that outlined his arm muscles. He stepped out into the hallway and shut the door behind him, readjusting his baseball cap. Marley bit her lip.

"Marley. What a surprise!"

"Yeah! I ended up falling asleep last night and wanted to make sure you knew I still wanted to take you up on your offer."

"That's alright." He shifted his weight from one hip to another. "I—" Thomas stretched his lips taut, revealing a clenched jaw. Aw. She made him nervous.

She stepped in front of him and looked up, their faces covered by the brim of Thomas' hat. "Silly man." She searched his eyes, but couldn't read them. "Aren't you going to let me in?"

Thomas reached behind him and opened the door. She stretched her hand out and pressed the two sandwiches into his hands. "Go find us some plates and we'll have a little breakfast. My breakfast sandwiches are pretty good, if I do say so myself."

While he complied, Marley took in the sights, noticing what she had been too sunstruck to see before: a couch that was sunk in from many an afternoon siesta, a widescreen television, a coffee table covered with ticket stubs, beer caps, event koozies, a deck of cards, a Rubik's cube, and dice. Baseballs stacked the shelving units, athletes' bobble heads in various states of nodding their heads. Something within her relaxed. It's not that Marley had missed it before; a woman definitely did not live here.

She walked around to the kitchen, cupping her cup of coffee, tightening her grip. He wasn't being himself.

"So how's your morning going?"

"Oh, fine," he said, placing the sandwiches on a plate and opening the microwave.

What was it about his back that she found so sexy? She stepped behind him and wrapped her arms around his torso, hugging him to her. He chuckled and placed his hands on top of her wrists. "You good, bobcat?"

"I will be once I have this sandwich in me and this robe on me."

Those were the magic words. He spun on his heels. "A robe, eh?"

"Yeah… and I realized something last night, that I couldn't wait to tell you. With a robe on."

"What's that?"

Marley grabbed the sides of Thomas' face. "I don't care if we don't get married. I don't even need to live with you. In fact," she looked around, "I'm not sure I'd want to. I realized that, what hurts more than not imagining you as my husband, is imagining my life without you in it." Marley looked down, blinking quickly as she re-engaged eye contact. She tapped her heart. "You're in here forever, you know. You've been my release from things I didn't even know were trapping me. I have had so much fun with you. You have given my life *flavor*." She looked to the side of him, trying to locate some spices that she could make a fun analogy with.

But a cream colored coffee cup from Café 43 caught her eye.

"Hold on a second?" Marley pushed on Thomas' hip and, though he was hesitant, he stepped aside. "We finally drove you to drinkin' coffee, huh? Let's see what kind you got." And though Thomas' hand almost intercepted Marley's, it wasn't fast enough to stop Marley from rotating the cup.

Bright red lipstick stared back.

Thomas started, "Marley, I—"

"If I didn't bring this, and you don't drink coffee, then…"

A balcony door slid open.

Marley's eyes widened. "Thomas, who is that?"

"I told her."

"You told *who*?" The redhead? The woman from El Bahama Club? Isabel?

"Marley, you should go."

Tears stung behind her eyes, but she stood her ground. "No. I'm done hiding. I'm done running. I'm done wondering." She wanted to know who or what was keeping him from being fully hers.

Stepping into the kitchen from the opposite entry was a gorgeous redhead. The sun glowed behind her. Her hair was tied back and her lean body was framed in a loose grey tank top, white shorts hugging her hips perfectly.

Thomas hung his head.

The floor rocked beneath her. She couldn't find the air. It was like someone had cut off her supply.

"Tommy? What's going on? Who is this?"

"Sofia, this is Marley, a colleague from work."

Sofia's eyes darkened. She wrapped her hand around the bottom of her ponytail and pulled on it. "No. You said it was over."

Words and memories, hopes and dreams swirled in meaningless nonsense in her mind.

Sofia stepped forward. "I can't believe you're doing this again. I leave for a couple weeks and… and you!" Marley lifted her head. Sofia was looking directly at her, an inferno in her eyes, like anger was incinerating her from within.

"Did you *know* he was married?!"

Suddenly, it wasn't Sofia looking at Marley, but Marley looking at her mother. And just like that, each stolen kiss, every hug that went on for a little longer than it should have, the night in the hotel, and each and every flirtation shared between them was not worth it. She had caused pain. She had created damage in the wake of her desires.

She could not lie anymore.

"Yes," she squeaked. Then, a little stronger. "Yes. I did." She quickly added, "Your husband is very attractive." She shook her head. Saying that made her sound like an idiot. Like that was reason enough to commit adultery.

What a dirty word. But it was time to call it what it was. What it had been.

Sofia scoffed. "So kind of you to say. Yes. Thank you. I know."

"And he has a lot of love to give," Marley added.

"Oh?" Sofia crossed her arms. "I'm glad one of us got it."

Marley looked helplessly at Thomas, who stared at the floor in front of him. Marley turned back towards Sofia. "He made it seem as if y'all were over. You in Toledo and he here in Granada…"

Sofia rolled her eyes. "It was a trial separation, but that didn't stop him from asking for pictures every night. Or sending messages that made me feel like…" Her voice trailed off. She looked back and forth between Marley and Thomas. "I didn't know he was actually…" Sofia shook her head, matching the bobbleheads on the shelves. Sofia drew her shoulders back, raising her chin. "You are *insatiable*, Thomas Elker," Sofia spat. "I deserve more. You know where to send my things."

Sofia stormed out of the room.

Thomas lifted his hat and ran a hand through his hair, rubbing his eyes with his fingertips.

Insatiable.

Marley understood. She and Thomas were cut from the same cloth. She couldn't get enough of Thomas, but it seemed like nobody would ever be enough for him.

The door slammed behind Sofia.

"I'm so sorry that happened," Marley started.

Thomas lifted his head and pushed himself off the counter. "I'm not."

Marley stared at him. "How can you say that?"

"Because…" He strode in front of her, cupping her face. "You showed me that it was possible to love and be loved in return. We obviously both had needs that we satisfied and now that it's over, no harm, no foul."

"What?" The question echoed like the crack of a whip. Marley took a step back and watched Thomas' arms fall. "You were *married*." As Marley's voice got louder, the pit in Marley's stomach dug deeper. "Knowing that it was possible to love and be loved should have been a given for you! I'm the one who needed the reminder!" She shook her head. Only a broken woman would still be here. Only someone like Peggy would still be standing after her world and marriage were blown to smithereens.

"So what happens next?" Marley demanded. "We're just going to live as if nothing ever happened? As if my world didn't completely fall off its axis because of you?" Marley threw her arms up in the air. Pretend normal suddenly didn't seem possible. "What was the point of all of this anyway? If you knew that this wasn't going to go anywhere, but you led me on anyway..." She groaned and ran her hand through her own hair, pulling at the ends. "Oh, my God," she cried. "You're *married*. And I *knew*. I'm a terrible person."

"Thomas. Say something. Please."

He squeezed the coffee cup lid. It broke it half. "I don't know what to say."

Coward.

"Say *something*. Say that you're willing to try. That I'm the 95% amazing you're willing to tolerate the 5% mess for. That I can make your life *happy* - not just this pretend shallow bullshit that you try to convince everyone of. That's so *fake*. Let people see the real you for once. Can't you see how much—"

"That's enough." Thomas stood straighter, pressing his palms against the table between them, leaning his upper body so all his muscles constricted. "You want honesty?"

"Yes." She looked up at him. "Please. Finally."

Thomas looked directly at her and said evenly, "I want to wash my hands of this. I want to be done."

Marley's breath left her chest.

And the treasure was buried forever.

Know When It's Time to Go

She wasn't sure how she got home.

After leaving Thomas', she meandered up and down the streets of Granada, throwing a middle finger to every convenient store and bar that had the audacity to be closed on Sunday, when she most needed her bourbon.

The typically crowded streets were desolate. The wind had started picking up and the sky was borrowing its purple from the lilacs surrounding the Alhambra. Sofia's face kept replaying in Marley's mind - and then Thomas' tired, worn out face, so over it all. So over her.

Putting headphones in her ears, Marley swiped to find "Natural" by Imagine Dragons. She pressed play. The melody hummed ominously.

The heat climbed up her neck and flooded her body. How did they get here? How did it get so messed up?

Nothing ever comes without a consequence.

And then his words: "I want to wash my hands of this."

The weight felt like Thomas had taken a baseball and swung it directly into her abdomen.

She took a deep, shaky breath.

That's the price you pay.

The wind knocked out of her left room for heat to gather in her chest. If she were in New York, she'd know exactly where to go. As it was, she had to make her own refuge here. Though it was almost noon, the sky had darkened with its rare threat of rain. Marley stepped over the iron trail blaze and onto the hard ground. It felt tougher than the cobblestones.

Rather be the hunter than the prey.

And the bass thrummed. She was a *natural*.

At what?

She scanned the park until she found what she hadn't realized she was looking for: lying beneath one of the eight Ash trees was a fallen branch. Marley grasped it and, with all the energy she had tucked deep within, swung at the tree trunk. The crack reverberated in her hands, vibrations running up her arms. She swung again, harder this time. She yelped, as the tree didn't provide much give and her hands slipped, a wood chip sliding into her palm. She lifted the branch over her shoulder and swung again. Again, and again, and again. The pain racked her from within. It was too much. It was too much.

'Cause you're a natural, Mr. Thomas Elker. *A beating heart of stone.*

She was mad that he had found her at Café 43 and pulled her away from Karl. She was mad that, even after he had told her the truth, that he had kissed her in the tea house. That she had kissed him back. That she had let herself become one of those women who revolved her life around waiting for the next embrace. That she had let herself fall.

She yelled, and the branch cracked in half.

But, mostly, she was mad at herself for being mad at the one who had filled up the part of her that she hadn't realized was empty. That she felt emptier now than she ever had.

And that's when she knew she wasn't mad.

Not even a little. Not even at all.

She set down the stick, dug the robe out of her knapsack, and threw it over her shoulders. It was getting chilly in the autumn evenings in Granada. It wasn't nearly as cold as it was in New York right now, but

November evenings compared to July nights left Marley's fingers a bit stiff - and the stick had made them raw.

Why did she even have a phone? Scrolling through her main contacts was like flipping through a yearbook. Most likely to ignore her for ignoring their advice? Zeke and Margaret. Most likely to never speak to her ever again? Lily Cromwell. Most likely to never forgive her for what she'd done? Peggy Harrow.

The song had changed. "Believer" was next.

Marley stopped and looked around her. The wind blew through the leaves, making them shiver. Marley pressed the robe tightly around her. The fear of judgment that used to paralyze her now taunted her. She had been nervous before, but at least she'd had friends to encourage her. She'd had a best friend who was getting married in less than a month. She'd had a job that was a dream come true: living abroad, experiencing a new language and culture... and now she was all by herself.

She thought being alone was the worst. But being stuck with the version of yourself that you hated was even worse.

I'm the master of my sea.

Maybe things would calm down by the time they went back to work on Monday. They could go back to the way things were before everything went haywire.

But before he walked in on her practice presentation, Thomas was basically a stranger to Marley.

Marley heaved. She didn't want that. She wanted to be his friend. Sure, being his lover had backfired. But imagining a life without Thomas in it? She couldn't do it. She couldn't see it.

So she pulled out her headphones, wrapped her hands around her head, her nose tucked into the space between her biceps, her fingernails digging into the back of her neck, and cried.

"Marley?" Margaret's voice rose above the heavy rain on stone and hard dry ground.

Margaret sat on the bench next to Marley. "I thought you might be here."

Marley turned to her friend, her bright yellow raincoat on, pink umbrella up and covering them, her pink boots crossed at the ankle and under the bench.

Marley sniffed. "Why are you here?"

"You butt-dialed me. I heard a bunch of violent snapping and then heard you crying and panicked. Are you okay?"

"How did you find me?"

"We're your emergency contacts, amiga. We see you on the map all the time."

There was too much to unpack. That's how they knew she was at the tea house. And at the hotel. And now here, witnessing where she had fallen apart.

"*Dime, amiga,*" Margaret said. "Tell me the weight on your heart." Margaret's voice reached within her, but it was Margaret's arms that pulled her in.

"I don't want to feel that way anymore. All of it was so intense. Simple and complicated, all at once." Marley dropped her hands to her side and picked up her head. "How do I stop feeling like this?"

Margaret looked around her room and Marley followed her gaze until both women were looking at a figurine of the virgin Mary.

"Do you pray, mija?"

Marley shifted uncomfortably. "For good grades and a parking spot in New York City, but that's all."

Margaret nodded, her lips lifting at the corners. "Those are good things to pray for. But I believe that we have someone for the big stuff, too."

"Girl, finding street parking in New York *is* a miracle."

They chuckled, the first time in weeks that Marley felt like the ice was thawing between them.

"And why would it seem like a miracle?"

"Because it seems impossible at the time."

"Exactamente. And how do you feel right now?"

"Like I'll never forget what it's like to be with this man - and that I'll never find anyone else like him. That it's impossible to feel the same way with someone else. Like he's the only one with the key."

"'Never' is a strong word, mija. It signals defeat before you've even tried."

"I did try, though." Marley gestured around her. "Look where it got me."

"Looks like it brought you to one of your best friends."

Marley hugged herself. "You're right." She sucked in a sharp breath. "So. Prayer. How does it work?"

"You've heard of 'Jesus, Take the Wheel'?"

"The Carrie Underwood song? Love her."

Margaret laughed. "Yes. Prayer is kind of like that. It's giving up control. It's both the most powerful and most invisible thing you can do. When you feel yourself getting full - whether it's of anxiety, or doubt, or fear - picture it as something that you can breathe out and put into God's hands. One of my favorite prayers is, 'Nope. I can't do this. It's too much. I don't know what to do with it. But you do.' And then I give it up."

"That's it?"

"Well. Sometimes I have to keep doing it. With every breath, all day long."

"That sounds exhausting."

"It sounds exhausting carrying all that weight around with you with it having nowhere to go, too. You have to choose the weight you want to carry. Hold it all yourself, or strengthen the muscles that take the weight from your heart into hands that will know what to do with it."

Marley considered it. To just give up control? Surrender it like that? That was as anti-Cromwell as she could get.

"Margaret, what's it like being in love with Zeke?"

"It's hard to explain."

Marley's laugh was hollow. "Yeah. Always is, isn't it? I thought what I felt with Thomas was the real thing. But if there is such pain and grief that follows a love like that... maybe it's easier to just not feel it at all. 'Avoid it at all costs.'"

"If I avoided all the negative that came with being with Zeke, I'd be missing the majority of the positive."

And suddenly, Marley understood.

The Cromwell Rules didn't guard against love.

They ensured the hurt would be worth it.

And this hurt was not worth it.

She wished she had never met Thomas Elker at all.

* * *

Marley stared at the ceiling. How was it Monday morning already? Marley pulled herself out of bed. She expected to be more tired. The exhaustion of the past few months - the relentless go, go, go and perpetual high - should have laid her out for the day. Instead, the anger of last night had rejuvenated her.

She didn't need a processing day. What she did need was to know that Thomas didn't hate her. Surely he'd want to talk to her and figure this out. They couldn't just leave things like this - so unsettled and so unknown.

She was desperate for one more hug. One more last kiss.

He hadn't *really* meant what he said. Had he?

She picked up her bright sundress from the floor. Maybe if she dressed how she wished she felt, he'd... She shook her head. No. She would put on the sundress because she liked the sundress. If he noticed, that'd be lucky for him. He wasn't worth rotating her world around anymore.

The walk to the office was quick.

Before long, Karl was at her cubicle with a cup from Café 43 in his hand. Her stomach turned at the sight of it. He scanned her from top to bottom. She tried to straighten her back and lift her chin. If he noticed anything, she hoped he wouldn't comment on it. She exhaled when he hooked his arm around hers, but then groaned when he turned to her with a smirk.

"We're going to go on a trip in style, I see!"

Marley stopped walking. How did Karl know that she had called her mother on the walk to work? True to Marley's suspicions, her mom had encouraged her to come home.

"What are you talking about?"

"We're going on our annual company field trip! 'Activity fuels creativity,' as *you* like to say."

Marley's jaw dropped and her hand flew up to hide her face. "Oh, no. I totally forgot." She pulled at her dress. "How am I supposed to..." Her eyes widened. "Karl. I can't go in this dress. We're hiking and - and - what else?"

"Rappelling down waterfalls."

"Who comes up with this stuff?!"

Karl laughed. "Didn't you? You were so excited about 'this stuff' that you made everyone else sign up for it, too."

"Yes, when I would be dressed for it. And mentally prepared."

Karl grabbed her hand. "I have an idea. Follow me."

As Marley followed Karl, her gaze flew to the space between the watercooler and the wall. Or pressed against the door frame of the room he'd invite her into. No box of Pop Rocks. Karl led them into the copy room and Marley felt every step heavier than the last. This was where she had imagined a future prompted by that heart-stopping moment when he had taken a knee. That would never be now. She didn't know which she wanted to give more power to: the anger that was just below the surface - or the heartache rumbling deep within.

Karl reached for the box on the second shelf of the storage rack. But all Marley could remember were the ways Thomas had breathed on Marley's neck and shoulders, the way his hands wandered when he had her pressed against the metal bars Karl was now trying to avoid. Would every inch of this place have Thomas Elker's tattoo on it?

"This should do it," Karl muttered. He pulled the box down and set it on the counter. Opening the flaps, he pulled out a bright orange t-shirt with Agencia del Tigre in bold print across the chest and a roaring tiger covering the back. After some additional searching along the bottom, he pulled out black drawstring shorts.

"There," Karl proclaimed proudly. "Problem solved." Marley's heart sank. If that were her only problem.

"Hey. It's okay. Go ahead and change real quick. I'll guard the door."

She forced a smile and grabbed the clothes. "Thanks, friend. I don't know what I'd do without you. Sit with you on the bus, yeah?"

Karl frowned, before turning to stand like a guard on the threshold of her bedroom. "The coast is clear!" he called over his shoulder. "I'm sorry! I can't. I told Mr. Elker I'd run through a few concepts with him on the way to Rio Verde."

She wouldn't make it through the next five minutes let alone the rest of this trip. Marley grabbed the corner of the box on the counter, positioning it so it'd press against her splinters, and pressed down until she felt a pain more intense than the constrictions in her chest. With Zeke mad at her and Karl talking to the very man she wanted to both avoid and also wrap her arms around, this trip that she had planned was now the bane of her existence.

"You good, Mar?" Karl asked, still not turning around.

She pushed into the box with everything that was in her. She released it. "Yes. Give me a second."

But she had to go. She lifted her dress over her head, the strap getting stuck over her ponytail. She shook her head to release it. She was happy to feel that, though the t-shirt fit snugly, the shorts gave her enough breathing room.

No more running away. No more processing days.

Marley needed to know that things would somehow be okay between her and Thomas. A heartbreak couldn't heal if the person who had caused it *had* to become a stranger. Right? That seemed backwards. Reconciliation brought healing. Once that happened, they could go back to at least being friends. Colleagues. Acquaintances, even. But not strangers. Becoming strangers would be the worst ending of all.

* * *

She held her breath, steeling herself as she entered the van. She didn't want to run or hide. She was the other woman and it was time to face reality. She nodded to Karl and offered a weak smile before making wide strides to her seat, third seat from the back. Curling her knees up to her chest, Marley watched as her colleagues boarded the bus.

Isabel stepped onto the bus, Maria right behind her. They were cackling about something Maria had said. Marley used to see a go-getter who always got her work done. Now, she only saw a tank top that boasted a lot of cleavage and pursed lips colored in red. She looked like she was going out to the club more than to rappel down some waterfalls. Isabel made a show of counting heads and strutted over to Thomas, keeping her hand on his shoulder longer than was appropriate between colleagues. Marley groaned and hit her head on the back of her seat.

Zeke walked up the aisle next. She wanted nothing more than to reach out, grab him, and tell him it was over and apologize profusely for dropping their friendship like it had never mattered; like it hadn't gotten her through so many days. The passionate romance hadn't been worth it. Though she stayed glued to her seat, she did lift a hand, hopeful that he'd see the desire to connect and sit with her. But he sat by himself a few rows in front of her. Tears burned in the back of her eyes, and she urged them away.

She sunk back into her seat and, before long, they were on their way.

It would take them a little over an hour to arrive in Otívar, a town just outside of the rural countryside that housed the waterfalls and rivers that they would get to explore. Marley had been on the committee to plan this adventure, totally in support of physical activity as a prerequisite to amazing creative ideas. But now that they were on their way, Marley couldn't think of anything less alluring. She frowned, thinking of Cilantro all by herself. She hoped the bumps along the way would lull her to sleep, but for once, she wasn't tired. Her mind was racing with ways to approach Thomas. What could she say? What was the right thing to do? How could they end this - properly?

Then, she heard Thomas' voice. She looked up at him through her bangs and over the seat back in front of her. He was speaking animatedly with Brandon and Karl. With his hair gelled back and his tan built up over the last few days, Thomas looked as perfect and polished as ever. He was unfazed. Nothing had changed. He was still the boss in charge, not a hair out of place.

Teflon.

How could she have put all her energy and love and hope onto a piece of plastic?

Memory upon memory stacked upon itself, the treasure chest begging to be opened again. She would have given up the passion and the intimacy if it meant that she could still have this man and call him friend. Memories often bolstered a person. But in this case, there were too many, and they were too heavy. She didn't have memories with Thomas in New York. Maybe it *was* time to go back.

The van came to a stop. The doors opened and a broad-shouldered man native to Spain stepped on, introducing himself to the group as Alejandro, their tour guide. Alejandro explained what the next few hours would entail: hiking, ziplining, and then ending the day with a ladder and rope down a cliff and along a waterfall to a bright blue pool of water.

After exiting the van and slathering on more sunscreen, Marley followed her team to the foot of the trail. She anticipated a speech of some kind: something that would encourage the team or remind them why they were spending a day doing this instead of working on Mariposa's project so close to the end of the quarter, but nothing came. They entered the trail as if they had been walking along it the entire time. Because Marley was always quiet, her colleagues didn't engage in conversation with her like they did with the others around them. They passed ahead of her quickly. This was fine. She was more interested in finding a chance to talk to Thomas. Alone.

Her opportunity finally came when the group had hiked a couple kilometers at a moderate incline and Alejandro commanded them to rest and rehydrate. When they were ready, he said, they would start the process of ziplining down, one at a time, to the cliffs. Maria and Isabel were freaking out about how high they were, pointing out the river rushing across, bubbling in with white water rapids. Ever the hero, Thomas offered to go first.

Which meant Marley would go next. She had ziplined a few times before in adventure parks tucked within woods in the north of New York state, so the apparatus wasn't new to her.

She closed her eyes, exhaling like Margaret had taught her. She gulped and stepped forward. She watched as the crew strapped him in, reminded Thomas to press the rope towards the end of the line, and reassured him that the gloves would be enough to keep his hands safe from the heat of friction.

She thought of the way they sat back enjoying the view and each other at Plaza de San Nicolas before everything became so complicated. Looking at him, even now, her body responded in ways she had never felt before. A simultaneous desire to cling on to him and run away kept her locked in place.

She hoped Thomas would understand the double-meaning when she said what she'd been chewing on for a few minutes now:

"It's a little more complicated than a hot air balloon, huh?" The "it" was them *and* ziplining. *Get it, Elker?* she wanted to say. *I know it's complicated and messed up, but surely we can figure this out.*

Thomas looked around, his gaze finally resting on her. *Please get it.*

"Need some Pop Rocks?" She smiled. *See? I understand you.*

"Nah," he said. "I'm good."

The crew said something to him and he nodded before waving casually in her direction.

"See ya."

And suddenly she couldn't imagine anything worse than being stuck with him on the other side while they waited for the rest of the team to zipline over.

She stepped back, allowing the rest of the team to disperse. She found a tree trunk and stared at the ground while she snapped the water bottle's push spout open and shut. She hated his ability to force the ground of her heart wide open. Each time he responded like he didn't care, the treasure chest sunk deeper. Her arms alone wouldn't be enough to lift it back up.

This relationship - whatever it was - was a two-man sport. And he had just abandoned his post.

It became clear then that remaining Thomas' friend wasn't possible. She didn't even know how she would be able to stay on at Tigre. All of this time spent yearning for a foreign adventure, and now that she'd had one, she longed for the steel and concrete assuredness of home. While she'd been searching for more, more, more, she'd missed what was right in front of her. How could she have given up so many of her friendships so easily? She'd gotten so swept away.

And even now, she hated that, if he had responded with an invitation to meet her at his house, she wouldn't hesitate.

How messed up did one have to be for *that* to happen?

"Hola, amiga."

Marley looked up and left the push spout open.

"Zeke." Her heart swelled, becoming a little wider in healing the hole that Thomas had left.

Ezequiel sat next to her. "I'm surprised you're not down at the other end by now."

"I am, too. I love this stuff. Usually."

"You still do. Let's go. I haven't rappelled down a waterfall yet, have you?"

Marley smiled, and felt that it was true. It was the first real smile she'd had in a while. "Todavia no. Pero estoy lista. Let's go."

The rush of the wind in her hair and the crashing of the water beneath her lifted Marley's spirits. She was flying. On the inside, heart ache was consuming her, but on the outside, the stark green ivy and leaves jumped out at her next to the dark bark of the trees. Even here, Marley could see the art and beauty around her. And maybe, if she looked deeply enough, she could make art with what had happened to her - what *was* happening to her - too.

Marley landed on the other side and, with the help of the crew, stepped out of the harness. She wrung her hands as she waited for Zeke.

When he landed with wind-scattered hair in every direction, she laughed - and it felt so good to hear him laugh, too. "Well, that was awesome. Thought I was going to die. But awesome."

But she didn't feel it was quite time to laugh yet. She had an apology to make. They walked together, heading to the top of the waterfall, where Alejandro was passing out helmets.

She took one and handed it to Zeke. "I am so sorry. I should have listened to you. You were right. I had no idea what I was getting myself into. I had so much *pride*. I was so wrapped up in how he saw me."

Zeke offered a small smile. They walked together to the side of the waterfall. They watched it surge from the rock beneath them, powerful enough to remind them they wouldn't want to be taken by it, but small enough that they could see through it as the afternoon light hit it, making small drops appear to be hopping from one rivulet to another.

"Tu eres como una cascada, Marley. We all are. We're not going to be the same at the top of the waterfall as we are during the fall as we are when we feel like we're being catapulted by the same thing that made us feel like flying moments before. You just had your fall now - and it might feel like drowning sometimes, but you'll find your way back to the surface. You just have to hang on."

They watched as the others were strapped into their harnesses and tied around with the rope.

"Oh, Zeke. I feel so used."

His lack of denial wounded her, but she felt his hand squeeze her shoulder. She leaned into him.

"We're using this waterfall, too. We're even going so far as to interrupt its natural flow by putting our legs or arm or face into its way. But it never stops being itself. It doesn't lose its essence. It finds a way to bend. To curve around. To push back." Zeke looked at Marley. "Which will you do?"

"I used to run, or hide, or wait for the storm to pass. But it's different when *you're* the one who caused the storm. I can't get over the fact that I had tossed away our friendship so quickly. I was an idiot."

Zeke nodded.

Marley laughed. "You agree? That I was an idiot?"

"La mas grande, si. Even Margaret thought so."

Marley's laughter faded. "Yeah. I'm glad I accidentally butt-dialed her. She came exactly when I needed her."

"She's so good like that." Marley looked up to see that familiar look. The same one Logan had for Lily. The one that had been captured in the photo of Sofia on Thomas' phone.

"I was such a fool to think that you wanted to ruin my life instead of protect me from hurt. I'm so sorry. I understand if you don't want me in your life anymore, but I really would love you to continue being part of mine."

Zeke grinned, and any of the worry she'd held about never being in Zeke's good graces ever again disappeared. "C'mere, chica." He wrapped her up in a warm hug. They were friends again. She melted into him and squeezed him tight.

Alejandro called them over. They disengaged and strode over together. The crew prepared them for descent, and Alejandro explained what they'd have to do. Marley could hear Isabel's laughter and Thomas' chuckle. Something within her curdled. Suddenly, she couldn't wait to be next to the waterfall; if they were one and the same, there was nothing to be afraid of. With the waterfall to her left, Zeke to her right, and the cliff's wall a firm base beneath her feet, she could be steady. She could be strong.

The sun warmed her skin and water cooled it down: a perfect balance. When was the last time she had felt such peace? She looked over at

Zeke, who was pushing himself off the wall, letting some of the rope loose, only to land a little lower, but still sure of himself, along the wall. It was like a trampoline park, but way more dangerous and infinitely times more cool. *This* was the kind of life she had wanted when she decided to leave the concrete jungle of New York City.

Isabel's giggle punctured the peace.

"Thomas, stop it!"

Mr. Elker was scooping up water with his hands and splashing Isabel. Isabel kicked from one side of him to the other, feigning annoyance but obviously thrilled that she had the boss's attention. Another woman forfeiting her mind to be led by her emotions. Marley had been there, done that. Marley looked over at Zeke, who gave her a wry smile. *This* was what being strong and sure of yourself was like.

Until she wasn't. She wanted to jump and play like Zeke had, but that meant she had let go of too much of the rope too quickly. The pressure of the waterfall pushed her down and against the cliff. She scrambled to find the rope, but with the water crashing against her, she couldn't grip it. Opening her mouth to yell for help, water rushed in through her nose and mouth and the force of the falls threw her against the jaws of the cliff, jagged rocks puncturing her skin. She could see Zeke's hand reaching out, but she had to climb back up the rope in order to reach him and gain traction.

Marley tucked her knees up to her chest, then, and upon making contact with her feet, pushed as hard as she could against the wall. The force pushed her away from the waterfall enough for her to zone in on the rope in front of and against her. She gripped it, hugging it tightly to her. Instead of bracing for impact on the way back, Marley pretended she was landing after having jumped to spike a volleyball. Knees bent and core engaged, Marley was perpendicular to the cliff. Alejandro yelled something like it would be okay to let go and fall into the water below, but she was *not* ready to be done with this experience. She had looked forward to it - and then had forgotten about it because she had become so wrapped up in Thomas. He was not going to steal her joy anymore.

Marley's jaw set, she hauled herself up, putting one hand on top of the other, using her core and chest muscles to lift her. She willed herself to walk up the wall, the water gushing over her feet, refreshing the cuts and bruises that were already in blossom. Pride surged within her. Her colleagues asked again and again if she was okay, but she whooped in victory. *She* had what it took. It was inside of her the entire time. The choices she had made related to Thomas Elker had totally wiped her out, but she was still Marley. She could still be good. She could still be her best self. Maybe it was a life's truth that a wipeout every now and then was the price to be paid for a heart that desired adventure. She was the captain of her own ship. And sometimes there would be storms.

And sometimes those storms could still be danced in.

Zeke and Marley played in the water, splashing each other and climbing up the rope just to fall and catch themselves again. The best part of the day was when she heaved herself up and over the ledge, took off her harness, walked 15 meters away from the edge, and then sprinted until she flew, flew, flew, and dropped into the crisp blue of the water.

It was easy for a man to splash someone, or slather aloe, or seduce a colleague into a copy room.

It was much more impressive if a man stayed loyal to his life and his ambitions.

And then, wading in the water until the final moments they had to leave, Marley knew. This would be her final Granada adventure. Marley couldn't be here anymore. Between the Café 43 cups that would trigger the way everything ended and the lack of Pop Rocks hiding in the office and Isabel making goo-goo eyes at their boss, Tigre wasn't safe for her anymore. It had lured her in with its promise of promotion and living abroad and making Spanish friends who'd help her feel cosmopolitan and well-traveled, but really, it had drained her of ideas, of joy, and always left her feeling like she was chasing her own tail. She couldn't imagine what her days would look like: the amount of effort it would take to keep pretending she was okay when her heart was pounding out of her chest with him just across the room. The amount of energy it would take to keep averting his eyes, when all she wanted was to get lost in them, again and again. She would take all that she had learned with her, but she needed to make new memories in a new place. Anything else would be self-sabotage. Thomas had been an aftershock of the earthquake that had already been her life, but staying would be an invitation to keep falling down the crevices, never having sure footing. And now that the aftermath had created so many crevices, she knew exactly where she'd make sure her cascada fell. New York City needed more naturaleza anyway.

* * *

It had been Marley's idea to plan this field trip on a Monday, hoping it would build creative momentum for the rest of the workweek - and the rest of the quarter. But looking around the table, people were spent. Maybe after a good night's sleep, it would work out how she had imagined. Too bad she wouldn't get to find out.

"Marley?" Karl scooted his chair next to hers. "Are you okay?"

Marley looked into Karl's eyes. So sincere. Always kind.

"Yes. No. Not totally. But I will be."

"How can I help?" She wanted to throw her arms around Karl and kiss him all over. What an idiot she'd been for looking for someone to comfort her when the one who always had, had been in front of her all along.

"Hmm.. you could tell me if Mariposa agreed to the terms of the deal."

"I do not have that information, but I believe they're going to tell us right now. Figures that they'd make us go on an adventure to test our cajones first."

But what difference would it make? She had played by her own rules, using her own compass. And now she had no one to blame but herself. Her selfishness had led her here. How she'd ever be able to make amends and feel redemption for the disgust she felt for herself seemed impossible. Lily would never speak to her again. Her mother would be so disappointed. Just thinking about Peggy sitting around the table, reminiscing on days when her home was full of Marley and Lily's antics made Marley's heart squeeze. How could she do this to her *mother*?

Karl interrupted her thoughts. "Mar?"

"It's like I'm having a conversation with myself for the first time in months. Does that make sense?"

"You? But you're always thinking and reflecting and wondering."

"I overthink and my reflections are all fear responses. I wonder how things could possibly go wrong. I don't actually live in the present. The only times I do are when I'm with Zeke, or Lily, or.."

"..or me!" Karl grinned.

Marley laughed. She brought her fingers to her lips. "Or you. I haven't actually been anxiety-free in years. And it's like, all of a sudden, it doesn't matter if a meteor crashes into me."

Karl furrowed his eyebrows. "Sounds serious. What the heck happened?"

"Do you want to go to New York with me?"

"Eventually, yeah. You know I've always wanted to go."

"Today. Now."

"What? Before the meeting? After rappelling down waterfalls? Are you an undercover adrenaline junkie? Don't you think you should sleep on it first?"

"Yes. Yes. Maybe. No. Who cares if Mariposa goes with the deal or not?"

"Uhm. We do. It's our livelihood. You're sexy enough to find an alternate occupation. I am *not*."

"You'll do fine. There's a place for everyone in the City. C'mon. If Mariposa closes on the deal, we can celebrate on the flight over and you can work remotely. If Mariposa doesn't, we can drink our worries away on the flight over and apply for new jobs. In New York."

"This is a very elaborate ruse to bring home a human souvenir, Marley."

"You'd be the best wedding date ever."

"Wedding?! You're going to a wedding?!"

"I'm the maid of honor. Well. I was. I need to find a way to convince Lily that I still can be."

"I *am* the king of persuasion."

"I know you are, but that's not why I want you with me. I don't want you to do anything for me. I just need a reminder that I can do it."

"Of course you can, Mar. You have everything you need inside of you. I've seen it since day one."

Karl wrapped his arm around Marley's shoulders. She tapped her head on Karl's shoulder and then lifted it, turning to him.

"Come to New York with me. We can stay with my mom. I have to make things right."

She felt another arm wrap around her. She craned her head back to see Zeke looking down at her.

"What a freaking tragedy I've written myself into, you guys."

Zeke squeezed again and let go. "If you can write yourself in, you can write yourself out."

Karl looked from Zeke to Marley and then back again. "I'm clearly missing some really key information. But that doesn't discount the fact that you can't just escape because things aren't going your way, Mar Mar."

"Plane ride?" Zeke asked. "Escape? 'Mar Mar'?"

"Marley's kidnapping me. Finally. But the timing is weird. Why not stay to celebrate here?"

Marley breathed in and imagined what Margaret had told her about breathing out everything she couldn't control. She *could* control what she did from here on out. She *could* control prioritizing her best friend and making amends. And as difficult as it was, she could also find a way to accept that, though Thomas was the yin to her yang, he did not know how to love. He had taught her so much just by being himself. But now she would have a lifetime of memories from a small snippet of time. She'd hug his ghost. And even though she had no idea how to be okay with that, she knew she had to find a way.

"I'm not escaping. I'm not running away. For the first time in my life, I'm doing what's best for me and those I love. I'm running *towards*." She grinned up at Zeke. "I'm pushing back. Even if it's the hardest thing I've ever had to do."

"Brandon!" Marley yelled across the room. The room fell silent. Marley never raised her voice.

He looked over curiously at her. Thomas' head jerked in her direction. *Relax,* she wanted to tell him. *I wouldn't rat you out.*

"Can you just tell us if Mariposa bought into the idea?"

Everyone turned to look at Brandon.

Brandon cleared his throat. "Well. Urm. I had this whole speech planned, but—"

"Aw, just tell us, man," Karl said.

Brandon grinned. "We got it. Our jobs are safe. Marley, without you…"

But she didn't wait to hear the rest. She leaned over Karl's shoulder. "I'll find the flights and text you. We're leaving in the next 24 hours."

She gathered her things and walked to the threshold, where Thomas had first walked in on her giving her practice presentation. She turned and looked one more at time at the colleagues who had, in a very short amount of time, become the closest thing she'd ever had to a dysfunctional family. Isabel was condescending and prideful, but she got the job done. Marley hoped she'd protect her heart better than Marley had. Hopefully Maria would help Isabel do that, with her reminders to take a nap on the couch, friendly, sincere, and duly ignored. And finally, with all the strength remaining within her, she forced herself to look at Thomas.

For once, he didn't look like he was putting on a brave face. He looked *sad*.

A surge of love threatened to burst through her. She did love him. And if it wasn't love, it was a deeper appreciation than she'd felt for many people. She loved him for all the ways he opened her to the world and to herself. For the ways he had taught her what love was not. She could write a book and there would still be things she'd want to say and things she'd want to do. So Marley breathed it out, and then she breathed out some more. Whoever this God was, Marley almost felt bad for him. That was a lot of uncertainty and angst coming in his direction.

Somehow, she believed he could handle it.

In the meantime, she had a flight to catch.

Reflect and Recalibrate

They had passed through security and run through the gates, just barely making the last flight of the night. Now they were finally on their way and didn't have any more distractions.

Marley stared in horror. "Karl. What are you doing?"

He turned to her while he untied his other shoe. "What does it look like I'm doing?"

Marley turned to the left, wondering if anyone else could see. "But we're in an airplane. A public place. People are here. That is, like, so unsanitary."

"And I took a shower. What gives, Mar? We're already 30,000 feet in the air. It's not like the pilot will ground us for wanting to be comfortable. Literally nobody else is bothered by this. I'm already traveling halfway around the world for you. Let me have my peace." He picked up the neck pillow from where it had been sitting on the hand rest between Karl and Marley's seats and slipped it behind his head.

Marley was in awe that Karl was sitting right next to her and they were flying to New York City together. She shrugged and untied her sneakers, too, careful not to bump Cilantro's carrier.

"Besides," he said. "You haven't told me *anything* yet. This is blind faith in action right here."

Karl was about to put in his bright pink earbuds when Marley stopped his hand.

And then she told him, starting from the very beginning, when Thomas had complimented her the first day he started on the Mariposa team and made her feel like she could really present.

"He called me a bobcat and, I know it sounds stupid, but it unlocked something in me. It's like someone really *saw* me."

"Yeah, I remember that day. You were all ready to go after spending a little time with him. It didn't matter that Zeke and I had encouraged you— *seen you*—for forever and day..."

Marley kept her hand on top of Karl's. "I know. And I feel so terrible about it. I don't know why Thomas..." She shook her head. "Mr. Elker, I mean, had such an effect on me. You and Zeke were nothing but kind and encouraging and *good* and the moment he stepped into my life, I suddenly felt like someone had infused me with, I don't know, this superhuman drug that made me feel invincible." The more she talked, though, the more it felt like excuses or justifications that would make it okay. She owed Karl more than that.

She squeezed Karl's hand. "I see you. You have chamomile tea in your office just in case I'm having a bad day and I know you hate the smell of it. Don't make that face. You try to hide it, but I know you hate it. You invite me out for coffee when you see I'm overtired and need a break. Shoot. You found a way for me to be comfortable in my own skin today - gosh, I can't believe that was just today - by pulling out Tigre merch. You have never once made me feel like I had to do anything on my own. And yet - I felt this stupid, stupid pull towards our *boss* when *I knew* it was wrong."

Karl withdrew his hand from beneath hers. "Yeah, it's weird. I'm not gonna lie. And hurtful. When you go out of your way to show real friend-ship - through actions - and all he has to do is, what, call you a nickname? Draw a picture of a lily on an index card?"

"What?" Thomas drew her a picture of a flower? Her heart sped up. When? It would have been something to hold on to. Something to remem-ber him by.

"The last girl I dated left me because the guy she had a crush on drew her a picture of a lily on an index card. Apparently that was all it took for her to go to his house the next week and totally forget about me. I hope the scraps are lying in a landfill somewhere," Karl added bitterly.

Marley lowered her head, biting down to stop her trembling bottom lip.

Karl reached past her head and lowered the tray in front of her. "Here. At least put your elbows on the tray and straighten your back. You can be sad and still hold on to your dignity."

Marley blew up into her bangs. "See? This is what I'm talking about. You're just so *nice*, Karl."

"Mr. Nice Guy. That's me. But the nice guy doesn't get the girl, it seems."

Marley sighed. "I'm sorry. I really am. But my heart is all sorts of messed up right now." And then Marley told him the rest. How she went out with him to Bahama Club, lied to Lily, and was found out by Zeke and Margaret at the tea house. She left out the part where she'd been mortified at the hotel; they weren't *that* close. But she did tell him that she had known about Sofia the whole time and chose to continue seeing Thomas anyway. And then she told him about how it all ended, including his stone cold reaction during the trip earlier.

"My head knows he's the worst person on the planet for me and my heart wants nothing more than to see if he's alright. And then the other part of me is like, of course he's alright. He's already moved on to Isabel. When he's done with Isabel, he'll have his alcohol and cigarettes and whatever else to keep him company. One addiction to another. And then I got caught up in it and now it feels like *I'm* addicted - to the high of feeling wanted, of being desired, of being acknowledged. It's so messed up. I know." Marley set her elbows on the tray table and ran her fingers through her hair. "I'm so messed up."

Karl lifted the arm rest between them and readjusted his position. Wrapping his arm around Marley's shoulders, he urged her towards him. She relaxed and let herself fall against him, her cheek resting against his shoulder.

"Hey. Haven't you heard that the only way to really connect with someone is by being vulnerable with them? And that only happens when you have the courage to share your truth. Like you've shared with me right now. I may not understand the whole addiction thing, but I do know that I'm kind of relieved that you're not perfect."

Marley laughed in between a cry, so it sounded like a snort. "What?"

"The luster is off. The sheen has been dulled around Marley's halo."

Marley expected to feel disappointed by such a statement, but instead she felt… relief?

She lifted her eyes, but could only see the black of his nostrils and feel tickled by the blonde of his beard. "And why does that matter?"

"Because if you accept that you're not perfect, you'll stop being disappointed when you make a mistake like the rest of us peasantry humans. "

"Sometimes it hits me so hard how much damage I've caused. The guilt hits me like a ton of bricks - and out of nowhere. And when I think about how I'm no better than the woman who helped my dad cheat on my mom? It almost becomes too much."

Karl lifted his hand to Marley's face and pet her temple like she often pet Cilantro. Marley would purr if she could. Instead, she closed her eyes and sighed.

"That's been a lot for you to carry, Mar."

And there was something in his acknowledgement of that that caused her to cave within herself. The crevices that had opened suddenly had space for more tears, and she let them flow. The sobs racked her. She had often been tired because of working overtime. But this was a different kind of tired. She'd have to call Dr. Deidre and resume sessions. She had so much healing ahead of her.

"I want to get better."

"You will, honey." Karl kissed the top of Marley's head. "Something about a caterpillar needing to shed its old skin to become a butterfly or whatever… You folded so many of those origami butterflies. You know it takes time. You'll create yourself into someone even more beautiful. I'll be here for you in the meantime."

Marley hugged Karl's arm to her chest.

Karl tightened his hold around her. Marley closed her eyes, settling into Karl.

"Just no more lillies on index cards," he said. "If you're going to fall for someone, fall for someone who shows up with more than words. Fall for someone who chooses you, above all else, and will stay."

"Yes, sir," Marley muttered. "And I know exactly who that will be."

Recover

"Does your mom know we're coming?" Karl's teeth chattered.

Marley shook her head vigorously and breathed out. White smoke from their breaths dissipated around them and landed on the frost tips of the lawn.

Karl held Cilantro's carrier while Marley opened the storm door. She stood in front of the bright yellow door - the only one in the neighborhood that wasn't dark maple or boasting stained glass windows. Peggy had it replaced after her divorce was finalized. Marley hadn't fully appreciated it every time she'd bust it open, relieved to be home. But now? This door had personality. Her mom had healed from what her father had done. There was hope.

"*Can* she know we're coming?" Karl asked. "What are w-we w-wait-ing f-for?"

I am the other woman, Marley wanted to yell. *I don't deserve to walk in like this is still my home.* Shame clawed at her insides. Cilantro meowed.

Marley grasped the knob, pressing on the nickel top that released the latch in the door. You'd think Peggy would keep her front door locked, but how else would her friends feel welcome? Marley pushed the door open and the security system beeped three times in recognition. They stepped onto the burgundy runner, the softness a buffer between their tired feet and the hard mahogany floors.

"One minute!" Peggy's gentle voice rang from the corner office. She heard her mother shuffling papers and the lid of the compost bin banging shut. Marley's lips lifted slightly at the corners. She wondered what bouquets she was working on today.

"Anne, I was just about to—"

Peggy dropped the bouquet at her feet. "My girl." She opened her arms and Marley ran into her mother's embrace. "You're home. You came home." Marley laid her cheek on her mother's shoulder as Peggy hugged her tighter, then took a step back.

"Let me get a look at you. You've gotten so tan. Your freckles popped up so beautifully. And your blue eyes..." Peggy paused. "What's wrong? What's happened?"

She looked up, finally noticing Karl. Marley turned around. "Momma, this is Karl." She blinked quickly, her eyelashes wet from the warm house after the cold wind. Marley smiled wide. "A really great friend."

Karl lifted Cilantro's carrier and bowed. "At your service, ma'am."

Peggy lifted an eyebrow, her lips parted, and then broke out into a smile, clapping her hands. "How adorable are you. Come on in, come on in. We have some catching up to do. I just took some cookies out of the oven." Peggy wrapped her arm around Marley's shoulders, guiding her into the kitchen and to the open seat at the round table. Karl stood in the threshold, still holding Cilantro. Once Marley had been seated, Peggy tapped Marley on the shoulders and spun to take Cilantro from Karl. "Please, do sit down."

Karl looked from Marley to Marley's mother. "Actually, I would be terrible company right now. My eyes are not adjusting well to this frigid air and if it wouldn't be too much trouble..."

"Of course! Silly me. Let me show you to the towels and the guest room." Peggy rested Cilantro's carrier onto the kitchen table. "I'll be right back, lovely." Peggy kissed the side of Marley's head. "Don't disappear."

Marley smiled and slid her arm across the table, letting her head rest on her bicep. She glanced up, the blue robin egg colored cabinetry the same. The smells of chocolate cookies, the same. Cilantro scratched at the black netting keeping her away from freedom. Marley lifted her head and zipped open Cilantro's carrier, scooping her up in her arms. She stood with Cilantro, the British shorthair placing her front paws on Marley's shoulder, purring in Marley's arms.

They walked together to the dark blue wall that had photographs in bright white frames hanging perfectly between the bright white chair rail and the stark white crown moulding. Each photo had a moment of Marley and her mother clasping onto each other, as if one of them would fly away at any moment. Only one photo had Marley all by herself, the day she'd decided to move to Spain.

"This was before you, Cilantro." Marley rocked Cilantro, pointing to the photo all the way to the right of the collection. Her belongings in one suitcase and a carry-on, Marley had a tight grasp around her backpack straps, but her smile had said it all: *I'm going on an adventure and I don't know what I'll find, but it's more exciting than what I have here.*

Marley turned around, soaking in the smells and sights of the kitchen. How grateful she was that she could find respite, recovery, and recalibration at home, surrounded by her mother's love. She hugged Cilantro tighter to her chest.

Three beeps resounded through the house.

"Peggy, darling, I'm so sorry I'm late! That Lily is changing her mind every minute, you know!"

Marley set Cilantro down. She inhaled deeply and looked once more at the photo of Marley from a year ago. She had been excited, sure, but she'd also been nervous and afraid and always worried of what others thought of her. It was time to face the most opinionated of them all: Anne Cromwell. Anne would be mad at her for messing up Lily's perfect wedding. Marley squared her shoulders, facing the facts: Marley deserved it. Anne would yell and then it'd be over and Marley would still be safe in this kitchen with *her* mother. She would be okay. If her mother was going to find out that Marley had become the black sheep, Marley actually preferred that Anne was the one with the spray can.

"Oh! Marley! How's our girl?!" It looked like Anne thought about coming in for a hug, but then kept herself back, tucking her gloves into the pockets of her fur coat. She walked over to the stove and lifted the cover on the freshly baked cookies, only to close it again.

"Oh, you know," Marley squirmed. "Figured it was time to visit Mom and start being present for whatever Lily needs!"

"Yes. It's such a shame that she decided to cancel her bachelorette party, but she assured me that that's exactly how she wanted it."

That wasn't true. Since they were teenagers, Lily and Marley had day-dreamed of the wedding festivities they'd enjoy together one day. Marley felt the ache in her heart. Maybe Lily hadn't told her mother of their drama.

"Her visit to Spain felt so short this time around, didn't it? I thought she'd take advantage of the longer vacation time. She had fought Greg about the extra days since she's worked so hard on the IceStorm launch. Tsk, tsk, tsk." Anne lifted the cover once more and withdrew a cookie. "Sometimes you just need to give in to the temptation," Anne winked.

Marley felt a surge in her spine. "Not all temptations are weighed equally," Marley said.

Anne cocked her head and looked at Marley as if seeing her for the first time. She nodded. "Those are the words of a wise woman. It sounds like they come from experience."

Marley looked down at her jeans and back up at Anne. "I've lost a lot because I gave into those temptations. I have caused quite the damage."

Anne nodded and pulled out a chair for herself. She sat down, elbows leaning on the table, a crescent shaped chocolate chip cookie in one hand and her other hand reaching out to Marley.

"You should talk to Lily. We'll be at the hotel later tonight to make sure the ballroom is set up the way we want it. Then, we will enjoy each other's company at *Paisano's*." Anne bit into the cookie and mused over her next thoughts. "I promise that you haven't lost everything. In fact, it might be now that you'll be able to see all that you do have."

Anne squeezed Marley's hand before releasing it, finishing her cookie.

"Delicious, as always," Anne told Peggy as she walked into the kitchen.

Anne knew, and she wasn't mad. The realization sunk in. *And* it sounded like Lily was open for reconciliation.

Hope sprouted in Marley - and with it came courage.

"Mom, could I ask you something?"

Peggy pressed the button on the electric kettle. "Of course, honey." Peggy pulled out a chair and sat down to the right of Marley.

"How did you really feel after you found out about Dad's…" Marley didn't want to say it, but she knew she needed to. She swallowed. "…Dad's affairs. And why were there multiple? Did you know about the first one? And stayed?"

Peggy leaned back in her chair, like a barrage of bullets had just missed her face by millimeters.

Anne stood and opened the cabinet doors, pulling out three glasses.

"We're going right for it, huh? Well. At first, I wanted to make it work. I offered marriage counseling. I asked what he needed from me to be happy. But he kept saying he didn't know. That it wasn't about me. At the end of the day, it just came down to me not being enough for your father. If he didn't treat me the way I wanted to be treated, it was my own fault. Why do you think we had those Saturday afternoons?"

"The Cromwell Rules sessions?"

"Yes. Those."

"Because you didn't want me falling for such shallow nonsense," Marley said, matter-of-fact. Her eyes widened. "Sorry, Anne."

Anne shrugged and opened the lid to the cookies, placing them in the middle of the table.

"No, honey." Her mother cast her eyes down. "What's the purpose of them?"

Anne pivoted, sploshing some of the brewing tea on the kitchen floor. Peggy lifted her hand. "Don't worry," she said. "They needed a wash anyway." Anne returned an encouraging smile. When had Peggy and Anne become friends? Peggy turned to Marley and repeated the question. "What's the purpose of the Cromwell Rules?"

"To keep yourself from getting hurt. Or at least to know that, if you do fall hard, to make the hurt worth it." Then, she paused, as understanding dawned upon her. "To keep yourself from getting hurt by always keeping a suitor interested. It's the chase, in rule-form."

Anne set the tea down in front of Marley and Cilantro leapt onto Marley's lap.

"Yes. I thought that, if I learned the Rules from Anne, then I'd know how to keep your father interested in me. And then I'd keep the family together. It took me a long time to realize, but it doesn't work that way. Why are you asking all of this now, love? What's happened?"

Marley and Anne made eye contact. Somehow, Anne's presence made it easier to tell her mother the truth.

She dug her hands into Cilantro's fur. She kneaded her short claws into Marley. "I knew my boss was married, but I got involved with him anyway. I can't stop thinking about him, when all I want to do is forget that it ever happened. And then I'm mad at myself for missing him and the way he made me feel."

Anne spoke. "How many women doubt themselves because the man doesn't know how to love them?"

Both Peggy and Marley turned to her.

"It's time to stop doubting yourself, darling. Your worth does not depend upon his inability to love you. You will find a way to love yourself and have that be enough. Mark my words: this will be the best thing that's ever happened to you."

And Marley couldn't find any reason to doubt her. No one argued with Anne Cromwell.

With her tea in hand, Anne pulled Marley up. "Take your tea. There's a good girl. Self-love and acceptance starts with a strong outfit."

Make Amends

The restaurant was washed in amber light. Lily must have allowed Logan to plan the details of the special guests' event; there was no way that she would have otherwise permitted a party in a restaurant that looked like the inside of a beer glass. Seeing evidence of Lily's ability to compromise made Marley's tension dissipate. Lily would forgive her, she kept reminding herself. Marley just had to keep being honest. Radical honesty, no matter what. It was secrecy that led her to lying - to protect what? Marley's image? At what cost? Even if Marley wouldn't be allowed to be Lily's maid of honor, at least she could be in the same space. In the back. Invisible. They'd never know she was there.

Anne greeted her at the threshold between the main restaurant and the stairway that would lead downstairs to the speakeasy room. Anne offered a warm smile and Marley threw her arms around her. It wouldn't have mattered if Anne returned the hug or not, but when Marley felt Anne's arms wrap around her, she knew that, no matter what happened next, it would be okay. Anne had been through loss and was still learning how to love. Marley wasn't even thirty years old yet and was still learning, too. Marley let go of Anne.

"Wish me luck," Marley said.

"No need, darling. You have everything it takes, right inside you." Anne shared a rare grin and tapped Marley's cheek with her fingertips. "Now go remind my Lily how to loosen up."

"Yes, ma'am."

Marley clutched the handrail, her feet wobbly on two-inch heels that she hadn't worn in a year. Last time she'd shown up for Lily was at the IceStorm launch party, and Marley was giddy, knowing that Lily would be excited to see her. But this time? What if Marley's presence was the absolute opposite of what her best friend wanted? Marley considered turning around, but the desire to make amends kept her rooted in place. She needed her best friend - not because Lily taught her who to be, but because Lily loved her through all the years that Marley had been trying to figure it out. Marley wasn't her mother. She wasn't Lily. And she wasn't her father, as similar as their stories may have appeared at one point.

Her father hadn't changed. And Marley was trying to.

Marley scanned the room, her fingernails digging into her palms. The bar was something out of a Victorian novel: red oak dominated the floor, bar, and ceiling tiles. A large roman numeral clock hung above the bartender's cove, mirrors extending from the center, framed by wood that dipped and danced according to the sculptor's muse. Three chandeliers hung from the ceiling. Servers in crisp white shirts and black bow-ties carried hors' d'oeuvres and glasses filled with champagne. She recognized Jeremiah and Hugo, Anne's unofficial beau sitting at the hightop against the wall across from the bar. A server passed in front of her, lifting the tray above both of their heads.

"Marley?"

Marley swung around, her arm making contact with the server's abdomen, causing the tray to go flying. Champagne and their flutes went flying, crashing against the bar and the floor. Marley covered her face, mortification flooding through her.

She let her hands drop and lifted her face to see Lily's mouth agape. They surveyed the damage around them. Champagne dripped from the bar stools, little pieces of glass shining around them, reflected light dancing on their dresses. Logan stepped into the room, his gaze fixed on Lily and how she would respond.

And then Lily threw her head back, laughing. "Marley Harrow, you are a mess."

All of Marley's nerves, fears, and shame erupted in a fit of giggles. "I want to hug you right now, but I'm afraid I'll make it worse if I do."

"You can't possibly make it worse."

And Marley realized she was right. Lily already knew the truth and was still standing in front of her with arms extended.

"Girl, we both have heels on. We've stepped on worse. Get over here."

Marley whispered quick apologies to the waiters, who were already mopping and sweeping. Marley took a step towards Lily and heard a crunch, but kept stepping over the mess she'd made on her way to her best friend's open arms.

They hugged like they hadn't seen each other in years. And it was true. They hadn't. Marley had held her best friend up on a pedestal, but here, hugging in a fancy pub in New York City, Lily was only a little taller than she.

"I'm so sorry," Marley said, squeezing Lily tighter. "I have so much I want to tell you."

"And I want to hear it," Lily said. "But let's enjoy this evening. We can go to your cave later to talk."

"You think it's still available?"

"I looked earlier this afternoon when Anne told me you were in town. It's a little overgrown, but open. We can talk there."

"Why there? We can go to your place."

"We always go where I want to go. If we're going to get into Marley's brain, we should go where she did most of her thinking as a kid, no?"

Marley stared at her best friend. "That's so kind."

Logan threw his arms around Marley and Lily. "About time I see you two together! Let's step into the other room, shall we? Dinner is served!"

Lily rolled her eyes. "Rib tips and fries and chicken fingers, oh my."

Marley laughed. "Your dream guy!"

Lily looked at Logan, her eyes full. Logan tucked a napkin into the collar of Lily's red dress, then bumped his finger against the bottom of her nose. She crinkled it and he laughed. "Let's go, girls," he sang in a mock Shania Twain voice.

Marley was home.

* * *

Marley clutched her sides. It had been a year since she'd eaten so many carbs. The cheese sticks, onion rings, and thick-cut french fries were coating her stomach and clogging her arteries with every step.

"It's gotta be around here somewhere," Marley called. "Not like it up and walked away." She giggled at the thought of the cave picking itself up by the edges and scuttling away. Maybe she should have stopped at that fourth flute of champagne.

Lily's high-heeled boots hit rock. Marley lifted her head to see Lily push aside the brush and step into the cave. Lily looked behind her "I think I've found it!"

Marley ran up to Lily and Lily pulled down her scarf, the bright white wool a stark contrast against her bright blonde hair and black nailpolish. She took another step and lost her footing. Marley reached out to catch her.

"Careful," Marley cautioned.

"Oh, you know me. Clumsy to the end." She laughed weakly and balanced herself upright by holding the wall next to her.

"You and me both, sister."

"Ew," Lily said, pulling her hand away from the moisture. "So. Tell me you're not surprised that it's still here, empty and waiting for you."

Marley tried not to smile. "Okay. Maybe. Yes."

They wordlessly scanned the interior of the cave, Marley's phone flashlight illuminating sections of the cave.

"It appears we are alone."

Marley sat down and Lily sat next to her on a rectangular stone. Lily loosened her boot. Marley cocked her head.

"What?" Lily said. "In case we have unwanted visitors. This heel can do some damage."

Marley laughed and shook her head. "You're not afraid of getting your coat dirty?"

"Nah. Logan says he likes a dirty girl."

"You're so much the same as you always were, but you're so different, too, Lil."

"Logan's a good influence on me." Lily bumped her knee against Marley's "You're a little different than you were a year ago too, you know."

"I know. I'd like to find my way back."

"No, no, no. We don't go back. We only move forward."

"I'm not sure where to go. I feel like there's still a lot *holding* me back."

Lily leaned her head against the cave, then pulled it upright again.

"Not *that* different," Lily chuckled. "When did you find this place again?"

"As a kid, you mean?"

"Yeah."

"When Dad still lived with us, but would be unavailable because of the late nights and weekend afternoons at the office. Or wherever he would go. Whoever he would do." She took another shaky breath in, extending her fingers out, bending them in, then extending them out again.

"How did I become my dad? How was I too weak to stop it? Why did I keep going back to him, red flag after red flag?" She hid her face in her hands.

"Hey," Lily said, pulling Marley's hands down and lifting her chin with a manicured fingernail. "We do not keep our heads down. Chin up, Cromwell. Keep telling me how you found this place."

"A bunny had sprinted past the bushes outside at full force, covering a huge stone. I thought for sure the bunny would have given itself a concussion." Lily started to laugh and Marley was surprised at the giggles rising in her throat. "I needed to check the little guy out. I pushed back a branch and was surprised to find the opening to a cave. I took out my flashlight -"

"Stop. You had a flashlight?"

"Duh. What if I had gotten lost in the park and needed to stay safe? Anyway. You're one to

talk - you have a boot in your hand."

Lily rolled her eyes, but Marley noticed that there was awe in them. "That's my Marley."

Marley cast her eyes downward. "I don't understand how you can still say that as if you're proud of me."

"Of course I'm proud of you."

"Still?"

"Still."

"How?

"Because you didn't stay on the path. You're figuring out how to recalibrate your compass. That matters." That gave Marley pause.

Marley smiled.

"I'm sorry," Lily said.

"For what?"

"For everything. You were right. I went straight into judgy-mode and assumed the worst instead of listening to you and giving you the benefit of the doubt. I was just so hurt that you hadn't trusted me with the truth."

"And I'm so sorry that I didn't know how to tell you. I was so afraid that, if I told you everything, you'd tell me to stop, and I was so blinded by what I thought I wanted." She paused. "By what I still, for God knows what reason, still want." Her heart dropped. "But I also know he's not good for me. He's not *for* me. Not the way Logan is for you." Marley turned her head to look at Lily. "Logan really is making you a better person, isn't he?"

Lily turned to her and scooped Marley's hands in her own. "Just like you always have, Stitch. Marley, you are my best friend. You have been since the day I told off Ashley for the fifteenth time and you kept double-checking to see if I was okay." She smirked.

"Because a confrontation like that would have paralyzed me forever, and that's, like, your M.O."

"Hey! I'm trying to have a sentimental moment here." Lily looked wounded. "It's not like I go looking for conflict. I just don't shrink and hide when I'm faced with it."

Lily was right. Marley always hid from adversity. If it wasn't free and easy-flowing, she didn't want it. *And yet?* that small voice from deep within whispered. *If this were true, how had she ended up moving so many times and to many different cities around the world?*

"I guess I got tired of being the boring one."

"Consistent is *not* boring, Marley. Consistent is dependable. Trustworthy. Reliable. Committed."

Marley winced at that word. *Committed.* Something her father couldn't claim and her lover couldn't promise.

"Tolerate the idea that you are a consistent, dependable, extra-super loving giver. And then tolerate the idea that other people would want to take advantage of that."

"Ugh. Like Thomas."

"Especially someone like Thomas. The guy has a wife. You knew. He was already emotionally unavailable and you were chasing someone emotionally unavailable. I don't know why - though I have my theories and *all* of them include your dad being emotionally unavailable for you. But Thomas *knew* that going after you—a colleague—was against the rules, too. All of it screams *exciting!* and is normal to someone who doesn't *know* the kind of love you provide. Awesome for him. Not so awesome for you. He went into what you guys had with 10% of his heart invested. But something tells me that, when you started to take a few steps back, he came on full force to remind you how much you needed him, huh? You deserve to have a man's *full* attention. Not just when there's something in it for him - but because he can't imagine anyone else by his side and he'll do whatever he can to keep you there. Even if it's scary and requires trust and commitment."

Marley had never heard Lily speak so candidly or emotionally before. "That's how you feel about Logan, huh?"

"The man's love has changed me. I was pretty freaking awesome before, but I feel like I'm an even better version of myself now. Does this Thomas guy make you feel better?"

"No." It surprised her how quickly and surely she said it. "Not really. In the moments we're together, it's exciting. He knows how to press my buttons so I relax completely in his arms. He takes my breath away. Literally. I gasp when he's holding me because it just feels so. damn. good. But when he's not near me? It seriously feels like a drug withdrawal. I know we'd combust if we were ever actually together; nothing would ever get done. I think that's also why I had to leave Tigre. If I were alone in a room with him, even now, it wouldn't matter that I knew how many ways this would end badly or how much my logical brain knows to stay away. I'd end up in his arms all over again. I've thought about texting him so many times since I've been home, Lil. He's like a freaking magnet. I can't do this. I feel so weak."

"But *have* you texted him?" Lily said plainly. "Even though you have felt like it and that makes you feel weak?"

"No."

"Then that sounds pretty strong to me." Lily smiled and squeezed her hand.

"Thanks," she whispered, but the praise didn't resonate. She didn't deserve it. A strong woman would have flipped him off and forgotten about him by now. She couldn't do that. She didn't know how to shut him out or shut off the memories that seemed to play on repeat. "I was so angry at first. But now, I'm just so sad. If we were meant to be apart," Marley said, "then why does being apart from him make me feel like - I know this sounds dramatic, don't judge me - a part of me is dying?"

"Which part?"

Marley watched a stalactite fall and crash to the ground.

"The part that comes alive when he's around." Her eyes brimmed. "The part that feels exciting when his arms are around me." She remembered how she had stared into Thomas' eyes. "The part that gives life flavor." She breathed in deeply. "I think I just want to be loved the way I love."

"With your whole heart."

The understanding that was threaded in Lily's voice made something within Marley crack.

She gasped for air. "Yes. And I don't think Thomas knows how to do that."

Lily wrapped an arm around Marley's shoulder and pressed her close. "No. No, he doesn't. And it was so unfair for him to make you feel this way."

"What if he breaks up with his wife?"

Lily held Marley an arm's length away. "If he broke up with his wife, what makes you think he wouldn't break up with you the moment he found someone else available to boost his ego? He avoids commitment because he's always thinking the next best thing is just around the corner."

Marley thought of Isabel and bit her lip. "You're right." She exhaled, feeling the familiar switch from desire to reason. "Sure, he made me feel good, but commitment is *hard* and he wasn't interested in that. Not with me, and not with his... wife."

"And look at you. It drained the life straight out of you. That's not *'alive'*, Mar. That's what we call a dopamine rush and crash. It feels like a drug addiction because he messed with your body, not caring what he did to your heart."

She buried her head into Lily.

Lily's hand rubbing Marley's head and shoulders was a balm, getting into all the cracks of her broken pieces.

"I hate that I know what being loved by him feels like. Not having it..."

Lily cut her off. "I'm going to stop you right there. What that man did — it was *not* love. Love builds you up and makes sure you're okay. It doesn't lie to you. It's not self-serving. It doesn't keep asking what you could do for it. It gives. It serves. It gives you what you give it and *more*. It commits. You don't hate that you miss him. You hate that the way you loved *him* revealed all the ways you never learned to love *yourself*."

The truth sunk in like a child who had finally allowed herself to fall asleep, the sheets rising around her as she fell deeper and deeper into slumber.

"You're right." Marley wiped her eyes. "You are so right."

Lily stretched her eyes open. "I'm so sorry."

"For what? Telling me the truth like the best of friends would?"

"Well. I guess so."

"Just because I didn't want to hear it doesn't mean I didn't need to know it. And you are right. I've been trying to find love by always pouring it out and hoping it would come back in. It's probably why I worked so hard, too. If I worked hard and others saw it, it would mean I was worthy and valuable. But I've never directed that energy towards *myself*. It's never what Marley wants to do - not in real, non-Thomas life, anyway. It's always revolving around what everyone else wants to do and Marley will figure out a way to blend in as to not create any conflict or perception of dissent. Jeez. Have I always been a people pleaser?"

"Hm. Not really. You don't aim to please *everybody*. If someone's doing something wrong and they ask you to participate, you don't do it. But if someone you love is doing something wrong, you'll bend over backwards to love them through it. You give more benefits of the doubt than anyone I know. But, at some point, Mar, you've gotta stand up for yourself. You have to say when enough is enough because '*I am enough.*'"

"Goodness, Lil. When did you become the philosopher?"

"Between Logan and my therapist, we're making serious strides to heal whatever broke when my dad had passed away and Anne tried to turn me into a master player. And, thankfully, Logan was successful in showing me why I deserved better. In a lot of ways, I was like Thomas, you know? Just going for what I wanted and not thinking about how my choices would hurt other people. I was in it for the next hit, too. I didn't need the confidence. I just wanted to feel good. Sexy."

Marley hadn't considered that. Lily as a female Thomas. But maybe the question that burned within her for so long would finally be answered by Lily, who was as close to Thomas' character as anyone else she knew.

"Do you think he loves me? Will miss me when I'm gone?"

Lily sucked in a breath. "Do you want The Truth or the kind of truth that'll make you feel good while not being the entire truth?"

"I don't know. Tell me what you think I can handle right now."

Lily exhaled. "That I can do. Okay. I think that, in his own way, he does. In his definition of it, where he doesn't have to be too close or too committed or 'robbed of his independence', he does. But your definition of love? I don't think he'd even know where to begin. He'd eventually have become smothered by your consistency. It wouldn't have been exciting enough for him. He's in it for the chase. For the dopamine. He's in it for the rush because, if he sits too long with himself, I'm pretty sure he doesn't like what he sees. And I would *never* want a man like *that* for my best friend. You deserve *so* much more."

The more Lily spoke, the more emboldened Marley had become. Maybe it wasn't who she *wasn't* when Thomas was around. Maybe it was all about who she could be now that he wasn't - and all the work she could do on learning how to love herself because he *had* revealed the holes in the boat, the knicks in the cave.

Marley spoke slowly, trying the words on for size. "I had fallen in love with the man I thought he could be. But he wasn't the man for me. And that's okay. I'm okay."

"Of course you are."

"It's not about how sad I am that he's gone. It's about how much he has lost now that I am."

"Yes, girl!" Lily pumped her first. "And I will hold up that mirror for you every time you forget how amazing you are. We can even break it down into Saturday morning lessons like we used to."

Marley laughed, taking a step towards the exit of the cave. "I've had enough of these Cromwell Rules. I was following them all wrong anyway."

"You *did* make fun of them while Anne was explaining why they were important. You didn't pay attention and then expected to pass the class?"

"I've always been something of an overachiever," Marley joked.

"Yeah, yeah. Save it for your speech."

Love Yourself

"**M**arley! Marley!"

The door that connected Marley's hotel room to Lily's flew open and Lily jumped onto the king-sized bed.

Marley used her grin to crinkle the tired out of her eyes.

"Perfect timing," she whispered. She dotted the last *i* before placing a period at the end of the sentence. She folded over the last page of her butterfly stationary from the Granada boutique with a satisfied sigh and then turned to Lily, who was coming at her with warp speed.

Lily threw her arms around Marley's shoulders and pulled her up before throwing her head back in glee and clapping her hands. "The day is here! It's a Saturday and I get to get married. I'm getting *married!* To the guy *I want* to get married to!"

Marley laughed. "You made it! You have found your forever man!"

Your person. Not a "maybe." Marley scooped her hair up into a bun. Where was the coffee?

Lily stood and opened the curtains. The soft glow of morning was reflecting from skyscrapers, making them look like knights preparing to watch over a royal wedding. "My mom is probably scared shitless, but who can blame her? The woman's main goal since my dad died has been to get me a rich husband." Lily bit her lip. Until that moment, Marley hadn't considered how Lily felt about her father not walking her down the aisle. Maybe Marley needed to start being a better listener, too.

Lily straightened her back. "But she'll find new goals tomorrow! We don't have to worry about Anne today. Today, we celebrate *love!*"

Marley looked at her best friend. Lily didn't have an ounce of makeup on her, but she'd never looked so radiant. Marley waited for the jealousy to sink in like the foundation would later, but none of it appeared. She had been so close to losing this friendship. Her heart swelled at her best friend, Lily's hands folded at her chest, like a little girl about to receive her favorite treat. What a fool Marley had been, choosing a man she had believed in over a woman she knew.

The morning passed in a blur, both because Anne was keeping them on a strict timeline and also because Marley was watching everything through teary eyes. When Lily was reading the note from Logan, or hugging sweet Genny to her stomach, Marley could see the joy that Lily's decisions to change the direction of her life would continue bringing her. Drinking mimosas with Vanessa was particularly entertaining while Lily had her long blonde tresses tucked into a thick braid that ran from her temple and gathered at the nape of her neck. The hairdresser was spraying the finishing touches and, before Marley knew it, silver, pink, and white confetti burst in front of Lily and Logan on the steps of the church, Logan's arm raised like he'd just scored a touchdown and both of Lily's hands clutching the one at his side. His pride. Her anchor. Marley's heart swelled, then deflated a millimeter, wondering how fragile this union was. Peggy had felt this way. Sofia had felt this way. Like they had won something that would never be taken away, until it was. Lily stepped forward, and Marley ran to Lily's train, straightening it and picking it up at the ends for the breeze to lift it just so.

Her best friend was *married.*

Marley's throat constricted. That meant Marley's hour was upon her.

* * *

"How are you? Are you okay? Do you need water?" Karl's palm was on Marley's bare shoulder. She hugged her waist and leaned over.

"There's gotta be like 300 people here, right? 300 people. Who knows 300 people, Karl?"

"Besides Anastasia, the rightful queen of Russia, I'm not sure, girl-friend. Your best friend is quite the socialite."

"How'd you know that's going to be their song?"

"What?"

"'In a Crowd of Thousands' from *Anastasia*. It's adorable. They've been practicing choreography and everything. Pretty sure Logan's swing friends are going to join in. It's going to be an event. Actually, would you play it? Maybe it would get me in the mood. I gotta get out of my head."

"Get out of your head? Is that even possible?"

Marley chuckled, swatting at the plastic water bottle at Karl's knee. He unscrewed the cap and handed it to her. She sat upright and took a few swigs, gesturing up the stairs that were to the right of them. "Would you get my knapsack? It's in the bridal room next to Lily's, right against the mirror."

"Do you want the knapsack or the song?"

"Both. Play the song while you're getting the knapsack."

"Commanding, Harrow." Karl growled and made a claw with his hand. "I like it."

"Oh, please. Don't make it a thing."

Karl rolled his eyes and spoke into his phone. He tapped Marley on the head before he leapt up the stairs, two at a time.

And the song played about a young girl, so 'proud and serene' in a parade, the boy who noticed her smile, and the man who helped Anastasia remember who she truly was.

She sighed. She missed him. It was in quiet moments like this - when she was afraid and nervous for what was to come - that she missed Thomas' presence in her life. She missed how he would make the scary seem like an opportunity and remind her of her strengths. Their encounter had been so brief, in the scheme of things, but it left an impression on her that she'd never be able to forget. Like a meteor. Or a shooting star.

Marley wiped the tears from her eyes, careful not to smear her eyeliner. Karl bounced back, holding out her knapsack. In the distance, she could hear the live jazz band play their trumpets, alerting everyone to attention, the deep voice of a soothing bass singer encouraging everyone to find their seats.

Marley stood and Karl grabbed her by the shoulders.

"You've got this, Mar. I am so proud of you. No matter what happens, I'll be here. I promise."

Marley reached up to hold the hands on either side of her and squeezed.

"You're amazing, Karl. This whole time. Never once have you let me down."

"Aw, shucks," Karl said, betraying a small smile, kicking his foot against the floor.

She slipped her arms around his torso and hugged him to her, lifting her nose against his Adam's apple, looking up at him.

"Thank you." Marley stood on her tiptoes and kissed him gently on the lips. "Thank you for showing me what friendship and forgiveness and love looks and feels like. I don't deserve you."

Karl blinked, then broke out into a wide grin. She kissed his cheek, then spun on her heel.She grinned over her shoulder, clutching the cotton knapsack against her, at the base the V-neck of her pink chiffon dress. "Time to crush it!" she yelled.

She kicked the material behind her. It was her time to shine.

* * *

Mr. and Mrs. West had been introduced, cheered, and accompanied by their wedding party and "Zoot Suit Riot" to the head table in front of floor to ceiling mirrors. The dancers from Logan's swing club were performing, dazzling their guests with twirls, jumps, flips, and kicks. Guests gawked, and maybe Marley would have been among them, but she was flipping through her knapsack. Where was her speech?! She blew up into her bangs, though every hair had been sprayed into place. She ignored the used tissues, a squeezed-out ukulele, her phone, her coin pouch, her pink lip gloss...

Lily's elbow hit the side of Marley's breast.

"Ah!" Marley gasped. "What gives?"

"Isn't this amazing?!" Lily yelled over the music.

Marley softened her eyes. "It all is!" she yelled back.

Lily squealed and returned to her place right next to Logan and Marley reached into the back once more, pulling out whatever she could on top of her charger plate.

A box of Pop Rocks. And an origami butterfly.

One reminded her of the potential within her and the other proved that she could.

The music stopped and a roar of applause erupted around her. According to Anne's itinerary, the emcee was going to introduce her - and soon.

She could spend the next few moments digging through the knapsack until she found the speech, or she could drop in a few Pop Rocks and hope they went down before someone passed her a microphone.

Rubbing the Pop Rocks box settled something within her, like she could feel the best of him coming through, loud and clear, looking at her like whatever she was about to say would be the most beautiful words ever spun. And running her fingernails against the origami reminded her of the hard work she'd put into Tigre, the labor of love she'd poured into believing that it could be the best agency in Spain.

Marley lifted her head and scanned the hundreds of people settling at their seats, ready for continued entertainment. She didn't have to be as good as a swing performance. She just had to be as good as she could be. And that was enough.

If Thomas had been her anchor, if only for a little while, she didn't need him anymore. The sea was still and she was in a rowboat all her own. It wasn't comfortable and it wasn't steady, but there were no holes in it, and she had the oars in her grasp. A wave might capsize her and lightning might strike, but odds were that she would make it another night. And then another. And another.

Each step she took towards the stage was another step more sure. Jeremiah handed her the microphone with a wink. Marley clasped it, feeling the fire lit and her eyes bright.

She tilted her head in Lily and Logan's direction and began.

"Lily." The way the light fell on Lily made her look so *young*. Lily's dress was sleeveless, her sequins glistening in the room whose lights had been dimmed for the speeches. "There is no doubt that all of us here are simultaneously in awe and also unsurprised at all that you've achieved in your 28 years of life. You've graduated from a prestigious school in a male-dominated field and traveled through the ranks of junior engineer to lead architect for a start-up that literally saves lives everyday. What no one ever expected, however, was that you'd marry someone who drives a Toyota Corolla."

Laughter surrounded them, and Marley eased the tension she'd been holding in her shoulders. Lily pretended to shield her face with her hand, while Logan threw his arms around Lily and brought her cheek against his shoulder. Marley laughed.

"Your achievements are great. But your most impressive success doesn't come through your career, or real estate, or education. It is that you let yourself be loved, and that you promise to love fiercely in return.

I have never seen someone look at anyone the way that Logan looks at you, Lil. That man melts everytime he sees you, like he can't believe that you're real. But every time he gets to hold you, it's a reminder that you *are* very much real - and that you're someone worth holding on to.

Logan, there's 5% of Lily Cromwell that you probably won't be able to tolerate, but I pray that you do. When she gets messy, like when she's ranting about work or the cab driver who ignored her *again*, let her rant. And do both of yourselves a favor and put your phone down while you pretend to listen. In many cases, she doesn't mean what she says. But make sure you pay attention to when her voice changes - and then you'll know she means business. You know what? Just do yourselves both a favor and keep the phones down when it's time to talk about your days. You deserve each other's full attention, and Lily is worth paying attention to.

We all break rules sometimes: I can't tell you how many times Lily looked over my shoulder in high school during exams when our teachers weren't looking. Sorry, Skittles." Marley made eye contact with Mr. Steel at Table 10 and waved. Mr. Steel, in his bright yellow shirt and bright pink bowtie, shrugged and winked.

Marley turned to the newlyweds. "But I think the name of the game is in the rules we don't break; the commitments we keep to each other because of the influence those commitments have on those around us. Logan, keep your eyes on Lily and only on Lily. Even when her 5% seems like the last mess on Earth you'd want to tolerate, keep tolerating it. Stay true. If anything threatens to tempt that loyalty, leave. It's not worth losing the love you have.

Lily, I know you. Logan is going to rile you up. He's going to press your buttons and hold you accountable and force you to see other people's perspectives. This does not mean that he's your enemy. This means he's *for* your best side - your best self. You, and those around you, deserve that best self.

Lily and Logan, though this wedding is for you, it's not about you."

Marley took in a deep breath and released it shakily. She hoped and prayed that this wouldn't be misinterpreted.

Marley couldn't keep Thomas from entering her mind. But instead of ushering him away, she wondered what she would say - and said it to her best friends instead.

"Your marriage is not about you. Your marriage is for the person whose hand you are holding. I pray that, when the days get heavy and you think you can't possibly do any more, your marriage will remind you that you can. When you want to be anywhere but your home because responsibility lives there, I pray that your marriage will remind you that love and laughter abides there, too.

And, when all else fails, Logan, draw a bath and pour some wine. Chances are high that Lily just needs to relax. Keep dancing with her in the middle of the street in Brooklyn."

Marley pressed the origami butterfly into her palm. "And may you always be each other's mirrors, reflecting the good in each other and bringing out the best."

Marley raised her glass. "To a lifetime of happiness. Cheers!"

* * *

Marley nodded and smiled her way to the bar. So many congratulations for a speech that had seemed too wordy and misdirected and without a point. But it was from the heart. That was undeniable. She squeezed past one couple here, a few larger groups of men taking shots of Fireball or cheering to the health of Lily and Logan with their mango-flavored Whiteclaws.

"Marley!" she heard coming from the side of her. She looked up in time to see Jeremiah, Lily's good friend from IceStorm, bouncing up to her like Tigger.

"Jeremiah!" Marley made a show of stepping back to admire his outfit: a bright orange shirt of a tiger lounging from behind the crisp black tuxedo. Would she never get away from the triggers? "Look at *you*."

"You are too kind, my bonny brunette." He bowed with a flourish, taking her hand in his and kissing the back of it. Lily had trained him well. He pulled her close. "Let's skip pleasantries and get straight to the heart of the matter. Who *is* that snack who is with you? I asked Lil and y'all are not together, so spill."

Marley laughed.

"That is Karl. He is one of my very good friends from work."

"*Friend…* from work. So no funny business?"

Something within her squeezed, but she stood her ground. "No funny business. He's free to explore the world as much as I am to journey through it on my own terms."

It looked like an electric current swam from the base of his spine through his extremities. Jeremiah shivered, "Ooh, yes. Do you think he would be interested in little old me?"

"If you couldn't make him gay, I don't think any other power on the face on the planet could. But I'd like to keep him for myself, if you wouldn't mind."

Jeremiah pouted. "But what if I showed him how much fun he's missing out on?"

"By all means."

Jeremiah twinkled his fingertips together. "Challenge accepted. But he can still be yours.

Tomorrow."

Marley laughed, watching him walk towards Karl, who was loosening his tie, gulping water down, ready for the next dance song to come on. Lily had ordered the slow, sappy songs to be kept to a minimum, so Aerosmith had two minutes to sing about not wanting to miss a thing, and that was it.

Her mother sidled up next to her, grabbing Marley's elbow and sliding Marley's hand into hers.

"Hey, Mama."

"Hi, cupcake."

"How'd it go?" Marley turned to her mother and set her drink down on the bar, grabbing her mom's other hand.

"I am *so* proud of you. I know how scary it must have been to stand up there in front of so many people, but if it tells you how well you did, Anne was *crying*. I haven't seen that woman cry in years. Decades."

"I feel like it was a bunch of mumbo jumbo. I had the speech written out, but I couldn't find it and then decided it'd probably be more authentic coming from the heart."

"And you were right to do so. I know I hated to have you gone, but that speech made so clear how much you've learned in your time abroad - about what it means to be in a relationship and, more importantly, what you want that relationship to bring out in *you*."

"You could say that again." Marley brought her shoulders to her ears and dropped them. "I feel like I've unlocked next-level Marley."

"That's how I felt after I finally let go of your father."

"Yeah?" Marley turned to reach for her drink, but bumped into someone else waiting at the bar.

"Oh! Excuse me."

He looked over at her and shrugged, a smile creeping into his lips, but then he looked back at the bartender, watching her flip over two tumblers and pouring in whiskey.

"Yes. I trust you, Marley. I trust you to make the right choices - not only for yourself, but for the people you love. Sometimes we have to royally mess up in order to see who stays and who is worth staying for. And sometimes, the heart has to break to make room for something more." Her mother nudged and lifted an eyebrow towards the man at the bar.

Marley rolled her eyes, but when she turned back, her mother was gone.

He had jet black hair and a black suit to match. The white collared shirt was unbuttoned, with a loose tie hanging askew. He kept staring ahead, arms on the bar, like there was no care in the world except that his drink wasn't coming fast enough. Something within Marley bristled.

"I should warn you," the man said. It took her a second to realize he was speaking to her. "I don't get with bridesmaids at a wedding. It's a rule of mine."

Marley raised an eyebrow. "So that's why you're acting like you don't care. It's good to know that you're not the type of man worth paying attention to."

"My, my. And you're the type of woman I should desire, is that right?"

"I know better than to tell a man what to do. But yes. That's right."

"Is that the last time you'll ever admit I'm right?"

"You catch on quick. What's your name?"

"Zach."

"Well, Zach, I have a question."

"Shoot."

Zach pulled up his two glasses of Jack and coke and Marley stole one, knocking it back.

"Thanks. What's with guys paying more attention to liquor than women?" she asked pointedly.

Zach laughed. "Have you listened to country songs, sweetheart? 'Whiskey and You,' 'Whiskey Lullaby'… Sometimes there isn't a difference. At least we know what to expect with alcohol." He drew in a breath and sang, "'Longneck, ice cold beer never broke my heart.'"

Marley's eyes widened. The man could sing. She thought of Karl's ex-girlfriend falling for a lily on an index card. Good singing was *not* enough. "Though nice, I can't stand a guy who uses 'sweetheart' like that. Man. Aren't you the whole package." She didn't hold back the sarcasm.

"Doesn't bother me a smidge, *sweetheart*." He leaned on the word as he leaned towards her and winked.

Marley felt something within her flutter. She also felt something within her strengthen. Her resolve? Her desire? She didn't push Thomas' memory away this time. Thomas had wanted her. Someone had desired her. She was worth wanting. She deserved to feel wanted. She didn't have to act on that; it was enough to enjoy it. "Well. I'm going to go dance. If that's something you'd also like to do, you're welcome to do so in the proximity of my own dancing space. But I have to warn *you*. That man over there? In the periwinkle suit?" She pointed to Karl, his arms wild above his head, bringing them down as he brought one knee up and then the other. "He's got some wild moves that I'm pretty interested in. *And* he's a great listener." Marley felt the blanket of song and rhythm surround her. She swayed her hips, kicked her legs, and found Lily in the center of the dance floor.

"Marley!" Lily squealed. She threw her arms around her as if Marley hadn't been by her side all night, and oh, how they laughed. Marley looked up to see the chandeliers sparkling and her best friend glowing.

And they danced until the morning's light.

Stay True

"Think fast!" Lily yelled, throwing a bag of Frito-Lays into the air. Marley caught it before it hit Karl in the face.

"Ugh, rude, Lillian!" Jeremiah scoffed, shielding Karl with his arm as Karl lay his head on the purple pillow on Jeremiah's lap. Marley rolled her eyes, and Karl winked at her. "We don't need people in Spain talking about how disrespectful the Americans are to their guests."

"Too late!" Karl said, picking himself up.

"No, don't move," Jeremiah sighed. He scowled in Lily's direction. "See what you've done?" He snagged the bag away from Marley and ripped it open. Karl took the bag and walked away with it, moving his hips dramatically from side to side.

Jeremiah bit his lip and Lily giggled behind her hand, hiding behind Marley.

It was Marley's turn to sigh. "Last night was a dream." She wrapped her arms around Lily. "Are you happy?"

The door opened and Logan walked in with coffees in styrofoam holders. Marley thought of Sofia's coffee cup, then pushed the memory from her mind.

"So happy," Lily said. Marley watched Lily as she watched Logan, with a softness to her eyes that Marley had never seen. He set the coffees down and, as everyone else reached for a cup, Logan kissed Lily's forehead.

Lily snuggled deeper into Marley's shoulder and Logan winked at them before turning to hand Marley her coffee.

"Latte, right?"

"Yes, thank you." Marley smiled and raised the cup in cheers.

"*But is it soy!?*" Karl yelled from the kitchen.

"I'm fine, Karl!" Marley yelled back.

Lily checked her watch and sat up. "Is your mom coming to brunch? Anne will probably be calling soon."

Marley's phone rang.

Lily and Marley made eye contact and burst out laughing. "It couldn't be." "I wouldn't be surprised."

"We could just let it go to voicemail."

"So that Anne could start her day with a heart attack? That wouldn't be good for her son-in-law."

"Yeah," Logan sat on the couch next to Lily, throwing his feet up onto the coffee table. "Because I'm scared of her."

Both Lily and Marley raised their eyebrows at him. "You should be."

Marley sighed and dug her phone out of her robe pocket.

Brandon?

She swiped the phone's screen to answer.

"Hello?"

"Marley. Come back."

"Hi, Brandon." She said his name so Karl would hear. It worked. Karl perked up and stuck his head behind the wall. Marley motioned him over. He dropped the bag into the bowl he'd been carrying and pushed the bowl into Jeremiah's hands. Jeremiah dug his hand into the bag and crunched on the chips like they were watching a movie.

Marley tapped the speakerphone option. Brandon's voice filled the space.

"Tigre needs you. We need you. What can we do or say to bring you back? You belong here."

"I'm sorry, Brandon, but I don't see how—"

"What if I told you that we were restructuring?"

"What does that mean?"

"We need a senior level creative to fly this butterfly."

"What about Thomas?" It hurt to say his name out loud. "Isabel?"

Brandon hesitated. "They've been… dismissed."

Karl's jaw dropped. Marley's did, too. "What?"

"Without revealing too much, let's just say that they revealed too much. Went way against company policy."

"Oh," Marley said. Images of her own back against the lounge couch or supply rack flashed through her mind.

Lily's eyes were wide, leaning in, while also motioning to Logan to open the champagne.

Karl grasped her hand.

Marley searched Karl's eyes, then looked above his head. Could she really go back there? Thomas' ghost already followed her across the ocean. She couldn't imagine going back to where it all started. This was her choice to make. There was no running from the consequences, or the fear of what she wanted.

What was best for *her*?

She squeezed Karl's hand and gave Lily her most dazzling grin.

"Brandon, I appreciate feeling so appreciated, and I'm so glad that Mariposa wants more of what I offered, but I'm not the only talented designer. Maybe you could find someone homegrown right in Granada to help you."

While Brandon rambled on about the reasons she really wasn't replaceable, Logan came in with the champagne. Lily gesticulated wildly for him to open it. Marley had no idea what waited on the horizon or who she'd become, but she knew that the Marley of the past deserved a Marley of the future who had the permission to be exactly who she was.

Though Thomas Elker wasn't everything she'd hoped he'd be, his presence in her life had made a difference. He had unlocked a version of herself that she'd always been too shy to show, but though he'd unlocked it, it didn't mean it was suddenly locked now that he was gone. He had left the key in her hands. That was the gift he'd left her with. The mirror might get covered by clothes and gather dust, but every now and then, she'd look back and appreciate how he saw her: brave, competent, bold. A bobcat.

She had quite the recalibration to do because of their love affair. And though her compass' needle sometimes yearned to point back in his direction, it was still very much in her grasp. She was the captain of her ship. Choosing to work in Granada had been Marley running from the version of herself she thought wasn't good enough, but now she saw that leaving Tigre and Thomas was running towards herself and those she loved.

"Thanks so much, Brandon, but I'm pointing in a new direction."

The champagne popped, and the cork hit the ceiling with a thud. Her friends hooped and hollered. Marley looked around at them, who were *for* her, cheering her on.

She was Marley freaking Harrow. She'd be just fine.

Author's Note

A big question that you may have asked Marley time and time again is *why*? How could she have *continually* explored relations with Thomas knowing that he was married and that she was losing those closest to her as a result!? I have tried to answer this question in the most human, understanding, and merciful way I could: the girl found herself in a self-sabotaging cycle of addiction. But how? We know love. We know lust. But what of limerence? Limerence is defined as "the state of being infatuated or obsessed with another person, typically experienced involuntarily and characterized by a strong desire for reciprocation of one's feelings but not primarily for a sexual relationship." If you, or someone you love, is "trapped" in this desire, I hope this novel helps show how one can get lost in it - and what is required to come out on the other side. If you're interested in reading more about love addiction, love avoidance, infidelity, codependency, and limerence, may I suggest Pia Mellody's *Facing Love Addiction* or AffairRecovery.com for further reading. Anyone in the thick of it, talk to others by checking out your local chapter of SLAA. I swear you're not alone. Going through withdrawal? Keep on going. If you're on the other side? Congratu-freaking-lations. You'll be just fine.

Acknowledgements

Nicolette Orlando, Kelly Vitatoe, Stacie Kemp, Susan Buss, and Cody Ray. Without you, I don't know that I'd have ever climbed out of my dark night of the soul. It was easy to write the first part of *Breaking the Rules* during May of the pandemic because everything was a mess - including me and, as a result, Marley. It took time to figure out how Marley would heal, but we figured it out together, thanks to weekly meetings with Nicolette in the early drafting process (*"But is it soy!?"*); frequent submissions and feedback chats in subsequent revisions with Kelly; writing sessions with Stacie that ended up being more therapeutic for me than anything else; actual therapy with Susan; and the hard, beautiful, rewarding work that is marriage to Cody. The moment Logan walks in, I can't help but grin. You and he are the same and I am incredibly lucky to receive your incredible love.

Alyse Bailey, you are the editor I have wished for. A digital nomad, editor, and coach all in one, you understand a heart that yearns for adventure and cheered for Marley as if she were one of your closest friends. Thank you for telling me things like "Zeke deserves a conversation" and holding me accountable to my characters. It's hard to tell who loves Karl more - you or Nicolette. I cannot wait to work on countless manuscripts with you in the future. Special thanks to Lauren and the Paperbacks & Co. community for bringing us together. The Instagram #writerscommunity is an amazing experience.

Fr. Ed Shea. January 23. Thank you for always asking about Marley. I love you.

Kristen Kaczynski and Daniel Pujol, thank you for your creative insight, knowledge, and work on the book cover. Kallie, you're my best friend - and now a model on a book cover *and* of what it means to treat yourself with self-respect. I am so thankful that we met in high school. And that you met Daniel in New York. You are the inspiration for Marley in the first book, but please know, World, that Marley and Kristen lose their common ground the moment *Breaking the Rules* begins.

To the students of De La Salle: I will miss your light in my life so very much. YOU are the hardest part of leaving the classroom. Thank you to my creative writing classes: the coffee cup with lipstick and countless "therapy" sessions we had in 314 totally have a place in this book. You made Marley better because you make *me* better.

To those I met through TLE and Quill & Cup: Michelle, Susan, Katie, Kendra, Holloway, Danielle, Amy, Morgan, Maria Elena, Mollie, and *so* many others… You have taught me more by simply being yourselves than I could have ever learned on my own. Thank you for lending your never-ending support, enthusiasm, and wisdom.

Kai and Joann, I swear that Hot Springs lake was my baptism - and the beginning of Marley's own journey back towards herself. You are lights in my life.

To my Arkansas family, thank you for understanding all the times I hid away in the sun room to write and for supplying so many hugs, words of encouragement, and Jack Daniel's Southern Peach. Y'all are the best.

To my family, both in Chicagoland and around the world… Mama and Tata, I'm crazy enough to believe I can do things like write books because you never whispered a word that I couldn't. Wojtek, Marek, and Rob - telling people that I'm your little sister still inspires more pride in me than saying I've written two novels. Angela, Danyelle, and Natalia - thank you for being a safe place for me to land. And to the kids? Thanks for not running away when I demand hugs and affection and boardgames. Kocham Was bardzo.